The REJECTED Lady

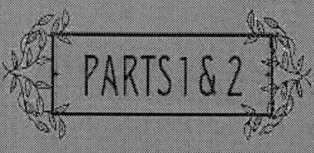

PARTS 1 & 2

Grandmother and Mother

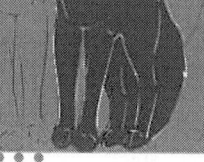

The Rejected Lady:

Parts 1 & 2

Table of Contents:

Disclaimer Notice:

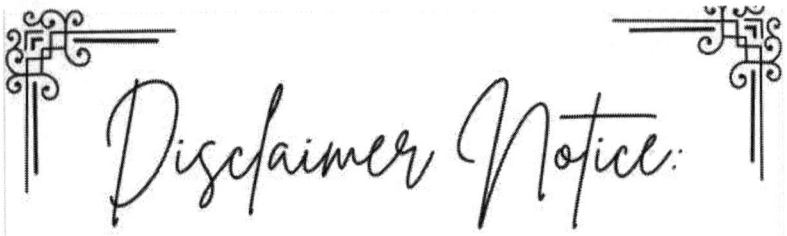

Disclaimer Notice:

All of the art in this novel series is drawn by the author, Kristen Elizabeth.

By no means am I a professional artist, nor do I claim to be, but I've always enjoyed the hobby.

I hope the drawings help you to integrate even further into this novel's world.

Thank you for reading!

Author's Warning:

This book contains trigger warnings and material, including:

Abandonment/Neglect
Forced arranged marriage
Bullying
Sexual Trauma/Assault
Trauma/Extreme depression
Still Birth/Miscarriage
Attempted Murder/Murder/Gore
Extreme Graphic Detail
Extreme Feels

Please proceed with caution, and if triggered by any of these themes or by the story, please seek the appropriate help or resources.

Be safe! Thank you!

The Rejected Lady – Parts 1 & 2 Muse Playlist–

<u>(Alphabetical Order)</u>

Book 1.0 theme: Within Temptation – Hills of Myst

1. 3OH3 ft Katy Perry – Starstuck
2. AFI – Girl's Not Grey
3. Amoebacrew – Drums of Drakkar
4. Apocolyptica – Not Strong Enough
5. Ashley Serena – Bayu Bayushki
6. Ashley Serena – In the Bleak Midwinter
7. Bad Wolves the Cranberries – Zombie (Metal Cover by Jonathan Young version)
8. Back Street Boys – Bye bye bye
9. Billy Squire – My Kinda Lover
10. Breaking Benjamin – I Will Not Bow
11. Bring me the Horizon – Throne
12. Disturbed – You're Mine
13. Doja Cat – Woman
14. Ernesto vs Bastian feat. Susana – Dark Side of the Moon
15. Ezio Auditore –

Legends Never
Die
16. John Legend –
All of Me
17. Kelly Clarkson –
Behind these
Hazel Eyes
18. Korn ft. Amy
Lee – Freak on
a Leash
19. Maneskin –
Beggin'
20. Peyton Parrish –
Battle Cries
21. Pitbull – Timber
22. Ruelle –
Madness
23. Sean Paul –
Temperature
24. Sia –
Unstoppable
25. The HU – Wolf
Totem
26. Within
Temptation –
Covered by
Roses
27. Within
Temptation –
Silver Moonlight

28. Within
Temptation –
Stairway to the
Skies
29. Within
Temptation –
Stand my
Ground
30. Within
Temptation –
Somewhere

Special Author's Note 1:

This novel saga uses an entirely different Calendar system, with different names of the months and days of the week. So, the Months and Weekdays are as follows:

January – Blizzard's Reign (30 days)

February – Nivis's End (20 days)

March – Seed's Sewn (40 days)

April – Rain's Fall (40 days)

May – Veras's Height (40 days)

June – Veras's End (20 days)

July – Solaris's Gifts (30 days)

August – Solaris's Reign (40 days)

September – Solaris's End (20 days)

October – Moon's Dance (27 days)

November – Folias's Blessing (30 days)

December – Year's Fall (20 days)

Sunday – Sun's Dawning

Monday – Morning's Stars

Tuesday – Seed's Rising

Wednesday – Sun's Reign

Thursday – Sun's Falling

Friday – Twilight's Reign

Saturday – Moon's Height

Spring – Veras

Summer – Solaris

Autumn – Folias

Winter – Nivis

Special Author's Note 2:

This novel uses multiple speech types! Here is an inside look to help you keep track!

"Speech"

"Pack link internal speech"

'Thoughts directed to wolf counterpart'

Internal dialogue

Wolf's internal thoughts

"Wolf's external/internal speech"

"Alpha commands"

"Moon Mother's speech"

"Ghost Speech"

PART 1

Grandmother

CHAPTER 1

Dove Terra...

Nivis's End, 1942 Imperial Lunar Year

It was in the Nivis that I was eleven years old that I saw *him* for the first time.

There was an important meeting between our two packs, because things had been quite tense and strained in the area, lately.

Our once large, formidable pack had split into two parts because of over-population and conflicts with the upper ranks, according to history.

This brother-pack was the one whom was here to negotiate terms for peace and unity against the opposing packs...or, at least, that is what father had said.

War was on the horizon for the territories, my father had told me.

I was standing there on the cliff that the pack-house sat upon, looking out over the territory, and admiring the forest being covered in the falling snow.

It was an idyllic scene, beautiful and pure.

I heard the crunch of snow, and thinking that it was my guard, I didn't respond to the presence at first.

Though, in hindsight later in life, I would realize what a fool I was, being so young. My senses as a wolf hadn't fully awakened and become in tune with me, so I had no business being alone on the outskirts of the area the way that I had been.

"It isn't wise for a female of your rank to stand out here, alone. Don't you know that war is coming?"

I jumped at the gruff voice, turning on my heel to see him.

He was beautiful, with dark grey hair and pale, minty-green eyes. He had an average skin tone, and he looked to be about my age.

From his scent and his demeanor, the way he carried himself, he seemed to be a high-rank.

Possibly a gamma?

The pack-ranks were fairly easy to keep up with.

There was the **Alpha**, the head of the pack. He would attract a powerful female, more powerful than any other female in her rank class, and he would find her scent to be most appealing—which was how it worked with all males, but only the alpha would be attracted to her specific scent, whereas it was possible for multiple males to appreciate a single female's scent in the lower ranks.

He would initiate a hunt, and they would play a game of cat-and-mouse. If she impressed him, he would try to get her to submit. The moon-mother, Selene, would have already blessed the union because she was the only female meant for the alpha, and he was the only male meant for that specific female. Then, he would proceed to mark her in front of the pack, claiming her as his alpha-female, or the Luna of the pack.

This was the greatest honor but biggest responsibility, and it could be a dream-come-true or a nightmare for the female.

There was the **Beta male**, whose position in the pack was to help with management of the pack, protecting the alpha, and raising a strong heir to carry on his place. If he had a daughter only—like in *my* family's case—he would have her raised in the most proper, high-standard ways and keep her under guard until she attracted a powerful male to take over the beta position.

She typically attracted another beta-ranked male, or a gamma or delta, depending on how desirable she was.

Beta females protected and assisted the luna, specifically dictated by pack law to watch over and protect her and be her best advisor.

There were *two* types of gammas;

First, there was the **Offensive Gamma**, who was the war-mongering, main warrior of the pack. He was to be the war general and manage the warriors and drills and training. He was also dictated by the pack ruling to protect the beta male, the same way that the beta male protected the alpha.

Secondly, there was the **Defensive Gamma**, who was dictated by pack ruling to protect the beta female and by extension, an extra defensive measure for the luna, as well, since most beta females weren't trained warriors. This role was even more important that the offensive gamma, because the beta female and the luna were not combatants.

Then, there was the **Pack Hunter**, who hunted down criminals and executed them, executed rogue wolves, and assisted the pack's discipline order. He was also dictated by pack ruling to protect the gammas, and have their backs when he wasn't already busy with his main work.

There were ten **Delta males** in each pack. They were keepers of the peace and order, our strongest soldiers. They were stronger than the omegas, but they didn't manage or run anything in the pack. They were more like police or military officers rather than pack officials.

● ● ●

Powerful in their own right.

Delta-ranked females raised up and protected the *pups* of the pack, protecting them and helping to start training for the young males. They ran the schools and other child-rearing activities for delta ranked and up pups.

Then, there were the **Omegas**. This rank made up the majority of the pack, and they helped protect and assist the deltas. Most of them held jobs like servants or assistants, and they made average lives in this manner.

They looked up to the ranked members because, in exchange for their work and assistance, they were protected and looked after.

Each ranking of the pack worked on a generational term, as well.

So, my job was to wait for my luna and then pledge myself to her service once she was brought into her position. Until then, I didn't have anything to really do except help out around the pack.

My guard, for example, was the defensive gamma heir, so he was already taking to his role of looking out for me.

Our Alpha, Alpha Falcon, already had an alpha heir, Finch Terra.

Because my father, the alpha's younger brother, was already his beta male, that position was taken by our family. So, gamma heir fell to the alpha's second son, Crow Terra.

Our pack did not currently have two gammas or gamma heirs as it should, but...we were a bit small for a pack.

We had lost many members over the years.

Our only gamma was the offensive gamma, and he didn't have any heirs.

I looked at the male before me.

He was from the brother pack, the **Terra-Stone** pack, because I didn't recognize him or his scent.

I was from the **Terra-Forest** pack.

"My guard is nearby, and I am right by the pack-house. The only pack around is an allied pack, and so I am well-protected here. I am high-ranked for my pack, and I doubt anyone would be stupid enough to attempt to harm me, if they don't wish to incur the wrath of my father or my uncle."

"And you don't think that a rogue could sneak in and kill you and be gone before your guard—who is likely your age—could even get to you?" He scoffed. "Who are your father and uncle?" He asked, smirking and crossing his arms.

"My uncle is the alpha of this pack, Alpha Falcon Terra. My father is his younger brother and beta, Raven Terra."

He looked surprised. "You and I are kin, then."

"Kin?" I asked, still not recognizing his scent.

"My uncle is Alpha Sierra Stone—your alpha's cousin. My father is the youngest cousin, Valley Stone."

"Oh," I said, stunned.

We were in a pack that had been split into two, I remembered.

The original Alpha of the packs had a pair of twin sons, Eagle and Amber.

These two brothers split the packs down the middle, making it into two separate packs.

Eagle became Eagle Terra, and Amber became Amber Stone.

Eagle Terra—my grandfather—had also had a set of twin sons of his own.

The first-born twin, Falcon Terra, became the alpha of the Terra-Forest pack. He was my uncle.

The second-born twin, Raven Terra, became beta. Raven was my father.

Eagle's eldest daughter, Daisy Terra, was the true mate of Eagle's nephew, Ash Stone, who would have been the alpha of the Terra-Stone pack.

That couple was killed in battle, though.

Amber's second son, Sierra Stone, became the alpha of the Terra-Stone pack.

Strangely enough, Eagle's first-born twin son, Falcon, was the true mate of Eagle's niece, Amber's eldest daughter, Basil Stone.

It seemed true mates didn't care about blood relation, as two pairs of cousins had been true mates.

The bond given by the moon Moon Mother was a precious gift, so they say, and it was nearly unheard of to reject it. Blood-relations included.

Amber's youngest son, Valley Stone, became the beta of the Terra-Stone pack.

So, *this boy* was the son of the Terra-Stone pack's beta...*my* rank, and my kin. Technically he was a *second-cousin*, because his father was my first-cousin.

He looked me up and down, studying me. "You are right, you aren't likely to be attacked with your rank. But it still isn't a good idea to be so far from your guard. It looks like your gamma heir needs some work, his scent is so distant that I can barely smell him from here. He wouldn't be able to make it in time to save you if I decided to kill you."

"You seem fascinated with me getting hurt," I huffed, crossing my arms. I already didn't like him.

Cousin or not, beta heir or not.

He scoffed. "I *am* the beta heir. It is my job to think about the protection of the pack, and management. Forgive me, oh snooty arrogant one, for being concerned about your safety," he sneered. "Our packs are discussing reuniting, and since you are the *only* child of your beta, that means that the title of beta will fall to *me* if our packs do happen to decide to join together again."

I startled, growling beneath my breath at the threat.

Since I was the only heir to my father's role, I was being trained to be beta until I could get married to a powerful enough male to take on the role.

"I might not be the beta heir, but I am still the beta's daughter. Who knows? The male I attract to mate might be stronger than you, and might just become the heir in *your* place," I said.

He shrugged. "I doubt it. *Most* of the packs in this state are enemies of our pack, and any male you attract would be unlikely to be stronger than me. I am the only beta heir in the state that is an ally of your pack, after all. You will likely be mated off to a delta—*possibly* a gamma, if you work on fixing that attitude and energy quickly. Though, I would hope for your sake it is *my* pack's gamma heir, because your pack's gamma heir doesn't seem to be very interested in doing their job properly."

"My pack is running just fine! We just have a lot going on," I grumbled.

"Your father is a beta, so I am sure that you are more in the knowing of how important this meeting today is. You are right, the packs are busy. But the sole job of the gamma heir is to ensure the protection of the beta's children. Looks like you're shit out of luck. For all he knew, I could have been an enemy."

"You're starting to *look* like one," I said beneath my breath.

I felt the breath leave my lungs as I was shoved against a tree nearby, his arm winding around my waist.

I looked up into his eyes, startled. "How dare you? I am the beta's daughter—"

"Do you know why it is so important for a high-ranked female to take classes on behavior, obedience, and helping the titled members of the pack?" He asked, pausing for just a moment. "Because the more obedient and helpful she is to the pack and higher ranks, the more *desirable* she becomes to a *potential mate*."

CHAPTER 2

Dove...

"...*Excuse* me?" I asked, glaring at him. "What did you say?"

He scoffed at me. "You know that, don't you? Haven't they taught you anything? Once a male locks in on her scent, his blood and his Moon Mother-given instinct will tell him if she is the right mate for him. He will already be going haywire due to 'the heat;' he won't be thinking about anything but instinct, for the most part. The Moon Mother will give him the knowledge to *know* if she is the right choice as his mate, and if she *is*, he marks her," he said. "Do you know why the mouthy, rude, disrespectful females end up with *weak* males? Because they are *last pick*. Males have already trained their instincts against that female's scent, to smell it as 'bad,' so that she does not attract him when our mating mind wakes up. *No* powerful male wants a she-wolf who *barks* too much, so even if he does become drawn to her scent, those females' true mates reject them and leave them as slim pickings for whatever male might be willing to tolerate her enough to take her," he sneered.

Tears pricked my eyes.

I knew, in that moment, that he was right.

My mother had been worrying herself sick over my mouthy, "lousy attitude" and "strongly voiced opinions."

She knew that I had the *potential* to be desirable, to be first chosen by my true mate because of my bloodline and my pedigree, *but*...

He let me go just as the crunching of snow alerted us to another presence.

"Miss Dove, mister Cloud, the betas have requested your presence," my gamma heir said, out of breath. Then, he noticed our *position*, going pale. "Miss—"

"Let's go, Crow," I told him, sighing. "We will need to talk later."

"I am sorry, Dove, father told me to stay near him because he might send me on an errand. I tried to stay close by in case you needed me, but—"

"How many gamma heirs *does* your pack have?" The boy—Cloud, Crow had called him—asked.

"We only have *one*," I said. "Our pack's only gamma, the Offensive Gamma, has no heirs. So, Alpha Falcon made his second son the Gamma Heir."

"Ah," he said. "My pack only has one gamma, also. Most packs have two, but it seems the roles divided evenly between the packs. And since he seems to be your guard, I take it that he is the *Defensive* Gamma Heir, right? Our pack's gamma is the offensive gamma...or, gamma heir only, now. But, once our packs join again, we will have two gammas, as is the norm."

I was basically just ignoring him, at this point. He was already thinking that he was going to take my position, and thinking badly of me as a potential mate.

I didn't want to talk to him.

We walked to the front of the pack house, and into the great-room, where our alphas and betas were waiting for us.

"Ah, good," his alpha said. "You have arrived. Thank you, young Defensive Gamma Heir," he said to Crow, who gave a nod and went to sit by his side.

"We have something important to discuss with you both," my uncle said. "As your fathers may have told you, the other packs in the state have been fighting over territory lately, and it seems that several of the packs have set their eyes on our territory," he said, looking grave. "So, in response, we have decided to reunite with our brother pack. However, there is a bit of a…stipulation to rejoining packs. No pack has ever had two alphas or two betas. Two gammas are standard, but no rank above that. Also, to rejoin, we have to…rejoin the bloodline entirely."

The other alpha spoke up again. "Because the original alpha of the joined packs had twin sons who then split the packs and married their own mates, it split the bloodline into two as well. To rejoin, our shaman has asked for a sign to learn how this will be possible in a peaceful way and not struggle with the ranking system. The first condition is something that we had never taken into consideration without it being the Moon Mother's choice, but…"

"There has to be a *marriage*," a male I didn't recognize said.

"A *marriage*, father?" Cloud asked, and I saw the resemblance as he said it.

So, this was their pack's beta male.

"Yes," he said. "Normally, we wait for a wolf to turn fourteen—age two, for your *wolf*—and let their senses given by the Moon Mother choose their true mates. As I am sure you both know, when you turn seven years of age, you awaken and meet your wolf, whom has just turned one-year-old, in your own body. Whatever female or male you may find as a mate will also start to seem more desirable and you will sense their presence around you or their scent might be particularly nice. When you turn fourteen and your wolf is two, the 'mating mind' awakens, and the instinct to mate with your fated partner drives you to find and accomplish this mating, immediately. An arranged marriage is highly unorthodox and considered rude to the Moon Mother…however, the only way to rejoin the blood and the pack together peacefully is through marriage."

It is rare for a true mate to be found outside of one's own pack, so an arrangement *was* necessary for this to happen...but...

"So, what does that have to do with *us*?" Cloud beat me to asking, deadpanning.

"*Well*," my father wouldn't look at me, and I understood even before the words escaped his mouth. "Both packs, we..." He sighed. "The Terra-Stone pack has a male alpha heir who is, unfortunately, weak and sick and isn't fit to command...so he has refused. But we *do* have a male beta heir, and male offensive gamma heir. *None* of those families have a *female*. The Terra-Forest pack has a male alpha heir, a male gamma heir, but *not*...a *female beta child*."

Cloud gaped, whirling his eyes to me. "You...you mean to marry *me* to *her*?" He asked, stunned.

His father nodded, looking at us sheepishly. "*She* is the *only* female close to your age who is of similar rank in *their* pack, son. We were also worried that she would feel intimidated by you joining their pack and taking her position from her—"

"I would *never* choose her!" Cloud said, a slight growl to his undertones. "She wouldn't be the Moon Mother's choice for me, either, I am sure of it. She might be *pretty*, but *no* self-respecting, powerful beta male would fall for a girl with *that* mouth or *attitude*—"

"We will spend the next two years working with her, *seriously*, fixing her behavior and attitude. She is ten now, but will be eleven in Rain's Fall. In two years, she will be turning thirteen. It is just only a year shy of when your wolves would choose mates anyway, so it won't be a drastic change to the norm. You will be given medication to keep you from smelling your mate, so even though you will come of age before she will, it will not become an issue for you to be concerned with, and we can proceed as planned—"

"But I—" Cloud tried, but his father glared at him.

"Father, you can't do this—" I tried.

● ● ●

"Stop it, Dove!" He scolded.

"But—"

"We *have* to reunite the packs," his alpha interrupted. "This is how we do it *peacefully*. You two are the key to that! A very important role! You should feel honored!" He said. Cloud and I glared at one another, and the alpha continued. "At the ceremony, the most powerful of the alphas will take command of the united pack, the most powerful beta will become the new alpha's beta, and *you* will be groomed to become the beta of the combined packs with your new beta female. As your alpha and as your uncle, I'm sure you know that I do not wish to have to use my alpha blood to *force* you into submission, but if I have to—"

"*No*," Cloud said, kneeling and baring his neck in submission to his alpha. "That is unnecessary. I will do as I am told. It is in my blood, as a trueborn beta heir, to obey the alpha's decisions."

Our alphas both nodded, before alpha Falcon turned his attention to me. "Is this going to be a problem, Dove?"

I glanced at Cloud, who looked up at me from the corner of his eye. A sour look crossed his face when I didn't answer right away.

"**Dove**!" Falcon said, and I could feel the pressure of force in his tone. What—?

He had never used his alpha pressure on me before, so I had no idea what it felt like and how to respond.

As it turns out, I had no ability to respond in any graceful manner, it seemed.

I gasped, collapsing to my knees...and I was shocked completely when Cloud quickly reached to catch me before my face hit the floor.

He helped me straighten a bit, waiting for me.

Why wasn't the pressure lessening...?

● ● ●

"…Bare your neck and submit," Cloud murmured into my ear. "You have to submit to the alpha."

I glanced at him, and he gave me a nod, helping me sit up a little more…and I bared my neck in submission to the alpha.

"…No, alpha. No problems."

As soon as I submitted, the pressure lifted.

I was successfully trapped.

I felt tears sting my eyes, even as I felt Cloud helping me to stand as we were dismissed, while my mind was stuck in a haze…and the cold wind blasted my face as he walked me outside. I gasped, struggling to breathe.

"That was your first time under the alpha command, I take it," Cloud said, soft. "It gets easier to take it, but the first few times—especially before your wolf fully awakens as an adult—is extremely difficult. You did fairly well, considering."

I didn't want to be comforted by him.

I wanted to shift, to run far away, but shifting was very personal.

Only your mate was supposed to see you strip and shift.

I was sure that this boy who disliked me would see me shift soon enough, anyway, since he was now my fiancé, but for now…I wanted to keep my wolf to myself.

A *mother* was there for her daughter's first shift, and a father was there for his son's first shift, but outside of that, the shift, itself, was private.

We did do pack runs often, admiring our beautiful wolves together, but shifting was painful and powerful and a wolf's basest instinct was to be alone during that change, unless their mate was there.

Wolves were at their most vulnerable during their shift, and it was one of the best times to kill one of us.

If you weren't *completely trusting* of whomever you were with, you didn't want to shift with anyone around.

I didn't think I would ever *want* to shift in front of Cloud, especially not right now.

"Are you alright, Dove?" Crow asked, flitting about me in a worried manner.

"Get her home," I heard Cloud tell him. "I imagine she's probably overwhelmed. I know *I* am not entirely pleased, but—"

"I won't get a Moon Mother given true mate," I whispered, voice trembling and eyes watery. "Even if I have one...I can't even be with him."

Cloud scoffed. *"That's* what upsets you? It isn't like *you're* the only one struggling. You're such a selfish child! How do you think I feel? *I'm* the one who has to be with a female I wouldn't have chosen! You are getting the better end of the deal, here! I am a powerful, desirable, attractive male! I am extremely popular and helpful to my pack. I would take care of you and honor you! You're so selfish! This is about much more than your petty *feelings*. It isn't like *I'm* thrilled, either."

I seethed, blushing hard as bristled and I glared at him. "I know you aren't happy about this, but *I* was raised being taught that I would be chosen by a powerful male if I worked hard to become his heart's desire, and that the Moon Mother would reward me for loving my pack with a male that was beautiful and powerful and would *love* me more than anything. That he would...see *me* as a Moon Mother, because I was given to him by the Moon Mother..." Tears started to spill down my cheeks, and I turned away. "That he would love me as much as my father loves my mother. That it would be an all-encompassing love, and that nobody else would ever be able to offer me that level of love. I just...wanted what he promised..."

He didn't respond to that.

● ● ●

"But as you have clearly stated, you would *never* pick me, and you seem sure the Moon Mother wouldn't pick me for you, either."

I whipped around to face him, and he gaped at me and my tear-streaked face.

"Dove—"

"That can only mean that *I* won't be *special* to you." I looked at him to see him look...almost conflicted. "It means that you won't even be *able* to love me the way that...well, even if I attracted a *weaker* mate, I am sure he would have at least *loved* me, wouldn't he?"

"Dove-"

"But *you*...you won't be able to give me love. You might act dutifully and you might take care of me and give me pups, but beyond that, you will spend your life resenting me...and I'll spend my life heartbroken with a male who can't even want me, let alone love me as the Moon Mother intended for me to be loved...I have to give up being loved, just to be of use to the pack. No other wolves will understand having to compromise that. Only us. And that's heartbreaking." I turned away again. "It was nice to meet you, beta heir Cloud. I will do my best to be less of a disappointment to you the next time we meet."

Then, I ran away, and I didn't let myself stop until I reached my bed.

CHAPTER 3

Cloud Stone...

I stood before the beta males of the packs, the meeting officially over, but the fathers of the couple in question wishing to speak with me.

I informed them of what had happened, but didn't mention all the things that the girl had given me to think about.

"So, she ran home," her father sighed, shaking his head. "I knew that she wouldn't be happy about this."

I stood with my arms clasped behind my back, listening respectfully.

I could see that Dove had gotten her father's tanned skin, and emerald green eyes, but her hair was far lighter than his dark, peppery-grey hair.

As grey-wolves, our people almost all had varying shades of grey or peppery hair.

Dove's hair was a beautiful, silvery-pepper, with lowlights of darker greys. It was luminous and shiny, luxurious, even...

Damn it, I didn't want to think about her!

* * *

She *was* beautiful, I would give her that. She had a *confidence* about her that was almost attractive, but it was a little too close to arrogance for my lacking. Still, she was self-assured, and she certainly had high self-esteem. She likely took good care of her hygiene and self-care, which was important in a prospective mate.

Her *mouth*, though...I almost shuttered at the thought of trying to tame *that*. No male wanted a female who would go against him, especially not so readily...and especially not because he had expressed concern over her own personal safety, trying to show care about her. It was in a wolf's basest nature to choose a female would submit to him, and let him keep her safe.

She had practically spat on my kindness...

A desirable female was quiet, listened well, and even when she had an opposing opinion on something, she was *calm* and *reserved* about expressing it. She wasn't always blindly expected to keep silent. She was just expected to not be hostile about it unless the situation actually called for hostility, and that situation most certainly didn't call for it.

That girl had *no* reserve about expressing attitude or displeasure.

She had been spoiled, more than likely.

'She is to be mate...?' I heard my wolf's voice flutter into my mind, and I sighed inwardly. **'What about <u>true mate</u>?'**

'Don't worry about true mate,' I answered.

'That girl takes the place of true mate?'

'Yes,' I answered. Then, I thought of her again, letting my wolf—*Slater's*—thought flow freely into my own. It was the only way to hear him—to not focus on him directly.

'But she was so upset...am I that bad? She was very sad.'

'Sad...?'

'Her wolf thinks we will hate them. Her wolf was sad. Her wolf was <u>scared</u>.'

● ● ●

So, she really *was* sad about it?

She wasn't just trying to tug at my heartstrings or manipulate me, then. This meant that she was genuinely upset. I trusted my wolf's instincts completely. He hadn't ever led me wrong.

Afraid, though? Why scared...?

'Scared to be her wolf with us, scared I would hate her like you hate her.'

Ouch.

That wasn't good...especially if she was my now-fiancé.

A wolf who was scared to be herself around her mate?

That was a very bad thing.

She needed to at *least* be *comfortable* with me...no matter how much we disliked one another.

"Please, *try* not to hold it against her, Cloud," her father pleaded. "As my only child, she grew up...probably a little over-indulged. Her mother has been working on her *appearance* a little too much, and how to be kind to others. I can tell you that her grades in school are very high, and she is smart and sharp as a tack on pack matters and volunteering to help tutor pups and she's already working hard in our community. She has gained quite a lot of popularity among the males of the pack, but she hasn't been taught enough about her *personality* behaviors, and that is our fault. She didn't have any siblings, and she was raised thinking that a high-ranking male would give his *all* to her, so..."

"She will need some more time, which is fine," my father waved it off. "Cloud will not go against the decision, even if he doesn't agree with it. He is a proper beta heir, and knows his place well. He will be loyal."

"My daughter is also loyal!" Her father rushed to defend. "She just—"

"Of course, of course. She was raised to think that she would be beta, until a powerful male mated her and took over with her as the beta pair. She is too full of herself to be a proper beta. With Cloud, however, I have driven it into him to follow his alpha to the letter, *without* submissive alpha force, and he has even had a great deal of combat training and obedience training already. We still fall short on *how to treat females*, though, as your gamma heir has pointed out," he glanced to the gamma heir of their pack, who shifted on his feet.

He had outed me out as soon as we had been called back in, telling the beta that I'd held his daughter to a tree by force and gotten in her face and been rude.

"She was running her mouth—"

"She is still technically not from *our* pack," father scolded, and I felt power in his tone.

Betas may not have the same authority as an alpha, but they still held a great deal of power to help manage and run the pack.

I felt my knees tremble minutely, struggling to stay firm under my father's force. He was angry that I was making him look bad, I knew...especially after he had been singing my praises before we got back in here.

Being my father, I knew his discipline would be way harsher than my alpha's, so I actually feared him more.

"Had you done that in *any other* pack, you could have started a *war*, you know. Kin or not, brother pack or not, disrespectful to *you* first or not...you should have told her father right away, rather than moving to handle it yourself. It was *not your place* to discipline her. She is the member of another pack."

"We are to be joined—"

"We aren't joined *yet*, boy!" My father shouted, and I flinched.

"...She is to be my wife," I reminded, softer.

He sighed, rubbing his eyes. "She *is* to be your bride, and your first meeting with her, you force her back to a tree and get in her *face*. You made to discipline her as if you were her beta and she was of lower blood. And just so you know—just because she is to be your wife does not mean that you are supposed to discipline her. She is to be your *partner*, not your child, and you've already made a horrible impression! You want to talk about *her* attitude? How about we work on *yours*?"

My face flamed.

It was embarrassing to be scolded so harshly in front of another male—particularly a fellow beta male—but it made it so much worse that he was to be my *father-in-law*...

Her father paced. "I *am* lucky to have such a strong male becoming her mate, but you...you *did* cross a line. I worry about leaving my precious child in your care. You know that she is descended from a line with Drakonian blood, don't you? She is of the highest pedigree, next to the alpha. She deserves love and proper care."

I felt shame well up within me.

Seeing it from *his* perspective, I could see why her father would be so upset. If I had a daughter, and she were in this position...I would be frustrated, too.

His daughter had been raised to believe that she would be her mate's *entire world*, worshipped the way that the males of our species and loved Selene—the progenitor of our kind, and seen as our "Moon Mother."

After all, without Selene's blessing, your chosen female couldn't actually become yours without force, which was against Selene's will. It was by her design that a female would submit to us during the initial mating, and let her scent draw us in the first place.

A mate was a *gift*.

There was no couple in the history of our kind who *didn't* have a mate given by our deity...Dove and I included.

All you had to do was find them.

A male would have an idea of what type of female he liked by the time his wolf awakened, and he would typically have a female whose scent he liked more than others by the time he came of age to mate.

During the pack-wide generation ceremony for all those who had come of age recently, they would hold the females and males in separate designated locations. Then, they would let the females go, and every one of them would shift. Their wolf forms were unknown to the males, and her scent was more concentrated in that form.

The males would be made to wait a while, and then...then, they let the males loose, to find the females.

Males typically looked for a submissive, quiet, but strong and giving female to choose. She was also usually of a similar rank to him, and that was instinctual, so that she wasn't likely to reject him because he was beneath her standards.

He would follow the scent he had always liked since his wolf had awakened from the beginning, and they would find one another at a special location in the pack, a place of significance. They would be in their wolf forms already, and wouldn't see one another shift until they had chosen one another and marked each other.

If the female impressed him and he felt a connection, desire for and compatibility with her, the Moon Mother would deem whether or not she was a good fit for him, and he, for her.

If they *were*, the scent would change as the *true mate bond* snapped into place. The scent would overwhelm the male, and he would claim her if she submitted to him.

She had the power to refuse, as did he, but wolves usually didn't *want* to. Of course, males could have intimate relations with females outside of their mates, but once a male met his true mate, his bonded female to be claimed, marked, and bonded to him...that was it.

Infidelity was almost impossible, as a female felt the betrayal pains in her soul when he mated outside of their union...and rejection was most improbable.

In our society, the males did all of the choosing. With the Moon Mother Selene's blessing, he would find his true love.

If he couldn't find it in his own pack—rare, but it did happen, occasionally—then the desire to locate her would be his goal. It would drive him all his life, and he could only hope that she was the one he had always sensed nearby.

Wolves, in general, woke up at the age of one, when our human selves were seven years old. He or she would always sense a presence, and when they were around their true mate, they would feel more at ease and smell their scent above all others...however, it wasn't powerful enough to actually pinpoint. You would have a natural gravitation to be around him or her, however...it wasn't certain until our mating mind woke up.

That happened when our wolves turned two, and we were fourteen.

On the rare occurrence that a mating was forced, they would hold a ceremony to appease the Moon Mother, as it was an unnatural bonding, and we would have to get her blessing, even still, just like a normal mating.

The difference was, however, that if she rejected the union, for whatever reason, and it was still made to proceed even against her wishes...the pair's lives would be cursed, and that curse had, in one case, traveled to be continued through eight generations of that family's direct descendants.

That family had eventually been cast out of their pack as Rogues—enemies and outcasts, forever condemned to live on their own, outside of a pack, and often hunted by packs because Rogues usually struggled to survive and would steal and kill from packs they came across...

It was a great sin to force such a union, and I could only pray that the Moon Mother wouldn't condemn us to such a fate.

I had to get my mind right, and be positive.

Perhaps if I stayed positive about my mate-to-be, and had good feelings towards her, Selene wouldn't refuse our union.

I knew, though, that in the eyes of this beta male, I had already expressed displeasure and contempt for the female that I would be mating through an *arrangement*, my instinct not leading me and driving me to love her, as he would have wished...

This arrangement, which was unorthodox and against the values of our people...and that female was *his* daughter.

"I assure you, Beta Raven, we will work on Cloud's behavior and attitude as well. I am sure that miss Dove will not be left disappointed."

Beta Raven's shoulders lost some of their tension, and he turned to face us, his eyes on me. "Let us both work to improve our children so that they do not disappoint *each other*, hm?"

"I can agree to that," my father said, and took Beta Raven's hand.

"I look forward to the next time we meet, Beta Valley."

"So do I," my father said.

Then, he grabbed my shoulder, and we turned and walked out into the cold.

Blizzard's Reign, 1944 ILY

"Now, we all know that this class will be turning fourteen within the next year. Do you all know why that is so significant?" Our teacher asked us, a pretty omega female.

"It is significant because when we turn fourteen, our wolf's mating instinct will awaken and we will be drawn to our mates."

"You are correct," the teacher smiled at the girl who answered. "Does anyone know how the mating practice works?"

"Aww," one boy had protested. "You mean we have to have *this* talk?" He groaned, and the girls giggled.

"Yes, Cinder, we have to have this talk. *Do you know?*"

He looked away, a blush on his cheeks. "Sure, I do. We just find a girl we like, who we like her smell, right?"

"That is only part of it," the teacher explained. "Throughout our childhoods, we will always find one particular person to be more enjoyable to be around, or always like their scent to be more pleasant...but it isn't pinpoint accurate. They are usually similar in rank to you, or at least won't be a hinderance to your wolf. You will enjoy that wolf's scent all of your life, and it will guide you two together."

"But my father said that a male will look for certain qualities in a female and then the scent will kick in," another girl commented.

The teacher laughed. "He was right. You see, each male will have an idea of qualities he likes."

"Oh…"

"It is, usually, the more submissive and calm natured, and compassionate and loving female who entices his wolf inside. Typically, he has already been drawn to her scent from childhood. When we hold the annual ceremony for our wolves who are coming of age, we have everyone shift into their wolf forms as we hold the males all together in one location, and the females in another. After everyone has shifted, we let the females loose into the forest. The males will then be released. They will follow the scent that they like best, and when they meet, he will confirm if she is interested in him as well."

"Then what?" Another girl asked, totally intrigued.

"If she does share his interest and finds him to be a good potential partner, the male and female will battle each other in a fight for submission. During this crucial dance for power, the Moon Mother will examine the couple together as a complete entity. If they are a good fit together, the female will naturally and instinctively submit to her male, releasing the mating scent—a special scent that only he will know means her consent—and she will accept him as her mate. He will be overwhelmed by this scent, and he will mark her with his wolf. Then, they will shift in front of one another for the first time."

"What about the *beta heir*?" One girl asked, and I flinched hard in my seat…because *she* had always been the female whose scent, *I* had always liked out of everyone I had met. I had always liked her scent, too.

Not that I could smell it anymore, though, now that I was on scent-blockers to keep me from smelling a true mate.

She was a cute little delta female, stronger than an omega but weaker than a gamma. She had always been sweet and helped take care of her younger siblings…and she had always obeyed authority the moment she received instruction.

An ideal prospective mate…and a girl I couldn't let myself get more attached to.

● ● ●

I tried my best to not look at her, forcing my eyes elsewhere even as her eyes bore into me.

"For the beta heir, he and his mate-to-be will have a *similar* ceremony, but it will happen with witnesses and he will mark her in front of *them*. She will still have to submit to him, but it may have to be a bit more forced, which is why the witnesses need to be there."

"W-why?" She asked, nervous.

"Because it is an arranged marriage, and they weren't initially drawn to one another, she may instinctually fight against him and decide not to submit at all."

"So...he might have to mate her by force against her will?" She gulped. She glanced at me again, and I felt her depression rising. "But...what about his true mate...?"

The teacher sighed, and gave me a knowing look. "He will have to reject her, if she ever pursues him. He will already be bound by a mark. There would be nothing that he could do. We wolves do not encourage infidelity, or cheating, one one's mate...whether it be by arrangement or otherwise."

"And what about *her*?" Another asked. "What if she already has a male interested in her scent, and then he comes for her? What if he is more powerful than beta heir Cloud?"

The teacher sighed. "It would be the same scenario. It is a sad but true situation that we are in. We have to join packs, and the only way to do so peacefully, without any disputes or fights, is to forge a union in a high-ranking couple."

"But why couldn't they have picked someone else?" The girl I had liked asked.

"Because she is the only high-ranked female in this age group who is unmated, and Cloud was the highest ranked male"

"What about the alpha heir?"

"Well, the alpha heir refused her hand because he is sickly and isn't actually pursuing the alpha title. *Cloud*...is the *only* male who matches her rank and *can* do this in the most honorable way..."

That shut everyone up, and there were no more questions.

Even I had learned a bit more about what would happen, but that just made me even more nervous.

Would I end up having to force a bond? Would I have to force my mark onto her while they pinned her down?

Would we still hate each other just as much after I marked her?

Rain's Fall, 1944 ILY

For the two years following our first meeting, my father and mother had really ramped up my training regimen to become a more powerful and a more...compassionate and loving male.

Mother seemed to be a bit worried, what with what my father had told her of my initial meeting with my betrothed, but she was at least partially satisfied by the improvements, which was saying a lot for my perfectionist mother's standards.

I had been taught self-grooming and hygiene, popular fashions among men lately, proper etiquette and social behaviors, proper demeanor around a potential mate, and so on.

My wolf's coat was much shinier and glossier, richer looking, than it had been when I had met her, so I hoped her wolf would like that when our wolves met. As well taken care of as her hair was, I could only assume that her wolf was as primped and preened as she, and her father had only confirmed that suspicion himself.

I would need to look good for her to impress her.

I fought, very hard, not to hate the need and drive to impress her...because we were going to be married, soon.

I had gained quite a bit of muscle in my training, as well, so her human form should be just as attracted to my human form as our wolves would be to one another.

I knew my wolf was larger than average for our age group.

I was taught dancing, *mating techniques...*

● ● ●

I was even taught how to *groom my female*, in the event that she became pregnant with pups and was struggling to do so herself.

I was taught that a male was reverent and honoring of his female, that he took care of her in all aspects, because she was the one who was given to him by Selene, and she was the one who gave him his pups.

Females may be the *submissive* role of our race, but they were in the inner workings of the pack and produced more males for the pack.

I had, indeed, learned that they were not simply supposed to be submissives in a certainly place. In fact, the females of our race were, truly, seen as almost holy beings, especially since males *outnumbered* females.

Many, many years ago, there had even been a female recorded who had been given *four* mates in a single pack, because there were almost twice the amount males in her pack than there were females.

Males were expected to keep their mates happy, because the females provide so much for the packs. They may be lesser...but in *many ways*, they were *more*.

Us males did our utmost to show them that and make sure they felt as important as they were.

"You need to remember, son," my father had told me. "Remember that a female is a gift in the first place, but a *beta's daughter*? She is to be respected, held in high regard. She was born to mate with high-ranked males. Most *alphas* are mated to former beta's daughters, you know. You are lucky, indeed, to get a beta's daughter."

"You also need to keep in mind, my dear, that she was raised by a beta couple, with the impression and belief that her mate would hold her in the highest light in his life. He would only put Selene, the alpha, and the luna above her. You may not be destined, true mates, but you will mate and mark her all the same. You must not let your feelings get in the way of honoring her the way that she deserves. Do you understand?" My mother asked.

"Yes, mother. Yes, father."

"Good. Now," father said. "Tomorrow is the arranged day. I expect you to give her the care and attention and respect that she deserves. If she gives you any problems—which I don't expect that she will—then trust her father to take care of it. Until you two are legally marked and mated, she is not yours to discipline—"

"She is my responsibility to *protect, nurture, care for, respect* and *love*. I am her mate to be, *not* her *parent*."

My father gave a tight nod, and straightened his back. "Stand proud, my son. Tomorrow, you will become a bridge to reuniting us with our other half—the pack will be united, you will become the official beta heir of the united pack, and the pack will be renamed. It is an extreme honor, and we must see it as such. Both packs have lost members to territory disputes over the last few years, but with a united pack, we will stand stronger than the other packs in this area."

I gave a bow, and a fist over my heart, as I had been taught to respect one of my own ranking or a similar rank. "Yes, father."

CHAPTER 4

Cloud...

The following morning, we set out with the entire pack, leaving the mountains to travel down to the forest where my mate-to-be lived.

My heart pounded in my chest, nervous and dreadful anticipation.

I had turned thirteen in Moon's Dance of the previous year, and she was turning thirteen this month.

In our society, one of our people was born with an inner wolf who would awaken when we turned seven years of age—or one year old, for the wolf. At age seven, we would have our first shift, name our wolf, and learn the history of our pack.

When we turned fourteen years of age—two years old for the wolf—we began our search for a mate, and I'm sure you've already grasped that concept by now.

To avoid my instincts to find my true mate, I had been given scent-blockers and a lot of training in preparation to become Dove's mate, and now, we were meeting to complete the mating before I turned fourteen.

The trip took a couple of hours, and I was suddenly overwhelmed by the smell of food floating through the air and decorations all in the trees and space around us, and suddenly...

Suddenly, I was hit with the reality.

It was not an idea trapped in my head anymore. No, no longer an idea or a thought.

I was getting married.

I would have to join her and two officiates out in the forest to the sacred circle, where all of the wedding ceremonies and markings were conducted, and we would shift in front of each other for the first time, to allow our wolves to meet one another...*and,* I would have to make her submit to me...either by instinct, or by force.

I shook off the thought of the girl whose scent had always appealed to me, pushing her cute, round face out of my mind. I hadn't been able to smell her scent in quite some time, so it wasn't as hard to let it go, now.

After that class had ended earlier this year, she had tried to approach me afterward, but I had turned tail and run. I ran, as fast as I could, out of the school and all the way home. I had rushed to my house and locked myself in my room, panting and gripping my hair in my hands, before I had taken my scent blockers so that the smell would leave me.

I couldn't let myself think of having a true mate, because I was already promised to someone for the sake of our combined packs. The poor girl that I had been drawn to would hopefully find another male who would take interest in her, and be able to bond to her and become her true mate. That wasn't set in stone, after all, until the Moon Mother finalized it during the mating.

The scent was just the start.

There was so much more to it, more complex things to consider.

The initial scenting interest, for pups, was to gain interest in a mate prospect. If you were meant to be true mates when your wolf had their second awakening, only then would the *mate* scent be picked up.

It was up to the individuals whether or not they chose to accept or reject their mates.

In ninety-eight percent of cases, they were accepted.

Hopefully, if I started pushing away the scent interest before we awakened, we might have a chance?

You and I—we will treat mate right, Slater's thoughts trickled in. *Mate will be pleased. She will see how strong we are, and that we won't hate her. Mate will submit.*

I could only pray that he was right.

'Mate still isn't the mate I would have chosen,' I grumbled to him.

My human thinks too much. Mate means partner, love will come later. She will come to love us; I will love her.

'Can I love her the same way I'd love my true mate?' I wondered.

Mate is mate, true mate or not, he growled. *Wolves only have one <u>marked</u> mate for life. She submits or not, I mark her either way. You told me so. Alpha orders us to. She is mate. I am beta. I protect alpha and mate. Mate gives me strong pups. Not complicated. Silly human mind stifles me with too much thinking.*

Perhaps he was right…perhaps I really *did* just think about it too much.

He seemed to be confident about the situation.

I hoped that meant that he knew what he was talking about.

We reached the pack house, and were welcomed by the alpha. "Welcome, Terra-Stone brother pack! This is truly a momentous occasion. A union to celebrate."

"Thank you, Alpha Falcon, for your warm welcome," my uncle said, nodding. "The prepared decorations and feast look and smell incredible, and we are very happy to see your excitement for this union."

"Ah, yes, well. Beta Raven and his daughter have already gone to the Sacred Circle and await us to join them. If you will follow me," he said, turning.

I gulped, and my father and I followed after him, even as my mother and my aunt joined the other luna and beta female.

I took deep, calming breaths.

It was about a twenty-minute walk to our destination, and we came through to a clearing of the forest. There was a fire-pit in the middle, with wooden benches spaced around in a circle around it. In front of the fire was a large, flat concrete circle on the ground, surrounded by planted flowers.

That is where Beta Raven and Dove stood, waiting for us.

There was a small, intimate fire going behind them in the fire-pit, and butterflies were flitting about in the bright sun-beams streaking through the trees.

It was truly a momentously beautiful sight.

I caught sight of my bride, in a pretty white sun-dress. Her sun-kissed tan skin looked ever darker against her lighter gray hair and her white dress.

She wore a beautiful, delicate rose-gold chain around her neck, with moon-stone embedded into a rose-gold casing that rested on her collar-bone.

I remembered my teacher going over this with me, telling me that the moon-stone was tradition for a beta or alpha couple to wear during the bonding ceremony.

It increased the odds of pleasing Selene, because moon-stone was her blessed gem.

Gamma females and lower ranks typically didn't worry about such a thing, but beta and alpha females believed in the superstition. As higher-ranked wolves, they wanted to be sure that their males, with their permission, had the blessing of Selene upon the union.

● ● ●

I noticed to the side that the pack's shaman also stood nearby, with a branch of sage and lavender wrapped in tiny beads of moon-stone lay in her hands.

"Welcome," Beta Raven said, baring his neck to his alpha and my own. Then, he held his hand out to my father and they grasped forearms—a familial greeting of friendship. Then, he extended the same greeting to me before he pulled me into the circle. "Today, we bear witness to a unique moment in history—a moment so rare that *each* incident of it has been recorded and kept track of throughout the couple's lifespan afterward."

I gulped.

I remembered having heard that before.

Almost every detail of those four couples' lives had been recorded, and it was terrifying to be under that sort of scrutiny.

"We gather here today," the shaman began. "To bind these two in a mate bond. They will shift before one another, battle for submission, and then the male will mark her...may we pray that Selene blesses the union so that it not be necessary to do so by force."

I could feel my gut churning at the thought.

If Selene was displeased at the idea of our union and didn't give her blessing, Dove wouldn't get the instinct to submit to me and they would have to hold her down so I could mark her by force.

Forced markings went against a wolf's instinct, because it meant she was always going to fight him and that meant a life of difficulty.

A forced marking was extremely disrespectful, almost akin to *raping* a female.

It was literally binding her to you in a marriage-type bond against her will by force, tying her to you.

It was also extremely painful.

If a female submitted, her body would relax and you could mark her in the correct place peacefully so as not to cause extra pain or trauma, and her body would accept the mark.

If she refused, her body would continue to struggle and you ran the risk of seriously injuring her during the marking.

Not only that, but her body rejected the mark and you would have to continue marking her *every year,* or until she accepts you *and* submitted, in order to keep her bound to you because rejection of the bond meant unbinding.

In the *mating ritual*, when it came time to have intimacy, if a female accepted your mark after submitting, she would mark you upon the physical act of mating.

Though only one case of *forced submission* had ever been recorded, the female had *never* marked her male, and it had caused her to be driven mad with anger and bitterness. She had died after birthing only one pup. *That* arranged marriage had been highly unwanted by both parties, and the male himself had struggled to mark her. They'd had to give him a drug to cause him to desire her, and she'd been held down.

It hadn't ended well.

Then, their entire line lad been cursed, and they had been cast out as rogues after multiple generations of extreme misfortune...in order to protect the pack.

I shook the thought from my mind, bringing myself back to the present.

I watched my bride, hoping against all hope that she had improved and that she matched me better now...and that I could please her, in turn.

I *needed* her to submit to me by her own instinct.

If she refused, a forced marking would only cause great strife and anger in our relationship and having pups would be much harder.

● ● ●

"We come together to join this beta heir and beta female heiress in matrimony, as bonded mates. We seek the favor of our great moon mother, Selene, and be for her blessing in this union. We seek protection against foes outside our territory, and justice for our fallen members to the violence of those seeking to force us out."

Our fathers and the alphas left the circle, but the shaman remained. "Face one another." We did so. "Beta male Cloud, do you promise to hold true and remain loyal and faithful to this female? Do you promise to protect and provide for her, and treat her as your true mate?"

I forced down the cringe and forced the tremble from my voice, straightening my spine, bowed my head before turning my gaze and looking down at my fiancé. "I promise."

"Beta female heiress," the shaman addressed. "Do you promise you hold true and remain loyal and faithful to this male? Do you promise to respect and revere him, and treat him as your true mate?"

I half expected for her to argue or pause, but without any hesitation or even missing a beat, she bowed her head. Then, her bright, vivid emerald-green eyes met my gaze.

"I promise," she said, and I felt tingles rush through my spine all the way down my arms and to my fingertips.

Her voice had changed, so much so that I struggled to believe it was the same bratty-mouthed kid I had met two years ago.

It was then that I really took in her body. Her hair cascaded in waves around her, her heart-shaped face framed by it. Her body was petite but gaining curve definition as she aged, filling out a bit more. She was shorter than me, but her back was straight and proud and she carried herself gracefully.

Indeed, I liked this girl much better than I had liked her initially. I hadn't expected her to answer so calmly and clearly. I could feel that my wolf liked the change, too.

● ● ●

I hoped, deep in my heart, that this meant that she wouldn't fight me when the time to mark her came.

"*Oh, blessed moon-mother, Selene*," the shaman spread her arms wide, and we started as the air in the clearing got dark. The sun was still shining, but it was like we were inside of a forcefield of darkness. One single, small orb of white, moon-like light lit at the top of the dome. "*We seek your favor and blessing*." She looked to us. "*Remove your clothes, and shift before the presence of our great mother*."

My heart pounded, and the alphas and our fathers turned their gazes from us, focusing only on the light at the top center of the dome.

I took a quick, deep calming breath before I untied the loop that held my shirt in place, and I pushed it off of my shoulders. I pushed my pants down, trying to ignore the discomfort of being naked before the shaman and this girl before me.

I waited, and after only a moment of hesitation and openly looking upon my form, my bride trembled slightly as she held my gaze and untied the straps of her sundress.

She pushed it down, stripping off her panties and standing bare before us.

She was beautiful. Her skin was free of scars, creamy and silky and smooth. She had not been trained for combat the way that I had, and it showed. She was actually rather dainty and petite.

She held my gaze defiantly, and that was a problem. If *she* couldn't be demure and submissive, her wolf wouldn't, either.

I could only hope that shifting into my wolf would help her get to the mindset she needed, because at present, it wasn't looking good.

Mate challenges us, Slater whispered in awe. **She isn't defying...she is asking us to rise to the challenge, prove ourselves to her.**

Another voice drifted into my mind when I watched her give me pleading eyes and clasp her hands...

A voice that I didn't recognize personally, but that my soul resonated with.

"Earn her submission and prove that you can earn the right to be her male...because I do not bless this union!" The voice shouted. "I gave you each a true mate, and you spit it in my face. Your union shall not be blessed."

CHAPTER 5

Dove...

I had to admit that his body was beautiful. I had already known about this part of the ceremony; my mother having told me how it would go just last night.

I had been taught, over the last two years, that holding my gaze on the ground or on his feet would be best, that I wasn't supposed to be defiant or rude.

I needed to be demure, so that his wolf wouldn't feel aggressive...but I needed to make him earn it.

I had been taught, over the last two years, that I was to hold my tongue, keep my opinions to myself, keep my emotions in check. I was supposed to let him have my body when he wanted it, and he would take care of me in kind.

I was to bear pups for him, and do so with honor. I was to be reverent and respectful and hold my beta male in high regard...as my mate.

In the deepest part of my heart of hearts, though, I needed him to prove to me that he deserved me. Not just because we were forced to do this, but because he was powerful enough to make me.

I was the daughter of a beta. I had been a spoiled princess for far too long, I admit that, but this wasn't from a place of being spoiled.

This was from a place in my heart of being a strong, desirable female, just as my parents had raised me up to be, and having a high pedigree and a powerful lineage behind me. I would provide strong, able, powerful pups for my male someday.

If this man was going to take the place of the male who had been attracted to me from childhood and given to me by Selene, then I was going to make him *earn* it.

I couldn't say why, but every instinct in my mind was telling me this was wrong. That this wasn't okay. This wasn't acceptable.

He hadn't been my original, destined true mate...so I needed him to prove to me that he could earn that place.

I only hoped that whatever male had wanted me to begin with could find a female as worthy of him as he would have had to be worthy of me.

I was the highest ranked female in my pack below my aunt and my mother, the luna and beta female. I was worthy of a strong, powerful, honorable mate.

I just was.

I knew what I had to offer.

So, I held his gaze with defiance.

'Please, please,' I pleaded in my mind. '*Please understand my intent. Please earn this role,*' I begged. '*Please prove that you can earn it and take the place of the male who was destined to truly love me, please Selene...*'

His eyes narrowed a bit as I pleaded with him with my eyes, and I slightly—marginally—lowered my head and turned my face, clasping my hands in front of me in a pleading manner.

His eyes widened, and he glanced at the fake moon at the top of the dome before looking at me again.

Then, I saw just the faintest hint of a smirk on his lips, and I heard the first crack, even as the moon faded, but the space inside of the force-field stayed dark.

● ● ●

"What's happening?!" Cloud's father gasped as the winds picked up inside the space.

"We were rejected by Selene! The beta heir will now have to fight to *earn* his place as her female and force submission!"

"Damn it all!" The alpha of his pack cried, covering his mouth. "She rejected us?"

"Selene does not like arranged marriages!" My father shouted. "It seems like this will just have to be done the old-fashioned way...by force," he said, voice grave.

I looked to Cloud, who was mid-shift.

I cringed as he growled beneath his breath, surprising me with how quickly the breaks and forming gripped his body. He made almost no complaint, which was highly impressive in its own right.

Within only three minutes, he stood there as a wolf.

For our age group, it was nearly unheard of to shift that fast.

He was a dark, glossy grey wolf. He was a large size for his age, already the size of an adult omega male. Considering that his wolf was only just under two years of age, that meant that he would be quite sizeable when he reached maturity. An admirable trait.

I could feel my wolf pacing in my mind, wanting to get out and meet him.

So, that meant that *she* liked what *she* was seeing, at least.

That was a good sign.

We had been rejected by moon mother Selene, so now, we had to fight it out, and he had to force me to submit.

I had to admit, I was terrified.

I pictured myself as my wolf, imagining the shift, and I felt the first cracks set in.

I did my best to contain my cries, but I had only shifted a couple of times, and it didn't seem to get any easier.

A sharp gasp left my throat, before I finally felt the form take hold, and I lowered to all fours.

I stood, shaking out my fur and stretching, before I stood before him in all my wolf's glory.

She was a beautiful, shiny, silvery-gray wolf, a bit smaller than average because I, myself, was short. She had perky ears and great posture, and she stood there patiently and waited for him to bask in her presence.

She was a bit of a drama queen.

Her fur was long and shiny and glossy, pristine. Her tail was poofy and swept with its long fur, and I looked well-brushed and groomed. Even her nails were trimmed and filed, the fur shaped up around her paws and hind-quarters, and her face held regality with the way her cheek-fur swept out. Almost like a fox. She was a very foxy-wolf.

She felt *rich*.

I had paid special attention to her lately, to be sure she was pleasing to the eye. I wanted for my mate-to-be to be pleased, at least.

He circled around me, and I could feel him looking me up and down, appraising me. I took the moment to see him from all sides too. His fur hadn't been trimmed or shaped, and his nails weren't filed—though they weren't long and jagged or chipped, either, so that meant that he at least kept those trimmed up and managed.

He looked like a darker, rougher, more ragged version of my wolf, but I was still impressed with how glossy and clean he looked.

He took good care of his wolf, and most males who took care of their wolves took good care of their mates.

It wasn't as if taking care of one's wolf was all that hard. Omegas helped each other with the task, but the higher ranked wolves had servants to help them with their wolves' upkeep. All you had to do was request it.

Generally, the more care that you showed for your wolf, the more desirable you were as a partner, because that meant you would care for your partner, too.

Still, many wolves didn't care much about all that.

As long as they were bathed and didn't stink, they called it a day.

Higher ranked wolves had to care a bit more, because we held the esteem of the rest of the pack...especially us females.

After a few more moments of checking me over, he *finally* gave me some feedback;

I could practically *feel* the small, purr-like rumbling growl that echoed inside of his chest as he looked at me...and relief struck me hard.

He was pleased. That was a pleased sound.

As we yipped and sniffed and circled one another, I could feel it as my wolf's tail wagged, and I rolled my eyes in my mind.

We could talk to our wolves and get a general sense of their emotions and desires, and sometimes they could give us instinctive or almost verbal responses to things, but we couldn't hold real conversations with them.

They didn't speak English to us or anything, like some novels and legends lead normal humans to believe. At least, to *my* knowledge, they didn't.

But with this pleasant, familiar greeting with this male, my wolf's emotions perked up.

She had been depressed, earlier, knowing the situation in a general sense. We were being married by arrangement, not by *choice*...

Now, though, that he was expressing his pleased feelings to her, she was responding in kind. She was much happier that he wasn't rejecting her.

My beauty queen had been quite worried that his handsome wolf wouldn't find her appealing, and I had thought she was crazy. If *any* wolf found us unappealing, I wouldn't understand it.

She was a stunning female.

I looked up at him through thick lashes, the black of my eye-lids a vivid contrast to the bright green of my wolf's eyes.

He paused in front of me, facing me again, and I could feel the air shifting. His instincts were shifting from greeting and familiarizing and play, to a more hazed, physical instinct; *the instinct to claim.*

His wolf was on board, then, and ready to act.

The air was changing as he stood taller, looking down at me, squaring his shoulders and rumbling low in his chest...a dominant sound, this time, more forceful than before. My wolf, however, was of the same rank as him and refused to submit so easily.

His head pulled back a bit, and he lifted his muzzle, making sure he looked proud and ready for me to give in to him.

My senses stirred and my fur bristled as my wolf, Silver, read his body language and responded, and I knew what his wolf was telling me.

'He is signaling for me to submit peacefully. One last-ditch effort to go without a fight,' I directed the thought to my wolf, even though I was sure she knew better than I did.

I stood strong and unwavering, however, and he cocked his head. He was confused.

I just couldn't.

Every instinct in me told me to fight him.

He didn't deserve me. Not yet.

He didn't deserve what belonged to another.

He huffed, giving a tight nod, but I didn't respond.

I watched him as he began to pace back in forth in front of me, coming closer slowly.

He tugged in a deep breath of air, puffing out his chest in an intimidating manner, but my wolf and I held our position.

He growled low again, the same dominant sound, but a bit louder and more gravely than before.

Again, I didn't move. In fact, I pulled my shoulders back, challenging.

I had already cleared this with his human, but the wolves had to settle things between *themselves*, separate from our human forms…and male wolves were much more obstinate about the submission than their human counterparts. His wolf would have to convince my wolf, herself.

This was now between the two of them.

Our human minds didn't hold a great deal of control over our wolves.

Wolves ran free and had their own instincts, so for the most part, as long as our wolves agreed with us and we agreed with them—we let them act of their own accord. They were their own beings with their own minds, after all.

I felt the instant he chose, and though I tried not to, my wolf ducked when he leapt at me, and she spun around on her heel, snarling at him.

She may like his wolf, but it seemed that she shared my sentiment from earlier—he would have to *earn* our submission, and she wasn't going to make it easy.

I dodged and parried him a few times, snapping at him and nabbing his fur a couple times.

He came closer and snarled an aggravated sound, getting frustrated with cat-and-mouse. His wolf wanted a fight, if I was going to be stubborn enough to fight against the submission physically this way.

'Fine,' I decided. 'I'll stay still, as he wishes,' I snickered in my mind to my wolf.

The next time that he lunged at me, he barreled right into me and took me off my feet.

He seemed absolutely startled, eyes wide as he rounded on me again, surprised that I had stayed still this time, and he skittered away in a cautious manner, trying to observe me...make sure he hadn't injured me.

He wanted for me to submit to him, not to hurt me. The entire goal of this fight was to earn my wolf and I.

He lunged again, and my wolf bit his shoulder.

He barked, shaking me off and pushing into me, before snapping at my face. I backed off, turning and lunging at him, trying to get to his back.

We continued biting and snapping, lunging and pushing, pushing and pulling...

Finally, after about an hour and with our witnesses getting restless, I was starting to tire.

My wolf was panting hard, struggling to remain focused.

I hadn't ever used her to this capacity before, and so her stamina was at its limit.

She had done well, all things considered.

He was tired too, but he could sense that my ending was near. The energy in the air changed, and he seemed more like a predator, now that he could sense that the end of the hunt was coming and that he was soon to have his reward for his perseverance.

As he lunged at me, I waited until the right moment before I caught him by the ear.

● ● ●

He yelped out a snarl, and I gasped in pain as I felt his paw slam down onto my shoulder and he latched his teeth into my neck...the only snag was, he missed my marking spot.

Though, I was impressed that he had finally landed a solid bite onto me.

He hadn't yet, just as I hadn't landed a *solid* bite on him, either.

A sudden calm, refreshing, amazing feeling swept through me in that moment, and I realized that my wolf was exhausted. She could no longer fight, and though she was a little frustrated that she had lost the battle, she was proud at her progress and ability...

Furthermore, I was proud that I had, in fact, made him actually earn it.

"*Now!*" My father shouted, and while I was distracted and tired, the two alphas and two betas grabbed me, each grabbing a leg and pulling them.

CHAPTER 6

Dove...

Like a tidal wave breaking onto the shore, my legs collapsed beneath me, and my chin slammed the ground as I began to whine.

I didn't like this...!

They were *making* me submit, by force!

My belly rubbed the ground, and I could hear the change in Cloud's snarl as he suddenly realized what was happening.

They popped open a small glass bottle of mating pheromones—or, more accurately, a liquid that the scientist of our pack had developed to help females struggling to enter heat for pup conception by boosting her pheromones and throwing her into heat—and they poured some onto me.

My body began to sting and thrum, and I panted hard as I struggled to glance up at Cloud.

It was time to mark me by force, now that my wolf was tired and he'd beaten the spirit from me.

Now, it was time to win the fight by marking me and ending it.

He let out a pleased sounding growl rolling out from his belly as he trotted happily over to me like some giddy puppy—all too happy to win the fight and take his prize—and he got into position, kneeling over me.

He nuzzled his muzzle into the scruff of my neck fur, sniffing and scenting me, giving me a good lick...he was deciding where to place it, trying to make sure he put it in a safe spot on me that wouldn't injure me.

Considering that I was already injured, I was having a hard time understanding why it mattered. I would already have to see the pack doctor after that bite from him earlier.

Though we had to mark in our wolf-forms, it *was* sometimes difficult—especially with *long* fur, like mine—to determine exactly *where* the marking spot was located.

I tried to fight, but the shaman got to my head and forced me still, holding my head in place with a lock-grab and hold that impressed me for her age.

I could not move in any direction.

He pulled away, meeting my eyes, and I looked away, as the shaman turned my head so that I was *forcefully* baring my neck—the uninjured side—for him.

He stepped around and came to stand over me again, his large paws on either side of my shoulders, and the shaman tilted my head to the side to give him the access he needed as she completed my submission for him.

His *instincts* told him—from my *body language and forced scent from the pheromone hormone booster*—that I was submitting.

That was the purpose of forcing me into this position and pouring that liquid on me, you see.

All *he* was seeing, in that moment, was my marking place and my body position. Smelling my scent, feeling my body's heat rising in response to him.

They may as well be invisible. They physically manipulated me to give all the signs of a submitted female, but he wasn't actually seeing them.

● ● ●

Now, I was held deathly still...because if I moved a hair, the results could turn fatal. Hinderance could mean injury, or even be fatal, if I moved at the wrong moment. I had to remain perfectly still.

He leaned in close again, and then he was sinking his fangs into my marking spot.

Selene had rejected our union, but he had managed to get my submission by fighting me for it, so it still wasn't as bad as it *could* have been.

I yelped as the pain set in, and I did my utmost best not to move.

The pain was excruciating.

Forced markings with forced submissions were always painful, and in that moment, I really resented Selene even more.

Not only had I been put into a situation where I couldn't have my true mate, but now, I was in a position where she hadn't even been gracious enough to bless my new union...?

Did she only wish pain for me?

My wolf weakened drastically at the thought, and I whimpered.

I shouldn't have thought that. Thinking horrible things about Selene and being bitter toward her weakened our wolves...

Though, I would be permanently weakened now, considering that I had proceeded with the forced marking with Cloud, and gone against Selene's wishes. We would be cursed for this.

He let out happy, contended rumbles. He had won, and he had made me submit. He had marked me.

He had been pleased.

I was pleased that he had earned it, at the very least, even if I was upset.

* * *

"The marriage and marking ceremony are now complete," the shaman said as Cloud released me, and he moved to lapping at the wound for a moment to clean it up before he backed off, stepping off to the side to allow me some breathing room. "Rejected by Selene, but called by desperate times to perform desperate measures...we plead to Selene, here and now, to forgive this transgression and to not curse us, at the very least."

The darkness cleared and the force-field dissipated, but the sun was setting, now. The clearing was growing darker.

"We will not force you to mate in front of us. The mating mark is enough. So, we will leave you two to shift and redress on your own," Alpha Sierra said. "We will meet you all back at the pack house."

They all turned and left, and Cloud and I just sat in our wolf forms, catching our breaths.

I couldn't move.

My body and mind were reeling, even as the forged mating bond continued stringing us together, tying us together.

I felt his feelings trickling in, I could smell his wonderful woodsy, musky cedar and pine scent with a hint of honey-suckles.

I could feel his power rolling off of him, his *strength*.

I could sense his concern for me as I continue to lay sprawled out, seemingly uncaring that we were expected to be somewhere.

My belly rumbled, hunger starting to take the forefront of my senses.

Irritation, as well, that I had been left here, injured, without even being shown concern by any of these assholes who had made us do this.

I needed to see a doctor, but I was so hungry and tired...

● ● ●

Hunger and sleep, that was what I wanted. I whined, too drained to stand but ready to eat and rest. My wolf had used up all of her power.

He stood, trotting to me and pacing around me, looking at me with worried eyes.

Wolves were generally much more expressive than humans, and thus more expressive than us in our human forms. They didn't hold it back or hide it beneath the surface or pretend...

They just let it all out.

He whined, nudging me with his nose and licking my cheek. Then he was pacing again, and looking after where our witnesses had left.

My belly rumbled, and I remembered that I was starving. I had been so nervous that I hadn't eaten all day, scared that I would vomit.

I *tried* to stand, but my legs trembled, and gave out beneath me. My marking and my injury both throbbed, and I whined pitifully. My wolf just wasn't having it.

His wolf whined again, panicked, and rushed to my side, crawling on his belly to lay out beside of me and nosing my mark with his snout.

I whined as he sniffed it, looking over the damage done. It had been a thorough marking; I could feel it. It would look so dark on my human self. It had been clean and straight into the muscles there, marking my wolf as being his forever.

Once a marking was placed, there simply was no way of undoing it. If it was a forced marking, it would have to be replaced every year, but if she submitted to him?

No taking it back, no making it go away or disappear. She would be bonded to him for the rest of my life.

Once a mark was accepted and the female willingly submitted, rejecting it was nearly impossible, and it also had to be done with Selene's blessing…but even then, it would only fade after a year. The affects would go away, but the scar would linger. Even then, you would still feel attachment and pain when you saw the ex-mate.

No, this was meant to be for life, and I had been forced to submit, but that didn't change anything.

My wolf was forever branded either way, though, because even if I never willingly submitted…he would have to mark me every year, until I did…

There was no going back, now.

He licked it and it tingled, sending pleasant little sparks through my body.

I trembled, my heart racing at the new sensations he caused.

Most of all, I was stunned by how he acted almost as if he…were actually, truly concerned. He acted like a loving mate.

Was this just a show?

Could I trust this to be genuine concern? Or was this just the hormones, because the pheromones that were rolling off of me due to that liquid told him that I was going into heat?

His wolf pressed up against me, nosing his snout under the crook of my front leg and helping me force them up. Then he helped me get up on all fours slowly, and with his support and leaning against his body, he helped me come to stand.

I took a deep breath, allowing my mind to picture my wolf turning into my human form again, and I felt the bones slowly shifting and popping as they moved again.

He watched me with concerned eyes, warm and compassionate.

I knew, vaguely, what he was thinking as slivers of thought trickled in through our bond.

● ● ●

Cloud knew just how tired I was, and shifting when you are exhausted is *much* harder.

I groaned, tears streaking my cheeks as the mark burned the base of my neck, where my neck met my shoulder.

It was *large* on my human body—the size still of his wolf-form's mouth on my skin. The top-jaw portion sat upon my collar-bone, whereas the bottom-jaw portion sat on my shoulder and shoulder-blade.

It was still bleeding lightly, but it was already on its way to healing. The other bite mark actually looked much gnarlier and like it would need medical attention.

He had been a little over eager for that bite.

Still, the mating mark itself? It looked like a clean job, which meant that I had stayed nice and still and he had been able to get to the correct spot properly without any blunders.

I was startled when he was suddenly against me in human form, holding me up and helping me to stay steady on my feet.

How...had he shifted so quickly?

Though, I had to remember that were talking about a beta heir. He had been trained since birth to fight and be strong and powerful, so of *course*, he had probably shifted *many* more times than I had.

It probably wasn't even painful to him anymore.

It *had* taken me much longer to shift earlier, I had noticed.

"Up we go," he said, his voice low and pleasant to listen to as it soothed into my ear. "There," he said. His eyes met mine, and I felt my cheeks warm up.

"Thank you," I said, baring my neck to him.

This is all because of the mating mark. I was convinced that it was.

He chuckled. "You submit so easily, now?" He asked. "You sure made me work for it," he said.

I didn't respond.

"I understand," he said. "I *needed* to earn it. I heard a voice tell me that," he said, and I gaped at him, surprised. He smiled at me. "You were right to hold your position. I needed to prove to you that I was worthy for you to submit to me, and I did. If I hadn't, you never would have felt the instinct to give yourself over to me, would you?"

I shook my head. "I d-didn't...I didn't...actually submit willingly, remember? They *forced* me to submit to you. As soon as I was tuckered out and injured, they..." I drifted off, ashamed and still reeling from the humiliation.

"They what?" He asked, cupping my cheek in his hand.

"...They grabbed me by the legs, and forced me to the ground. They held me still the entire time, even turning my head into submission position for you. They doused my fur in pheromone booster..."

He startled. "*What?*"

"I know you didn't see them. You only saw my wolf, my submitting...but it was forced."

"Oh...oh, no," he said, soft and face full of regret. "*That's* why you were in so much pain...?" He asked, taking my face in his hands, and lifting my face to look him full on in the face. "Dove, I'm so sorry...I didn't know."

I shook my head. "Don't worry. The submission might not have been natural, and Selene might not have blessed the union, but..." I sighed. "You *did* earn it," I said. "I was about to submit, and my wolf is satisfied. She just...didn't get to submit because they interfered. They must have thought I would keep fighting if they didn't stop me."

"I am sorry that you were forced into it...but I am glad that I earned it, in your eyes."

● ● ●

He grinned a bright grin at me, and surprised me when he brought my dress to me, helping me get it onto my body and tying the straps in place.

"You seem to be particularly tired," he noted. "And I mean beyond your being injured. I am sorry about that, by the way."

I nodded. "I don't shift very often," I admitted. "Silver isn't used to getting out much."

He looked at me. "She likes her name," he told me, a small smile in place. "Your wolf told my wolf that she loves her human, and that he would have to get through her to have you."

"You knew her name?" I asked.

"When you shift as often as I do, you learn to understand more of your wolf than a lot of our kind do. That's why alphas, betas and gammas are so powerful. It is more like a *thought* in your own mind, a whisper. Asking them *directly*...doesn't work. But the thought will just come. Go on, try picturing my wolf in your mind and think of his name. I am sure you will know it."

I pictured his dark grey wolf in my mind's eye, and remembered his actions and lunges and attacks, the light green eyes he had...

Slater...

The name startled me, popping up out of nowhere and in my own mind's voice.

"Slater," I said.

He nodded; his eyes warm. "Yes, his name is Slater." He dressed himself, and then he turned to me. "And just so you know...he likes your wolf." He cleared his throat. "...And you.."

I blushed. "I-I'm glad..."

He cleared his throat. "Anyway, I guess we should join the others back at the pack house, huh? You sounded hungry earlier."

I blushed, and he turned around, walking away.

Maybe being his wife...wouldn't be as bad as I had thought, after all...

CHAPTER 7

Dove...

We arrived back after a twenty-minute walk, but by the time we arrived, he had to have my arm wrapped over his shoulders and he had to help me with my steps. My legs were barely hanging on, and I was struggling to hold on to my conscious mind.

I wanted sleep...but there was still one major detail that we hadn't been told, yet.

"Ah, they've returned," Alpha Falcon exclaimed. "We were just telling everyone the exciting news about the submission and how hard he fought to earn it. What a power couple!" He laughed. "And so, now we can all discuss how things will go from here. Now that our beta heir has his beta female marked and ready, we can decide where to go from here."

I was thoroughly perturbed that they made it sound as if the union had been blessed and I had submitted...but that hadn't been the case.

They're omitting details to help morale, I see.

My injury and the marking—which were being eyed by pack members—were throbbing in pain as their lack of care resonated in me.

I had always been so special to my pack. The beta's only child, his daughter...

● ● ●

To be so disregarded stung more than I could ever put into voice.

Cloud hugged me a little tighter.

"We have decided that for the time being, each ranked family will be staying in the Terra-Forest pack's pack house until a new pack house can be built between the two packs, and we can section off the completed territory. We will begin construction on new homes closer to this new pack house, and this pack house will become a guard station."

"What about the alpha and beta and gamma?" The gamma asked.

"The Alpha title will fall to the stronger of the two alphas...Alpha Falcon. He is, I am a little embarrassed to admit, physically more powerful and mentally better prepared than I am," Alpha Sierra said. "He also has more experience. Therefore, I will become the Defensive Gamma for the combined pack. My son, who already forfeited his rank as my alpha heir, will become a delta, and any future son I may have will become a gamma heir for whichever gamma needs an heir."

"As for beta," my father spoke up. "Beta Valley and I have discussed it, and I will remain beta for the pack since I am already Beta for Alpha Falcon. He will become the Offensive Gamma for the combined packs. The Terra-Forest Pack's former Offensive Gamma will become a secondary Pack Hunter, and will work strictly with our warriors and head the deltas."

"The future beta and beta female are Beta Heir Cloud, my son, and his new bride," my father-in-law said. "The Defensive Gamma Heir that she has will pledge to her, and I will pledge to Cloud and the alpha."

I suddenly felt a strange prickle, and I glanced down the table to see a cute, round-faced, young-looking female staring at Cloud.

I felt...strangely uncomfortable, oddly enough. Why was she bothering me? Well, it was simple. She wasn't just simply looking with a passing glance, no...

She was outright staring, to the point of being rude, almost.

I watched, intrigued, as Cloud went out of his way to avoid looking at her, and it suddenly clicked.

That was his true mate; the one who *would* have been, anyway.

She was cute, in a childish kind of way. She noticed me staring and immediately looked down, staring at her plate.

Ah, so she was a submissive, the thought floated through my mind. **She likely would have submitted right away instead of making Slater earn the right to mark her.**

I was surprised by the thought, and I realized that Cloud had been right. When I thought of *wolves*, in general, my wolf would let her thoughts drift to me. I couldn't converse with her directly, but if I didn't focus on *her*, my mind let me understand her thoughts.

I couldn't believe Cloud had helped me connect with her when I had thought that wasn't possible.

"So," Alpha Falcon's luna, Basil, said to us. "As for the matter of where you two will be staying. For now, you may stay on the Beta-floor of the pack house. There are two rooms there, and the former beta couple of the Terra-Stone pack will be sleeping there for now. It will be fine if the two of you share that space, as the beta heirs of the pack."

"Thank you," Cloud said, nodding to her respectfully before looking to me. "Is that alright with you?" He asked, and I startled.

He was...actually asking for my thoughts?

I nodded. "Yes, that is fine with me."

"It is settled, then," she said, clasping her hands. "We will adjourn there once the feast is over."

We all set to eating, then, digging into the wonderful spit-roasted meats and sauteed vegetables that were offered at the table, before sleep started to overtake me.

● ● ●

I heard a small sigh and a soft, single-scoff chuckling sound, before I felt my body lifted.

I fought for a moment, before his voice reached me, low and right at my ear. "Easy, easy. I am just carrying you to the pack house to go to bed. You are exhausted, and it is time for you to get some rest."

I let my body relax a bit, but I was still too uncomfortable to be completely at ease around him.

I may have marked by him, but I didn't trust him completely.

I was starting to lose consciousness, but my wary mind forced me to keep some awareness of my surroundings as I felt us arrive to the pack house by the cliff-side. I heard some deltas welcome us and let us inside, telling us the area was secure and that the beta floor was on the second floor. I heard Cloud asking them to retrieve the pack doctor, and send him to our room to tend to my injury.

Then, we made our way to the beta-floor of the pack house.

The alpha level was in the basement; the most protected space. The gamma and delta floor was the ground-level floor. The second floor up from the ground floor was the beta and pack-hunter level.

Cloud carried me up the stairs, and I heard him request to one of the maids that she bring me a spare set of clothes and a pair of pajamas, as well as a tooth-brush and tooth-paste.

After setting me on the bed, he took off my shoes and necklace, before the omega girl returned with what he'd requested and he dismissed her, shutting the door behind her.

Then, I felt him come over to me and sit on the edge of the bed.

"Dove," he said, his voice quiet. "May I take care of you?" He asked. "If you say no, I will respect that."

He is truly trying to do right by us, now. He might not love us, but he respects us for making him earn our submission. Slater told me he will take care of us.

I knew that Silver was right.

I barely opened my eyes, and I saw him watching me quietly.

"Is...t-that...okay...?" I murmured in a slur.

"Of course, it is," he told me. "May I?" He asked again.

I gave a single relenting nod, granting permission, and bared my neck to him—the spot that he'd marked.

I vaguely felt him moving me, heard his voice murmuring the steps he was going through.

I felt him hold my mouth open and brush my teeth. Then, I felt it when he made too change my clothes and slip me into some silky-feeling pj's, and I even felt him brush out my heavy, thick wavy hair as he told me that he was thankful that, even if Selene didn't bless our union...he wouldn't ever hold that against me.

He wouldn't disrespect me. He wouldn't make me regret being with him, and he wouldn't let me be bitter.

He would take care of me from that point forward.

How thankful he was that I trusted him enough to *let* him take care of me, and that he wouldn't hurt me.

I heard as he brought the pack doctor in, and he was attentive and paying heed to what he was told as far as my care...and how regretful he was that I needed stitches, because the wound had been so jagged and torn, and was at risk for infection.

I heard him walk the doctor out, before he lay me in bed and tucked me in, stroking strands of my hair out of my face before he got into bed beside of me.

I felt him curl, minutely, toward me, in a protective sort of way, but not touching me. Giving me my space.

• • •

Finally, in that moment, I felt Silver let go.

She let my body relax entirely, and I slipped into sleep. I was no longer holding onto consciousness, and I felt nothing but peace.

It was something I had never anticipated.

I awoke to the smell of bacon and eggs and toast, teasing my stomach as it rumbled in hunger.

I heard a light laugh—a woman.

"He said you would be hungry," she said.

I peeked my eyes open, and saw a young omega woman there, wearing a maid's uniform. Her voice sounded familiar.

"Ah, good morning," she said. "You must be wondering where your mate is," she said. "He had a meeting this morning with the alphas and—I mean, alpha, beta, and gammas. He said to let you sleep until you woke up and then to feed you well, before you go to join him at the meeting."

"I see," I said. "Thank you," I smiled at her.

I didn't remember her name, because she normally took care of cleaning the pack house, but since everyone was so busy with other business, she must have had to do the servant work, also.

"Of course, beta heiress," she smiled.

"Has everyone else eaten breakfast? Is there anything that I can help with?" I asked, ready to help.

I would usually offer help around the pack, trying to help everyone out and lessen the burden around the pack.

"Anything I need help with?" She asked.

"Direction or overseeing? Any extra work?" I asked. As the beta heiress, it was my job to help out with things around the pack and running the pack, and when the alpha heir chose a luna, I would be assisting her directly with taking care of the pack.

Until then, most of that work fell to the beta female and heiress.

She shook her head. "No, miss. Everything has been taken care of today, the beta female took care of it all today. Your father and mother and your mate all said that you just need to get to the meeting after you rest and eat." Then, she bowed her head, hand over heart, before she scurried out.

I ate my breakfast in peace, enjoying the flavor of the amazing omelet with bacon and herbs I had been given and toast with butter on the side served with orange juice to drink, and I stretched, flinching at the pain in my shoulder.

I stood, making my way to the dresser against the wall where a large mirror stood beside of it in a frame. I looked at myself, my eyes zeroing in on the large, thick-scabbed, purple and black area where Cloud had marked me.

It had, been a forced mark, but it hadn't been as bad and horrible as it could have been.

Furthermore, when I thought of him... imagining him changing me and wiping the blood away himself, even brushing my hair and my teeth...changing my clothes...

I felt myself almost...pulsing. What was this?

What was the pulsing?

It was strange. I hadn't ever felt this way.

My heart beats felt sluggish and thick, sloshy almost, and my body felt tingly as my belly throbbed down low.

What was this feeling...?

Imagining him taking care of me, it...made me blush and made me feel...hot.

Was I embarrassed? Where was this feeling even coming from?

I could feel my wolf in my mind, her tail wagging so hard I could practically hear it thumping the ground.

Was she...happy when I thought of Cloud?

Then, there was Slater...

He had been quite pretty, for sure. His coat was pretty, though it wasn't as glossy and shiny as my own, but he looked like he took good care of it.

How had he known how to brush my hair and to brush my teeth? Or wipe me clean? Did he just do it because he felt obligated, or had he wanted to take care of me?

Too many questions swirled around my mind as my fingers danced over the burning, tingling mate's mark on the base of my neck.

When I thought of him and his wolf, the mark throbbed and heated.

Was that normal...?

Silver's words replayed in my mind...

Slater told me he will take care of us.

A blush spread across my cheeks.

CHAPTER 8

Cloud...

She arrived about two hours after I had left, and I smiled to myself. She had slept for thirteen or fourteen hours, and I knew that she needed the rest. She had clearly worn herself out the day before.

When she had clasped her hands together, in almost a pleading fashion, I had suddenly heard a warm, deep chuckle and a sweet voice tell me that she wanted—needed—for me to earn my place as her male, to prove to her I deserved her and what she had to offer me.

I, of course, had obliged. I couldn't fault her for that. I wasn't originally the male meant for her wolf—that much was obvious by the fact that the Moon Mother had rejected our union—so I couldn't get mad at her that she wanted to have me earn that position.

It had been a grueling battle, shockingly; I had to admit as much. She was impressive, considering that I knew for a fact that she had never had any training.

That was the beta blood in her, making her stronger than average females.

She would certainly produce strong pups.

She had finally been worn down, however, when I had managed to inflict a pretty serious wound on her, and then...

Then, all I that I could remembering was having had seen her in a submissive position.

I hadn't realized it was forced, but as I thought of it now...her scent hadn't changed naturally. She wasn't at the age for her mating scent to produce naturally on its own, and the liquid they had put on her may have stimulated that scent in her body to be released and throw her into a pre-aged heat, but it wasn't natural...

Naturally, her scent hadn't truly changed for me until I had placed my marking on her.

Indeed, she smelled quite...pleasant to me, whereas *before*, I hadn't cared one way or the other about her scent.

Now, she smelled of wildflowers and pine with a hint of cinnamon, and I found that I really quite enjoyed the scent, relished in the smell.

That *hadn't happened until I marked her.*

I was concerned that Selene hadn't blessed the union. It was known that she wasn't fond of blessing arranged unions, but to reject us, only to tell me I had to fight Dove and *earn* the submission?

That was even more than just forcing a female still and marking by force.

That was an actual *fight* for the marking.

I was still bothered that they had literally forced her down for the marking...that turned my stomach and made me uncomfortable. They had interfered too soon because she had been ready to submit on her own.

Interfering and making her submit had actually made things worse.

When we all sat together, the alpha and beta waited for us to settle before addressing us.

"Now that the two of you have both arrived, we need to begin discussing the future of this pack. You both know that you are the beta couple of the future, once the beta retires and the next alpha takes his place, but today is another day filled with symbolism. There have already been some...*growing pains* among the deltas and omegas, wondering about rankings and who would be taking over in the future," Alpha Falcon explained.

"And so, we have reached a solution. Today, the future ranked members will go before the pack and make their vows of loyalty...today."

"*Today?*" I asked. "That isn't how it normally works. Normally, the oaths aren't taken until we take those roles, because of the bonds that form with the oath."

When a beta swore his oath of loyalty to his alpha, it created a bond that caused you to be close to them, and going against them would be excruciatingly painful...and in the event of their death, you would feel their death in your own body. It could drive one mad, potentially.

It was a serious, not-to-be-taken-lightly bond.

"We need to show the pack the new generation and let them know that we have order and stability. They are all restless. Because the union was rejected by our matron, well, it seems that the more...*lunar-biased* wolves are upset that it wasn't a *natural* union forged by the Moon Mother's design. They are furious that the union was completed without a blessing."

I glanced at Dove, and she lowered her eyes, timid...I could almost imagine that there was a faint blush on her cheeks, but I couldn't let myself believe that it was really there.

She has grown, the thought flittered through my mind from Slater. **Bashful, timid, and nervous around us. Her wolf is very happy we are her male. She is embarrassed that her submission was interfered with and they got in the way.**

Embarrassed...?

Her wolf is...happy?

'Are you sure?' I asked my wolf, thinking again of the sleek, beautiful silver wolf of my mate.

Her wolf likes us, and so now she starts to thin of us the way her wolf does. She is nervous about being mates but likes that we are her mate. She is hurt that she was forced to submit before she got to herself. Betas and alphas made a mistake. They hurt mate.

I contemplated what that really meant. Did that mean that she could grow feelings for me?

Would she?

Furthermore, I was even more bothered that she was upset and embarrassed. She had truly been ready to submit on her own before they interfered and forced it, and had hurt my mate.

How could we fix this without growing resentment and bitterness toward the alphas and betas?

"Alright," Alpha Falcon said, standing up. "Let's proceed."

We followed him outside, and he got everyone gathered together faster than I had thought.

"As you all know, yesterday we joined and became one pack again. I remained the alpha, and Beta Raven remained beta. We added a second gamma and gamma heir to the pack. However, that wasn't enough to root out the growing pains and ease doubts among the pack completely. We understand the reluctance to accept unions that aren't blessed by Moon Mother Selene...however, this was a necessary move for us to make. It is a heavy burden we must face. All we can do is ask for the Mother's understanding and forgiveness."

"So, today, we will have the Alpha heir, Beta heir, and Gamma heirs step forward to give their oaths to one another and proclaim their future positions," Beta Raven said.

The crowd murmured as the group of next generation leaders stepped forward, and I waited to hear what was said.

● ● ●

"I, Finch Terra, son of Alpha Falcon and Luna Basil, do hereby proclaim my position as Alpha Heir in front of the pack and by the blessing of Selene. I vow to look after the best interests of the pack, protect the pack, and love the pack as my brothers and sisters. I vow to find a suitable luna to help run the pack with me, and to respect my luna, my beta, my gammas, and my deltas. I also vow to respect the omegas who make up the bulk of the pack."

"Thank you, Alpha Heir Finch," Alpha Falcon said, proud. Then, he turned to me, and I took it as my cue.

"I, Cloud Stone, son of former Beta, now Offensive Gamma, Valley Stone and his mate, Violet Ivy, do hereby proclaim my position as Beta Heir in front of the pack and by the blessing of Selene. I vow my loyalty to my Alpha Heir, Finch Terra. I vow to have his back, help him manage the pack, advise him, and protect him."

We both gasped, and I collapsed to my knees and bared my neck to him on instinct, pledging myself as his beta.

I could hear vague thoughts from his wolf conversing with my own, but I let them have their own moment.

I chose, instead, to continue my vow. "I vow to be a guiding, protective force for my fellow pack members. I vow to honor, respect, protect and love the pack as my brothers and sisters. I vow to honor and respect my beta female, Dove Terra—now Dove Stone—and to be available to you all as a united beta couple. I vow to respect my Alpha, future luna, beta female, the gammas and the deltas, as well as the omegas."

I felt the overwhelming surge of energy as my soul's strings reached out and touched the strings of all of the other souls around me, and I took a deep breath, steadying myself.

I felt the bonds forge within me.

My already-started bond with Dove strengthened even more, and I felt her emotions within me, if only slightly.

● ● ●

I knew that mated couples forged a bond even deeper than those between regular pack members, but none of the mated wolves had told me what it was like.

Now, I understood why; because it couldn't be explained in simple words.

The feeling was...incredible, invasive, and vaguely terrifying...

"Thank you, Beta Heir Cloud," Alpha Falcon smiled. "Beta female heiress?" He asked, turning to Dove.

"I, Dove Terra—I mean, Dove Stone—daughter of Beta Raven and Beta Female Jade Rose, mate of Beta Heir Cloud Stone, proclaim my position as Beta Female Heiress. I vow my loyalty to my Alpha Heir, Finch Terra, and his future luna. As Beta Heiress, I vow my service and protection, as dictated by the Beta Female position, to the Luna. I vow to protect and serve her, to have her back, and watch after her. I vow my loyalty to my mate and Beta Heir, Cloud Stone. I vow to honor, nurture and support my alpha and luna, to look after my gamma heir, and be here as a comforting nurturer for the pack. I vow to love the pack, and honor you all. I vow to submit to my alpha heir and my beta heir, and honor their decisions, though I also vow to help advise and support them when they make those decisions."

"Thank you, Beta Heiress Dove," Falcon said.

My heart thumped wildly in my chest, playing over her words.

She vowed to honor and support me, *submit* to me...

I wished that she could have submitted to me naturally. Slater really wanted that, and it was a constant thought in my mind.

I was a little bothered by it, but Slater made sure that I knew that I couldn't feel negativity toward the alphas and betas about it...or else I risked looking disloyal.

Alpha Falcon just continued on down the line.

● ● ●

"I, Crow Terra, son of Alpha Falcon and Luna Basil, proclaim my position as the Defensive Gamma Heir. I vow my loyalty to my Alpha Heir, Finch Terra and his future luna. I vow my loyalty to my Beta Heir, Cloud Stone, but most of all, as my position strictly dictates my protection and service to the Beta Female, Beta Heiress Dove Stone. I vow to protect her, have her back, support her, honor her, serve her, and watch after her." I heard her sharp intake of breath as he said this, and he gasped as his knees buckled, forcing him to kneel.

It was a powerful thing, to have a definitive, dictated task-given position.

Because there was no luna, yet, Dove hadn't been made to kneel, but because the gamma heir had a beta heiress to pledge to, it brought him to his knees as his vow took hold.

Taking a deep, steadying breath, he continued on. "I vow to coordinate with the Offensive Gamma Heir, to protect and defend the pack, and support them. I vow to honor, protect, and respect my fellow pack members, the deltas, and omegas."

"Thank you, Defensive Gamma Heir Crow," the alpha said.

There was only one final oath to hear, from the gamma heir that originally came from my pack.

"I, Granite Grove, son of deceased Defensive Gamma Cotton Grove and Gamma Female Lavender Stone, proclaim my position as the Offensive Gamma Heir. I vow my loyalty to Alpha Heir Finch Terra and his future luna. I vow loyalty to Beta Heir Cloud Stone, as is my dictated position, and to help with offensive battle strategies and war for the pack. I vow to honor, protect, shield, and kill for this pack, to love this pack and all of its members. I vow to look after them and watch over my deltas. I vow to respect all ranks of the pack, from alpha to omega."

I felt the bond snap into place yet again, and I was better prepared this time.

● ● ●

"I, Sparrow Onyx, son of the former Offensive Gamma, now Secondary Pack Hunter, Terran Onyx and former Gamma Female Robin Rose, proclaim my position as the Pack Hunter Heir. I vow my loyalty to Alpha Heir Finch Terra and his future luna, Beta Heir Cloud Stone and his female, Dove Terra...Dove *Stone*," he grumbled that bit. "I vow to perform my duties and protect and honor the pack and all of its members. I vow to respect members of all ranks."

That final bond snapped into place, but this one...felt a little different.

Something about him stuck out to me, something about his smell...he smelled good.

Did I usually think that?

CHAPTER 9

Cloud...

"As of now, we are, officially, the **Terra-Forest-Stone pack**. I, Falcon Terra, am your Alpha, with my Luna, Basil. We have Beta couple, Raven and Jade Terra. Defensive Gamma Sierra Stone. We have our Offensive Gamma, Valley Stone. We have our Pack Hunters Olive Rock and Terran Onyx. For our next generation, we have Alpha Heir Finch Terra, Beta Heir and Heiress Cloud Stone and Dove Stone, formerly Dove Terra. We have Defensive Gamma Heir Crow Terra, and Offensive Gamma Heir Granite Grove. Our Pack Hunter heir is Sparrow Onyx. Welcome, one and all, to the Terra-Forest-Stone pack, nestled into the mountains and forests at the heart of Tennessee. You are all dismissed, please report back to your homes and await further news via mind-link."

The final pack-bond snapped into place with the announcement as we all accepted his proclamation, and I struggled to remain composed. It was a dizzying experience, and I reached out to help steady my mate.

Crow came over to her side, smiling at her. "Congratulations, cousin," he smiled at her.

She rolled her eyes, but smiled and brought him into a tight hug. He laughed, before giving me a nod. "Beta Heir Cloud," he smiled.

"Defensive Gamma Heir Crow," I laughed.

"I will know if you ever make my dear beta female cry," he promised. "I am her official body guard, you know," he smirked.

"I will do my utmost not to hurt her," I vowed...and I meant it.

I noted, out of the corner of my eye, that she gasped and stared at me in awe for a moment.

"Alright, everyone," Alpha Falcon refocused our attention. "Now that we have the positions set and secured, and we have the new pack-link in place, we will host our very first formal pack run this morning. We will use this as an opportunity to hunt, to learn one another's wolves and learn about each other's strengths. Let us all adjourn to have some lunch, and then we will meet this evening at sunset. All awakened wolves are encouraged to participate, but if you fear for your child's safety, they may remain behind with the delta females who are watching the young pups."

There were murmurs and chattering among the pack, and most of us seemed to agree that a pack run—especially our first run as a whole, united pack—was important for us.

Pack runs were a bonding experience.

A pack who ran together were close to each other.

For a newly formed pack, it was very important to use this time to bond and learn one another.

Although we wouldn't see each other shift—each of us would do that in private with our parents or mates beforehand and then meet at the pack house to set out for the run—we would still be able to recognize one another by our scents.

As wolves, we each had an individual scent characteristic; no matter how slight the difference may be, we would be able to smell it.

Just as every human smelled different to dogs, the same could be said for our kind.

In our wolf forms, our scent was marginally stronger, easier to recognize. That, and most of our wolves resembled our human forms. Our fur as a wolf was, ninety-nine percent of the time, the same color as our human form's hair. Our eyes were brighter, but they were still the same general color.

Most of all, it was important to let our wolves meet each other and build bonds of friendship and potential mates as their own form, because they had their own individual minds from us.

Even if I, for example, disliked someone, my wolf may very well like and be on great terms with their wolf.

Our wolves needed to know each other so that we could protect each other in case of attacks, too. We wouldn't want to accidentally hurt one another because we didn't recognize someone from our own pack.

We were all dismissed, and Dove and I walked in a peaceful silence back to the pack house for a light lunch.

It would be our first pack run and hunt as a couple, which was yet another huge milestone for a wolf.

Pack runs were a good chance to demonstrate how fast and strong you were, and hunts were to prove how cunning, skilled, and powerful the wolf within you was. As a newly mated male, it was even more than that;

It was a chance to prove to my mate that her submission to me was not given error, that she could trust me to provide for her.

In the lion pride, it was the females' jobs to hunt for the pride...but in the wolf pack, it was a male's job to provide for the pack.

The only exception to this rule was if the males were busy and unavailable, or if the delta females were hunting for the mothers of newborn pups while they nursed their young and hunted for the weaning pups.

"Are you excited?" I asked Dove off-handedly, making light conversation.

• • •

She gave a nod, a small smile gracing her lips. "Yes," she said. "It has been a while since the last pack run. Silver has missed her friends lately, so it'll be good to let her out with them for a while."

The thought of her true mate struck me, and I forced myself not to pause. "That is good, then. I am sure she will enjoy seeing them."

I knew that there was still a male out there whom had always liked her scent; a male whom would have claimed her as his own, a true mate.

He may even possibly approach her still, when he comes of age.

The idea of a pack run with a wolf that would have been her true mate...made Slater a bit uneasy.

Mate is ours, now, Slater's thoughts drifted through, a snarl to his tone. **Let another male come, see my mark on her...he will know who she belongs to.**

'She wouldn't have, though, Slater,' I reminded him, picturing her sleek, beautiful silver wolf with some random gray wolf in my mind. 'She might belong to us through these circumstances...but she would have belonged to another—'

Too bad for him, then. His loss, my gain. I will take care of her; prove she doesn't need that male. You will be good to her human and prove to her we can provide all she needs.

There was no convincing him otherwise. His thoughts were firm and solid in his head.

He was right, in a sense, though.

There was no taking back my mark.

Any male who came for her and realized she was claimed would more than likely be upset...there was a small chance he could turn violent.

Most of the arranged marriages that had taken place in the past, were with males and females who hadn't ever been drawn to anyone and seemed to be mate-less.

The one case where a potential mate did show up later, she had turned aggressive and tried to attack the other female to claim the male.

Such a violent reaction from a female, I could only imagine how a male would respond. He might attack me, or *worse*...he might even attack *her*.

It was especially worrisome because the union had not been blessed. That meant that Selene still favored him as her true mate. It was completely up to Dove which way she would choose to go.

"Cloud?" I heard Dove call me, as if she had said my name several times.

"Oh," I said, looking to her and chuckling. "Sorry, Slater's thoughts were coming through. What did you say?"

"I asked if you were feeling excited for the pack run?"

"Ah," I said. "Yes, I am. It will be nice to meet everyone's wolves."

She gave me a shy smile, before turning to her plate.

When had we been served food...?

I shook off the question, reminding myself that talking to my wolf put my human body into auto-pilot.

We sat and ate peacefully, and Crow finished his lunch early and went to stand by the wall, waiting in case Dove needed anything.

After we finished eating and the omegas took our dishes, I stood. "Come with me, please," I told Dove, and she gave me a confused expression before she trailed after me to the bedroom.

I turned to face her once we were in the bedroom. "Let me see," I said.

She blushed, gasping with wide eyes, and I realized what she thought first.

● ● ●

"I mean the *mark*," I said quickly, my cheeks heating up. "Of course, I meant the mark." I cleared my throat. "I want to make sure it is doing alright. You..."

Crow crossed his arms, leaning against the wall nearby, as Dove cocked her head at me. "I...?"

"You looked...tense earlier," I said, rubbing the back of my neck. "I just wanted to make sure it was okay."

She gave me a surprised look, before a shy smile. She turned her back to me, pulling the loose neck of her top to the side and down her shoulder, baring it for me.

I stepped over, looking over the bite.

It was nice and clean with no jagged edges or traces of infection...though, it was still bright red and scabbed more than I would have thought.

Her wolf was struggling to heal it properly, it seemed.

Most markings healed within a few days, only leaving a scar behind.

Crow whistled from the corner. "Look at the *size* of that jaw! Holy-moly, Dove, how did *that* feel?"

She made a begrudged, groaning laugh, short. "It hurt. A *lot*. But thanks to them all holding me in place, I stayed nice and still for the marking, so it didn't turn out as bad as it could have."

"But that jaw set, wow, look how big it is. How large was his wolf?"

"Much bigger than average for our age," she smiled, shy. Her cheeks flushed with a blush. "He was...quite impressive, I admit."

My wolf's tail wagged and chest puffed up with pride at her praise.

"It seems so," he commented. "Goodness. One of the cleanest, best, well-placed marks I've seen. A good testament of the amount of control his wolf has, especially since it was a forced mark."

She flushed a bit darker. She knew it was true.

I leaned over her, and I felt my eyes burn as I summoned Slater forward, concentrating on my tongue.

I had been working on using my abilities as a wolf-shifter for years—ever since he woke up, when I was seven.

I was determined early on as a child that I wanted to be close to my wolf and to have great control over his power. A determination that many wolves my age did not share.

I met her eyes, her wide gaze meeting mine, and I lapped my tongue over the wound.

She hissed out in pain, before I could feel the teeth markings against my tongue heating up, and her groan turned into a moan of confused pleasure.

I could feel the tingles in my own tongue, radiating out into my body from my mouth.

Our wolves were still under the mating age, but we were close enough to the age of awakening our mating senses to connect through the sparks the bond forged within us.

She would be fourteen in a year, and I would be fourteen in just few mere months.

"Does that feel better?" I asked her, and she nodded.

"Yes, oddly..."

"I am glad to hear that. I wanted to use my shifter abilities to help heal it and comfort you a bit."

She nodded. "Thank you," she said, looking away with a blush on her face.

The day continued to pass, until it was time for us to get going.

Crow went out into the edge of the woods, and I followed Dove out to a good spot that was clear of witnesses.

She took a deep breath, and I heard her murmuring to herself. I focused, and I could hear whispered self-encouragements.

I had noticed, when I saw her shift before, that her shift was slow and she seemed almost...apprehensive about it.

"Do you...struggle to shift?" I asked her.

Her eyes whirled to look at me, shocked. Then, she looked down to the ground, pushing her toes into the dirt and looking sheepish. She gave a single nod. "Yes. It seems to drag out too long. When I've seen other wolves shift, it doesn't seem to hurt them as much or take as long."

I gave a thoughtful nod. "Yes, it does seem to be particularly difficult for you. I noticed that Silver was a little smaller than average for our age group..."

Though, I wondered what that had to do with anything.

'Any ideas why she may be struggling?' I asked my wolf.

He was quiet for a long, long time, even as I thought of her and her wolf. I was just beginning to think that he wouldn't respond at all, when I finally heard his thoughts.

Mate is disconnected from moon, he said, his voice sounding sad. **Mate's spirit broke when she felt the loss of the future with a true mate. That is what Silver told me.**

'The loss of true—**oh**,' I realized.

It all went back to when we had learned that we were to be in an arranged marriage, *two years ago*.

Learning that she wouldn't be able to find love the way that our Moon Mother intended, especially at her rank...it broke her spirit.

That was also why she had fought submission so hard, making me earn the right to be her male.

Then, the interference and forcing of the submission had broken her even further, going against the moon mother and cutting her further off.

So, in a small sense, it was our fault. We had both been victims of circumstance, but I was the highest ranked single male who could marry her and forge the alliance of our packs. I was the male she was bonded to.

I pictured her wolf, standing alone and struggling on her own, wondering how I could help her.

Our duty, Slater said, determined. ***We protect mate, teach mate. Comfort mate, reassure her. Encourage, touch her while she shifts so she feels better. I will help Silver.***

I gave a nod, in response to him and in affirmation of what I needed to do.

"Slater wants you to begin your shift...I think I can help you."

She glanced at me, nervous. "A-are you sure...? Shifting is so painful, and I—" She paused as she held my gaze, and she finally nodded, baring her neck in submission to my demand like a good girl for me. "Okay."

She took a deep breath, and I began hearing the pops start, a pained groan erupting from her.

"I-I'm scared," she admitted, whimpering.

I took a deep breath myself, placing my hand on her mark. She startled, looking at me.

"You can do it. I am right here, right here with you. You're a brave girl. Don't fight her."

Her eyes wide, cheeks flushed, she watched me. "I can do this..."

"You've done it before," I reminded, as gently as I could. "Silver needs you to let her out. Come, now, good girl," I said at some particularly loud pops.

I watched as the bones shifted, and she whined softly.

"Such a good girl," I said. "You are doing well."

"It...doesn't hurt...as bad as normal," she panted out.

I smiled at her, and I was thankful that as usual, Slater had been right on target.

Keeping physical contact with her helped to lessen the pain, because of the good feelings the sparks brought.

I heard the spinal crack, and as she sobbed, I pulled her into my lap, letting her lay back against my chest.

"Easy does it," I tell her. "It's almost over," I told her as her wolf began to take shape in my lap, her hair shortening and turning into long, soft, silky fur.

It almost felt like plush, and I could barely contain the purr Slater let loose in me. So, so *soft*...

One final crack with a small, terrified yelp as I stroked her fur, and there she was.

Silver was a beautiful wolf, indeed.

"Good, good girl," I told her. "You did well. It didn't take you as long this time, and it didn't hurt as bad, did it?"

She stretched, shaking out her luxurious fur, before she gave me a small yip and a happy wag.

I was curious to get to know this wolf.

Each wolf had its own mind, separate thoughts from their human, their own feelings and personalities. Whereas Dove was still a bit shy and uncomfortable, wary almost. I understood why. It would take time for her to feel comfortable and open with me.

This wolf, though, seemed chipper and happy to see me.

"You are such a *pretty* girl," I commented.

She huffed, plopping to a sit, and looking to the side, sticking her nose in the air dramatically.

She is a lady, Slater scolded me. **Beta daughter is high rank. Beta female higher rank. Lady, lady! Not girl, amateur.**

"I'm sorry," I said quickly, amending my statement. "You are such a beautiful *lady*," I amended and emphasized.

She turned her snout to look at me and gave a happy yip again, wagging before she came and nuzzled my hand. She stuck her nose up again as she presented her back to me.

What...what was I...?

Fool human, stupid! Pet her! Slater groaned. **She deemed you worthy to touch her, touch the female! Touch mate!**

'Alright, alright,' I laughed. 'Goodness, you're almost as dramatic as she is.'

Not dramatic, he thought as I began to stroke her wonderfully soft fur. **High standards, high maintenance. High class for high rank.**

'Snooty, is what you both seem to me,' I snickered to him.

After a few minutes of me petting her, she stood, hopping on her front paws and trotting in a circle before her chest pressed to the ground as she looked up at me, butt up in the air and wagging side to side with the force of her tail.

At least Silver seemed to be a pleasant wolf, I observed.

Dramatic, maybe, and possibly snooty, but happy. I hadn't ever seen her human this happy...

Would I ever see her human this happy?

I took a deep breath as I felt Slater pacing in my mind, knowing that he was telling me that he was ready.

● ● ●

I let the shift happen, barely feeling the pops and shifting of the bones, letting it flow naturally.

I'd never struggled much with it, but I had been made to shift so often for training that I just got used to it after a while.

It was obvious that Dove's family had let her remain in her human form as much as she wished, with no training for her human form nor her wolf form.

She was stronger than I would have anticipated, considering that this was the case, but she was still very weak in comparison to wolves who had training...and most of the delta females and other ranked females had training.

Considering her role to protect and serve the luna, I was shocked that she hadn't had physical training.

I took a back seat to watch, almost like it was a film that I was watching through my wolf's mind's eyes, as he took control of our wolf-form.

The two trotted around one another, sniffing and panting and yipping.

Slater immediately set to licking her face and shoulders, her neck specifically, to groom her and help heal the mark.

Mates were supposed to help with grooming, especially around the mark, but mates also had the ability to help heal one another's marks on their partners.

She began to pant heavily as he lavished his bite on her with attention, and I could feel his tail swish with his heavy wags as he felt the instinct to mount and hump her like a puppy.

'No!' I told him. 'Down. She isn't ready for mating yet. We must wait. We're also about to be around the pack.'

He huffed and I could practically feel him roll his eyes at me, but he resisted the urge, opting to continue his attention to his sealing mark upon her body.

We continued to circle one another for a minute before we played chase for a minute, and I chuckled as I watched him play with her.

They weren't even quite two, yet, so I supposed that it was okay to let them play this way.

They were basically pre-teens, the same as we were.

When they turned two—when the human form turned fourteen—they became adolescents, able to mate and reproduce and start their own families.

Most wolves waited a while, to let their wolves enjoy each other for a while first, usually waiting until they were about to be adults. By twenty-one—three, for our wolves— most of us had just had or were about to have pups.

We heard the summoning howl and the call of the alpha through the link to join up at the pack house, and so we bumped into each other playfully before we trotted out of the woods and back to the pack house building, where the pack was gathering together.

The alpha was a rough, sizeable grey wolf—his fur different shades of gray and streaks of silver, like pepper. His jade green eyes were even brighter than usual.

I could recognize members of her family, even as Crow's dark silver-grey wolf, with black hairs interspaced in his fur, trotted to us. He was larger than Dove's wolf, but a bit smaller than I was.

He sniffed us and bared his neck, showing us his submission as dictated, before the alpha barked to get our attention.

"Tonight, we run. We run, and we hunt, together. One pack. Terra-Forest-Stone pack, altogether." The Alpha finished a short speech via pack link in our minds, before he pulled back his head, letting a joyous and happy howl ring through the evening air.

We all joined in, and I listened as I caught sight of my mate howling, trying to single out her sound.

She had a soft, melodic tone that was just as beautiful and soft as she was.

How had I ever disliked her...? I had to wonder.

Wait...

What...?

I was just starting to contemplate how terrifying that thought was, when it was time to move.

Then, we set off, starting in a trot for a while before we ran.

CHAPTER 10

Dove...

I could hardly believe how much less pain I'd felt during this shift.

I could hardly believe that my mate actually sat there, comforting me, and staying at my side as I went through it.

That, and how at ease and happy his wolf seemed to be with mine.

They seemed so close already, it was baffling to me.

'*Silver seems to really be smitten with Slater,*' I thought, a bit sour about it.

I was still embarrassed and shy around Cloud. It was awkward, but he was so good looking and even though it was by arrangement and circumstance, technically...he was mine.

Did that mean that it was okay to want him...? I wasn't entirely sure.

Mate likes us, Silver thought, insistent. **Mate wants to provide for us, protect us. Mate wants us. I like mate.**

Well, at least *she* was happy.

He'd already managed to get on her good side, it seemed, so the next natural step seemed to be for me to get on board. I was a little annoyed about it, but that was because...I wasn't actually entirely bothered by it.

I was annoyed that this young man who I was in an arranged marriage with, I actually...didn't hate him.

I remembered all of the extensive training I had received, all of the work and effort and "education" I had been put through in order to be his wife...I was so angry about it for so long, but marrying him, I just...couldn't hate him.

He wasn't going anywhere, and neither was I. Mates, but especially arranged mates were for life.

I was mad that I wasn't angrier about it.

As the pack began to trot up to a run, together, I kept glancing at my mate. I noticed many others glancing at him, too.

Males and females alike, noting his size and power for our age range. It was unusual, admittedly, and something about that had me even more bothered by him...in a romantic way.

My mate was a strong male, and I was fortunate that even if he couldn't love me, I had an honorable male who would treat me the way I was supposed to be treated, and he was obviously strong and well-trained...

He seemed to respect me, if nothing else.

Though, he had been quite kind to me already. Hopefully, he'd noticed my much-improved behavior and manners and my controlled mouth.

Slater and Silver already liked each other...all that was left for the both of us to follow their lead, right?

I hoped it would be that simple.

We began to branch off as males began to track and stalk prey.

This was going to be a competition; I could tell already. We would see which male could prove his worth the best, what kind of prey he could catch, and how quickly.

Slater led us to a fallen log, where I heard his voice tell Silver to lay low and wait for him.

We sat, holding our position as we watched him hunting.

Within moments, he had a large hare in his hold, and he bit through its neck quickly before bringing the carcass to me in his mouth.

I picked it up by the hindleg in my teeth, and followed after him as he continued onward into the forest.

I had to admit that he'd done well on that hunt. He'd tracked it well, stalked it to its home, and killed it in just a few minutes. He was good.

He could hunt.

He continued catching and killing prey, and once he had landed a sizeable porcupine without a single quill injury to himself...I was sure that he could, at least, easily physically provide for me and our future pups.

My wolf wagged her tail, happy and content with his skills, and he in turn panted happily and gave her a timid but happy lick to the cheek.

They both froze, staring at one another for a long moment. Dark, shiny slate-grey against bright, white-tinted silver tones...

Light, pale green eyes against bright, vivid emerald eyes.

Large against small.

We were opposites of one another, but our wolves were very attracted to one another.

After a moment of deciding, Silver decided to wag her tail yet again, giving him a tentative lick on his cheek in return, and his tail wagged as well.

A sudden soft but sharp bark brought us back to ourselves, and I glanced over at Crow, watching us with a bored, withered expression.

I barked out a laugh, and I followed Cloud, Crow following me, as we carried our prize back to the pack house.

I noticed, after a moment, that only a few servants and a couple of guards remained.

"Where is everyone? I just realized that after we were told to stay here...only a few servants and guards remained." I asked Crow via pack link.

"Well, you did just...marry and get marked, so..."

"But why would that mean that they needed to stay—oh," I realized. They were giving us privacy, in case we wanted to...what? *"But don't they realize that this was an arranged marriage? Besides, the mating instinct isn't even fully awakened yet."*

"I don't know, but that was how they were thinking. The rest of us were told to steer clear if we didn't want to hear anything...strange."

"Oh, good gracious."

That did, however, let me know that I would need to request to my parents that a separate house be built for us.

My parents stayed at the pack house often, for business proceedings; that was why there was a designated floor for each rank, of course.

Each family, though, had their own home, just like humans.

Most of our homes were built into the ground, like wolf-dens, so they weren't very large and they were usually compact and cozy.

I glanced at Cloud, who was scanning the area as if he had noticed the same thing, turning to look at me.

• • •

"*Do you wish to stay here for the night?*" He asked me tentatively, but his voice was gruffer and thicker than his human form. This was the first time I was hearing his wolf speak via pack-link, and it took me a little too long—embarrassingly—to realize he was the one speaking.

"*Can we...find somewhere else?*" I asked. "*We are putting the others out, it seems. I have just been informed that the others didn't return before, because it was the day of our marriage and they thought we...*"

"*Oh,*" he said, barking out a laugh. "*Sillies,*" he scolded the pack's thinking lightly. "*I will search for a place. Stay and wait with the food, I will return.*"

I gave a nod and tail wag, and off he ran.

He was fast, and I realized with surprise that I had been holding him back earlier. I had been moving fairly quickly, but it was like a turtle in comparison.

He really was a beta, it seems.

I waited for him to return, even though I was hungry and I wanted to start eating.

Eating went by rank—so if I didn't have expressed permission to eat the food before he left, I was supposed to wait for him. It was a sign of respect.

As my mate, he was absolutely to eat before me, especially because he was the one who had hunted and killed the food. I couldn't eat until he told me that I could.

He returned as the sun was setting—about thirty minutes later. It took a moment, though, to realize it was him. As he was getting closer, Crow went on the defensive like the good gamma heir that he was.

Crow blocked me and snarled out a warning, but we heard a sharp bark and Crow put his belly to the ground, letting out a grumble.

"**Your gamma has gotten better. That is good**," Slater noted to me. "**I found a place. Come on, I want to make it before dark.**"

● ● ●

I lifted a few of the hares and Crow lifted the porcupine—carefully—and the other couple of hares.

Over all, we had six hares and the porcupine, so we had a good amount of good food to get us started.

I followed after Cloud, and after a while of walking deep into the forest, we reached a large burrow that went up beneath a large, thick oak deep in the forest.

There was a stream nearby, and the location was surrounded by flowers.

I went slack-jawed, staring in awe at what he had found for us.

Could this...really be real?

It was perfect for a new wolf couple starting out.

I gaped at him, and I saw him standing there, looking almost shy. He didn't look cocky or proud as I would have expected.

"This...this is amazing. *Can this be our new home?*" I asked him, and he startled a bit, eyes wide with surprise.

"*You...really like it?*"

"*It is perfect,*" I told him, walking toward the hole beneath the tree. Even the hole was covered well by shrubbery, and if it hadn't been for his moving it to the side, I wouldn't have noticed the entrance. "*It is well hidden, in a great location, a good size...great to start a new family.*"

If he could have blushed in this form, I was sure he would have been by that point.

He grumbled, clearing his throat, before he nudged his snout out toward the den, motioning for me to enter.

I picked up his kills again, stepping through the brush still covering the hole and into the den, before I set it down on a bed of leaves he had gathered by the entrance. Then I turned, looking around.

● ● ●
114

There was enough space for us to stand in our human forms, going deeper into the earth beneath the tree than I had thought.

I could already imagine a small, cozy home with two bedrooms built into the space, and a small cooking/sitting area for the family.

I could picture us painting it in here, and setting up our amenities...

"This is perfect," I reiterated to him, my heart pounding.

Surprising me, he came and gave my marking a good, loving lick, and I almost shuddered.

"I am glad," Slater, in control of the wolf now, told me. **"I hoped you'd be pleased."**

"What does Cloud think?" I asked Slater separately.

"He is satisfied, and even if he wasn't, I care not. I am wolf; I like this den. This den is good for mate and future pups. It took a lot of effort to find."

When his wolf spoke that way, my heart raced all the harder.

I glanced at Crow, who stood awkwardly by the entrance, looking to one of the walls.

I giggled a bit in my mind. *"Go on,"* I told him. *"You can find something nearby or go back, until I have your own space set up here."*

He gave a nod and quickly—a bit *too* happily— rushed back out.

Romance wasn't quite for preteen boys, obviously, though Cloud seemed to be decent at it so far.

"Shift?" Slater asked, looking to me as I faced him again.

I gave a nod. *"You first,"* I told him.

I heard the pops and cracks as he quickly began to return back to normal, and I turned my head so he could pull on some loose-fitting pants and a tunic-top.

Then he was at my side, sitting down on the earthen floor with his legs stretched out, waiting for me.

I lay on my side with my head on his thigh, facing his feet, as he petted my fur.

I took a deep breath, letting the breaks set in, groaning in pain as I let my human mind and human body be in charge once more.

As my vocal cords changed over, I could hear the sobs starting, but Cloud just waited patiently for me as he stroked my hair.

"Good girl," he said. "You are doing well."

I took a deep, steadying breath, focusing on his praise.

I couldn't explain how much his encouragement meant for me. My mother had been with me for my first shift, but every other shift after that, until my wedding day had been spent alone and in utter, sheer agony.

Cloud being here...it not only helped us bond, but it helped me trust him more.

Finally, I lay in my human form, trembling...naked.

Cloud kept his eyes on my face, save for one glance at my shaking body. Then, he stood, going and getting something from the other side of our new space and bringing it over.

It was my bag, I realized quickly.

The one that the servants had brought from my parents to the pack house while the meeting was taking place.

He'd gone back and gotten it even as he had found this place...?

• • •

He turned, and I sat up with a throbbing belly and chest as I pulled on a loose, soft night-tunic. My version of pajamas.

He turned to face me again when I told him I was finished changing, and he turned to the meat. "I will get these skinned, processed, and bleeding out," he said, taking them and hanging them out before he came back into the den. "Do you want to return to the pack for a while to get some cooked food, or would you like to just eat one of these without bleeding and curing it first? Have you ever had it straight wild?"

I realized what he was asking me.

Most wolves had eaten food straight from the hunt, but many preferred for it to be properly bled, cured, and cooked to make it much tastier.

If I wanted, we could go back to the pack and have a good meal that had already undergone that processing before we returned to our new den.

"I am fine with wild, if you would rather stay here. We will go with whichever you prefer, I am fine either way. Thank you for asking," I smiled at him.

Because many males don't bother being courteous enough to ask.

He gave a nod. "We can go back to the pack, then, and we can get some supplies while we go. Are you alright to walk that far? I know that shifting takes a lot of your energy and is painful for you, so if you want, I can shift back and carry you?"

I gaped at him for a moment, stunned.

Most wolves—especially high ranked wolves—would *never* offer someone a ride on their back.

Oh, how far out of the way he was going to be nice...

It made me feel my heart thump harder than usual, and my cheeks heated up.

"Oh, that isn't necessary, but thank you for considering me. I can walk, that is fine."

Cloud hadn't needed to carry me back to the pack house, but after a good meal and gathering supplies, as well as leftovers for later to take with us, we turned with some deltas to help us set up our space a bit more.

There was a thin mattress that would serve the both of us, some blankets, our toiletries, some lanterns, and a couple of cookware items.

We were also given a few gallons of clean drinking water.

We were well on our way, and the whole pack was excited to hear that we'd already chosen a den...because most wolves don't choose their own den until they are ready for mating.

There were several implications behind us getting our own den.

I was almost asleep by the time we got back, but it wasn't until I started stumbling along the path to our den that Cloud passed his arm-load to a delta and took *me* into his arms, instead.

I'd blushed, embarrassed, but Cloud hadn't seemed to mind it.

He knew that I'd had a tiring couple of days, and he made no complaints about my lack of energy.

In fact, he encouraged me to rest.

When we reached our space, the deltas set to helping us set up at Cloud's instructions right away, and we found out, as Crow appeared, that he had found a small den nearby himself and was taking care of his own needs but that he was just a mind-link away if needed.

Once the deltas left, I took a sleepy glance around at the space.

There was a lot of work left that needed to be done to turn this den into a home, but for now, it was more than adequate.

There was a mattress in the corner of the den, complete for now with blankets and pillows. Nearby were the jugs of drinking water, and Cloud had managed to have the deltas build a smoke-escape for a self-made cut out in the wall where he was building a fire-pit.

In essence, a fireplace that actually had a chimney.

Beside of this space sat our pot and pan with a couple of plates, a bowl, and a fork and spoon.

Over by the entrance sat our toiletries, so that when we needed to go out to do our business, we could just grab what we needed on the way out.

I saw that there was even a couple of towels there.

For now, we had a small old cooling box set up for our meat—I wasn't sure when or how that had been retrieved, but it was just an insulated metal box that was full of ice cubes. It didn't run on electricity or anything—it was just a cooler.

At least it wasn't like the cooling boxes that we used to have, before we found a wrecked shipping container full of these coolers.

We were pretty behind the times, it had seemed, when we found that truck. We had never seen anything like that before, but it was already wrecked when we had found it.

Although, to be fair, most shifter-packs were rumored to be very behind on modern technology.

I wouldn't know, because I had never been out in the human world outside of our packs, but I had heard from a few adrenaline adventure-addicts that they had been out in the human world, and that we were several decades—in some areas, even centuries—behind in technology.

Most shifter packs, however, were content to be so.

Our meat sat inside, and the box was latched and locked shut, stored in the far side of the den.

During the deltas' time here, they had even managed to install a frame around the inside of the entrance—which was like a fox-hole tunnel to the outside—and put hinges and a door, so we at least had somewhat of a manner of protection.

It was temporary for now, but all we had to do was open the door and crawl out of the tunnel to get outside.

Cloud lit the lantern and set it up by the bedside, a few feet away. Then, he came to my side after he had lit a fire and gotten it going well.

"Come, you need to get to sleep. Your eyes are droopy," he commented with a small smirk, teasing...though my yawn made me not care so much.

I glanced to the mattress, before I looked back to him. "So..."

"So," he repeated, glancing at the mattress before he met my eyes again. "Are we doing this?" He asked, as if he was guessing my question.

I nodded. "Yeah," I said. "How, though?"

"Take whichever side you prefer. I will sleep on the other side. If you prefer, I will put a blanket rolled up in the middle to separate us, but—"

"I'm not worried about that," I said. "Are you...sure you want to share the same bed?"

He looked a bit baffled by my question. "It isn't a problem. Besides, you and I are mates now. If we can't even share a bed for sleeping, how could we ever expect to be able to do more intimate things?"

I nodded. "Yeah. Okay. Yeah. We're good, that's good. Okay," I said, yawning again before I climbed into bed. "Good night, Cloud."

"Good night, Dove."

I slowly let myself drift into a fitful, light rest, though I felt strangely...safe.

CHAPTER 11

Cloud...

She fell asleep rather quickly, and I was surprised by how at ease she seemed. I truly hadn't anticipated that she would like the den at all, growing up in a high-status household, but for her to be comfortable and feel safe here...it made my wolf particularly pleased.

Though being able to find a good den in a good location was an excessively coveted quality for a male to have, I had been worried that she wouldn't be satisfied with what I would choose.

Perhaps she was a little less spoiled than I had thought.

Her breathing evened out quickly, and I smiled in spite of myself.

She liked the den.

She liked the den!

She was impressed by my hunting, she specifically requested a space to ourselves, and *then,* she actually liked what I had found for us?

It was a male's ego dream-come-true.

Before bed, I went out one last time to take care of my business in the woods nearby, so that she wasn't left alone.

Then, I went back to the den with Dove and allowed myself to crawl into bed.

She hadn't put anything between myself and her, and I was impressed by that, too.

I was almost asleep when I felt Dove's body instinctively turn to face the heat that had joined her in bed, and she cuddled into my side for warmth.

That was Silver, I knew. It was a wolf's instinct in sleep to be warm and protected, and most of the time, wild wolves huddled together in their dens.

Despite that it wasn't a cold time of year, it was still chilly during the nights, and we were underneath the ground. Of course, when the sun didn't hit any of this place, of course it stayed colder than anywhere above ground.

Shifter-wolves ran with hotter temperatures anyway, so it was a good thing that our hidden, earthen homes were so cool. It helped us not to be so hot.

I let Dove cuddle closer to me, not moving an inch as she brought herself over to my body.

When I felt that she had relaxed some, I smiled as I brought the blankets up to cover us before I gave a final glance at the makeshift door of our den, making sure for my instincts and my sanity's sakes that we were safe.

Then I finally allowed sleep to take me.

It was a light and restless, being that as the male— and a newly mated male, at that—protection of my den and female would fall to me first.

Dove was what packs would refer to as a last resort defense; only to fight if all of the males were unavailable, or...dead.

I wouldn't want for her to have to fight unless she had no other choice.

● ● ●

She was a beta's *daughter*, and since they didn't inherit the title of beta, they were usually untrained in anything beyond the basic wolf skills, self-defense, and light fighting strategy in an effort to protect the luna.

However, beta females were expected to and trained to sacrifice themselves for their beta male, luna and alpha, if it came down to it. Because of that mindset, they were used as a *last resort* method of protection, and males of the pack strove to protect the females anyway because males outnumbered females by a shocking amount.

Moreso than that, females were the future of the packs. They were encouraged not to fight unless they had to.

If anyone attacked the pack, she and the other females would be expected to hunker down in a den somewhere to hide.

The pups would be put at the very back, the luna and beta female in front of them.

The defensive gamma would be in front of those two, and then the omegas.

In front of everyone would be the delta females and the offensive and defensive gamma females, who did have a bit more training...just in case.

Being in a new place was always difficult when it came to sleep, but I was, even in my unconscious mind, glad that Dove seemed to be resting fine enough curled against me.

Some amount of time later, I heard the birds outside singing, and the pilfering of rabbits as they hopped past the den.

I heard a fox huffing and sniffing—likely smelling our meat—and then I heard a light growl and the pattering of feet as the fox took off in fear.

It sounded like Crow's growl, and I smiled to myself.

He had been much improved compared to when I first met him.

As the defensive gamma heir, it was his job to start watching out for the beta female and her den—most defensive gammas actually had a permanent home inside of or directly next to her den with his mate and pups as well—and anything that came too close that seemed like it would want to steal from or harm the beta female was ran off or fought.

I looked down to find Dove's leg thrown haphazardly over my own, but her torso was curled in to herself and her own space, arms up in front of her like a barrier of sorts, and her head was tucked into my ribcage, making my heart pound.

I gently disentangled myself from her, bringing the blankets back up to cover her as she stirred but remained asleep, and I stretched and took a good sip of water before I put on a tunic and pants and opened the door, crawling out of the tunnel and into the early morning air.

The air was crisp and cool, sharp with the smell of pollen, dirt, and evergreens. The sun was just peeking into the forest, coming up from the horizon to the west. Birds chirped and landed to eat from the ground before flying off. The bees were starting to stir.

Crow sat outside—in his wolf form—and looked to me as I stepped out.

He gave a huff and a nod of his head, and I gave him a nod in return.

• • •

"Thank you for your diligence," I told him. "I am glad Dove has such a capable defensive gamma. You have really improved, and I'm glad she has you to rely on." He gave a nod in response. "Was it a fox?" I asked, grinning at him. Another nod. "I thought so. Must have smelled the meat. I'm glad it wasn't a bear. We'll have to be a bit more careful about our hunting, it seems." I glanced around, taking a deep whiff of the air.

When it smelled clear and I didn't sense any danger, I looked back to him, still looking up at me for direction.

Wolf-shifters were quite a bit larger than wild wolves, so his shoulders reached up to my hips, his head and ears up to my abs...and he was *smaller* than *my* wolf form...

Yet, both of us were still smaller than adult males.

"Do you mind if I go for a quick run? Slater needs to stretch his legs, and he wants to patrol the area. He's still on high alert, what with a new den and a new mate to protect. It has been quite an adjustment. I'm sure you can imagine."

He gave a nod, and I let the energy flow through my body as I allowed myself to shift seamlessly.

When Slater was standing there in the space my human form had once occupied, he stretched, shook out his fur, and yipped out a greeting to Crow's wolf, whose name I didn't know yet.

He yipped softly back to me, before standing and moving over, taking a seat at the entrance to the den, ready to defend the beta female if someone came to disturb her.

"She is still resting, but she will likely wake soon," I told him through the pack link. *"I will try to return soon."*

When he gave me a tight nod, I turned and took off into the woods at a trot, letting Slater take over while I took a back seat ride.

Slater relieved our bladder and bowels before we shook off the dew from the bush leaves we'd brushed up against, and then we were off again.

I came across a few other wolves who bowed their heads and bared their necks before going on their way, but nothing beyond that.

By the time I got back to the den, I had determined that everything was indeed safe for now.

The only ones around were random small wild animals, and other members of our own pack.

When I returned, Crow and I both shifted back.

"Has she woken yet?" I asked him as he pulled on his clothes.

He shook his head. "I haven't heard her yet, but she may be awake in bed. She does that often, laying there lost in thought."

That had me slightly concerned.

Being idle was not common for our kind, and it left me wondering why. Still, I gave a nod. "You're welcome to come in and have breakfast, if you're hungry? Just keep it down so we don't accidentally wake her."

"Sure," he smiled, following me into the den.

We were quiet at first, until we saw and took note of the state of the female occupant.

She was actually already awake and cooking, putting together a quick meal.

As we stepped closer, she plated up a couple of dishes and handed them to us.

"I hadn't expected you be awake yet, let alone cooking," I smiled. "I figured you would still be resting."

"Well, I am used to getting up early and helping around the pack, with the warriors and whatnot. Please don't worry...my mother made sure and taught me well what is expected of females with my rank. I will do my very best to not disappoint you."

...She was a bit...different today...

I wasn't that worried about her disappointing me. In fact, I had actually anticipated that I wouldn't be very happy in this marriage.

To be fully honest, she was already doing much better than I had expected, and I was already more pleased with this situation than I had originally thought that I would be.

I gave a nod. "You are doing well," I told her, before I took a bite of the food. "And this," I said, pointing to the plate of food, "This is good," I said.

"Oh, thanks. I am glad you approve," she smiled softly. "It smells good," she complimented. "I will eat once I finish the dishes."

I watched her as she worked like a whirlwind around me, tidying and putting things away before she cleaned mine and Crow's dishes as soon as we had finished.

Then, she was finally able to sit and eat a little something, though admittedly...she barely ate enough to compensate for all the energy that she was expending, and I wondered if she would always put everyone else's needs before her own.

Was she getting enough protein and calories to make up for what she was using?

My mother only acted this way when my father was otherwise busy with business around the pack, but whenever he was home, at the den...he took care of the cooking and dishes himself, massaging her shoulders and kissing her collarbone, licking her mating mark—

He had taught me well how males should treat their mates.

Would I seem strange to her, if I wanted to do that for her? I was certain that wouldn't be very well received, considering that we were still in the early stages of this arranged marriage.

We weren't very close, yet, after all.

Still, seeing her working so hard to feed us and clean up after us before she even got to eat did something...unexpected to me.

"I was surprised to see you gone so early, so I wanted to go ahead and make busy myself," she smiled at me. "I hope that doesn't bother you."

One look at Crow's face was enough to let me know that this was unusual behavior. In fact, he looked...almost concerned, and more than a little...akin to sad?

I shrugged. "It isn't a big deal. I already went on patrol around the area, and everything is calm and safe. You should go for a run this morning; I am sure that it'd be good for Silver."

She shuddered, looking at her bowl with focus as she ignored my statement.

She was still having a hard time with shifting, but I was positive that the more she connected with Silver—and with me—the easier it would be for her.

After she'd eaten the little amount of breakfast that she wanted—a fraction of the portion that she had served Crow and myself—she had moved quickly and washed off her dishes.

"Do you want to go for a run?" I asked her, and she froze in the corner as she put away the dishes on a table we'd had brought here.

"I...guess that I should," she said.

"Come on, I'll help you like before," I said. I sat down, and I let her lay back on my lap as she shifted.

I noticed Crow's concern for her, but I quietly explained the reason behind the struggle as she shifted and he gaped at us.

Most wolves didn't suffer this way with shifting. To be so disconnected from your wolf because your wolf was disconnected from the moon...that was scary, and hindered your spirit.

Finally, she was shifted, and Crow and I both took to our wolf forms quickly ourselves, before we were all out of the den.

"I need to find an omega to come stay at the den when we get more settled and get this place more home-like. I don't like leaving the den unattended." I mentioned to Crow via the pack link, communicating with him alone.

He barked softly, acknowledging me in agreement.

"Is Dove normally like this?" I asked. "I don't understand why she is this way."

"...We had to...go through very extensive training after your engagement was initially set," he informed me. "Her parents pushed her to help around the pack, doing any and every chore, giving her all to be as humble, available, and useful as possible. She was taught to keep her opinions to herself, unless asked directly, and that she exists...solely for this pack...and for you. I watched them figuratively and literally knock that into her."

I froze for a moment, almost tripping over my own paws as I startled at that.

"What?"

I could hear him huff out a heavy breath. "Her free time, when she was finally left to herself, was staring at walls and crying for a long time. At least she doesn't cry all the time anymore."

Well...that was horrifying and made things a lot bleaker.

It was also no wonder to me that she had been so particularly agreeable.

His words echoed in my heart, and Slater whined in my mind, his tail hanging low and ears drooping as he took in this information.

We reached the pack house, and found it full with our families.

They smiled at us and they were out in the forest in moments to shift to their wolves, before they all came back to us.

"A morning run, darling? You haven't run in quite a long time, huh? Not since we told you about your engagement, at least. It feels like I've only seen Silver a couple times," I heard Dove's mother address her over a group pack link chat—just our direct small group, which included Dove's parents, my parents, Crow, and the alpha and luna.

Silver huffed, but Dove felt embarrassed. "Cloud has been helping me shift."

Beta Raven looked at me, eyes wide with surprise. "I've struggled to get Dove to shift for quite some time. How did you manage it?"

"We figured out that physical contact between the two of us makes it not be so painful to her," I told him, and they all looked at one another, my father sniffing the air.

"But you two haven't—"

"We haven't copulated," I told him, rolling my eyes. "We aren't ready for that. But I can still keep my hand on her shoulder or hold her hand while she shifts."

He nodded with a yip, happy that I've been getting along with her.

We could feel the pleasant buzz in the air.

We all trotted around and stretched, before I looked to the alpha.

"Can we get one of the omegas to move to our den? And can we get some builders? We are ready to get the den prepared to live in."

"I've already made a note about it," Luna Basil said when he glanced to her. "The deltas and omegas are scheduled to come out today and begin construction. We are impressed you managed to find and secure a den of your own so soon. Do you have a floor plan?"

• • •

I nodded, showing it to her in our mind's eye. "*I would like four bed chambers, with a bathroom and a kitchen and living room space. It will require quite a bit more digging, but the den is large enough that it shouldn't require much expansion, honestly.*"

"*What a magnificent find!*" Alpha Falcon praised, looking at the images in my mind as I projected them to the group. "*You have quite a talent,*" he said. "*You did quite well hunting, also, so that is very good. I am sure that you will be a fantastic beta when you are appointed.*"

I smiled in my mind, flushing at the praise. "*My father has raised me well.*"

"*That, I can see,*" the alpha said. "*What a good beta couple we have to look forward to.*"

I could feel the tension in Dove's body as her fur bristled, but she huffed out and let herself stride forward faster, away from us. She moved to go off on her own for a bit, a bit further from the group.

This seemed to put her at ease a bit and I was happy that she seemed a little more comfortable...at least, until her father barked at her—a scolding sound—and she shrunk in on herself, slinking back over to the group to fall into place behind me, head lowered and ears drooping, tail swishing low.

Her father huffed, rolling his eyes and shaking his head, and I could vaguely hear through our private mate-bond channel that he was yelling at her in their own private pack link.

I had to refrain from growling at him as she shrunk even further, Silver whining and tail starting to pull in between her hind legs.

If it were not for the fact that her father was higher ranked than me and that starting a fight was definitely not my plate—nor was it a good look to our newly united pack—I would have stepped in to defend her right away.

We all continued on, and after a good run and working up a sweat, we went back to the pack house after shifting back and dressing so that we could all have lunch, before a large group of omegas and deltas met us out at the den.

Construction began, and we all pitched in to help.

Though, through it all, I noticed one of the deltas staring at Dove with intensity.

He didn't come *very* close to her, but I suddenly wished she wasn't wearing such a high-necked shirt that covered my mark on her.

I was actually feeling self-conscious.

I didn't like the way that he looked at her.

I also didn't like the way he looked around the den, almost in a way like he was sizing it up, and glancing at her to see how she felt about it...before glaring at me.

Mate's *true* mate, Slater snarled.

I startled, looking at him again.

Yes, I realized. *I could see it on his face. The way he tried to lift heavy things when she was looking his direction, but was lazy when she wasn't. The way he kept his eyes trained on her. The way that he, subtly, scented the air whenever she got within a couple of feet of him.*

Slater's fur bristled inside of me, hackles rising and snarls threatening to spill out vocally.

This male *was* quite attractive, I had to admit, and powerful for a delta.

I could sense it.

He had lighter grey hair and tan skin, with jade green eyes. His eyebrows were a dark grey, though, and he had thick, thick black eyelashes.

He was handsome; as handsome as Dove was beautiful.

'*Who is he?*' I asked, trying to picture his wolf.

He seemed familiar, but I didn't see him often enough to know right away and I was still new enough to the pack that I wasn't overly familiar with everyone yet. '*I don't—*'

Pack Hunter's son, Slater rumbled, and I startled again. That was why he was so strong. **He would have been future beta because beta only had daughter**, Slater told me.

He was the next to succeed the Pack Hunter...the most powerful of all the delta males, and more powerful that the gammas because of the Pack Hunter title.

If I remembered correctly, his father had originally been the previous Offensive Gamma's son, but his father had been made into the secondary Pack Hunter because my father had taken the Offensive Gamma position. So, he was originally born with Gamma ranked blood, making him much stronger than the other deltas. He had been demoted, but he was still stronger than they were.

Mate would have been Pack Hunter's mate, Slater grumbled, a bit flustered and perturbed by the information.

Pack Hunters, as the law enforcers of the pack, had to be stronger than the deltas and gammas.

He trained excessively, became almost *feral* to become powerful enough to take on higher members of the pack, to enforce our laws.

It was more than being disturbed by the news, though.

Deep down, I could even feel Slater's guilt in his emotions.

He felt guilty that he had taken a Pack Hunter's true mate from him, and a powerful mate from Dove.

From the look on *his* face, he would have chosen her. He would have accepted her and taken her. He would have loved her and given her his all.

It wasn't common for Pack Hunters to have natural, born fated mates. Most Pack Hunters had to have an arranged delta female give him an heir, because his position was so dangerous that permanent mates are usually not wanted. After all, if anything killed him, the mate would suffer, too.

Pack Hunter heir is strong...he might fight me for her, Slater said, fur bristling again. I felt prickly all over.

The male had the good sense to feel the shift in the air, and his eyes, wide, whirled to me. I pulled Slater forward, staking my place as the male of this den and her mate...

He didn't, however, look away and bare his neck to his superior as I had expected and hoped that he would.

No.

Instead, he held my gaze, his eyes sad as the truth set in.

He must have already turned fourteen and just realized who Dove was for him, I realized.

The den was full of deltas, omegas, and the leaders of the pack, so he couldn't start a fight with me over her here.

Suddenly, Dove was coming up to ask me a question, and his gaze snapped to her.

The scent in the air changed, and I could tell that he'd unconsciously released his seeking-scent...letting her smell him in return. He started to bristle when I pulled closer to her, blocking his path to her, and he wanted to move me out of the way, I knew.

This scent that he was releasing was the way that our kind's males made sure that their chosen females knew our preference for them, and could scent him, too.

Think of it as a dog pissing on a tree to mark his territory, or a male cat spraying to attract females.

His "calling card," if you will.

● ● ●

"Cloud," Crow said, stepping over to me. "I mean, Beta Heir...where you would and my Beta Heiress like this?" He asked, holding up a random item as he shot a glance at the Pack Hunter Heir.

He asked the question very obviously, and loud enough to be heard.

I glanced to the Pack Hunter Heir, who looked between Crow, Dove and myself quickly.

His eyes got wide as he gaped, looking down at himself before he looked at us again.

It wasn't on purpose, Slater grumbled. *He needs work on self-control. He released his calling-scent without meaning to, and now he actually knows who we are. He did not know mate was ours and claimed. Mate—*

Before he could finish, I heard her as she took a sharp breath, looking at him, her eyes wide.

I worried, instantly, as I saw the recognition and the spark of heated interest in her eyes.

Slater was practically pacing in my mind as he waited to see her reaction to her true mate.

She stared at him for a long moment...before her hand drifted to her neck junction where my mating mark rested.

The Pack Hunter heir looked alarmed, almost, before she gave him a sad smile and she shook herself, remembering where she was and what was happening, and she looked back and forth between him and I, noticing how tense and tight my body was as I stood there, completely rigid.

She came to me, gently squeezing my hand before she, very subtly, bore her neck to me—and pulled the neck of her top down, letting part of my mark on her show.

I noticed how he stood there staring at her with eyes wide, expression a mixture of sadness and horror, and then looked back to me with understanding dawning on him.

She looked to the male, taking a step away from Crow and I, both. "Sparrow…"

He flinched at the sad tone of her voice, glancing between her and I.

He now fully realized who we actually were, our ranks, our identities, the fact that we'd already become a married mate couple, and that I'd already marked her.

I wasn't entirely sure how many members of the pack knew that the union wasn't blessed by Selene; as far as I knew, that information had been kept rather secret…but he certainly didn't look happy.

He looked to her neck, then back at me…a snarl in his throat as he clutched his hand over his mouth to keep it from escaping, giving her one last look of horror before he turned tail to run.

He was out of the den in seconds, as everyone looked around at the situation and started murmuring.

My father came up to me. "What—"

"That was her true mate," I told him quietly, and his eyes dawned with the realization.

"He is already of age, and he realized who she was," he said, sad.

I nodded. "He is the Pack Hunter's son," I told him.

He looked disturbed by this. *"Watch out for him,"* he told me privately in our private pack link. *"Because you two weren't blessed by Selene, **technically**…he could actually challenge you for her. He has the right. If he won, he could take her and you couldn't do anything. The alliance has been officially forged, so we can't break it just because you two get separated. That was our forging of the packs, but the contract stated that in case of death, warranted divorce or separation, we couldn't protest it. It was a clause."*

I gaped at him, realizing that if Sparrow challenged me and managed to win her…pack law wouldn't be able to help me, as I would have thought.

All because she and I hadn't received the blessing of the moon mother to become mates.

If we *had*, then pack law would have dictated that he couldn't do anything about our union.

The lack of blessing actually put our laws on *his* side, if he chose to do something about it…but that was only if he found out that we hadn't received a blessing from Selene.

Not to mention that a warranted divorce only counted for infidelity cases, or for high ranks such as gamma, beta, and alpha, the inability to produce a pup…

Separation—a male challenging me for my female, and me losing—was perfectly legal in the pack's eyes.

We need to train, Slater growled. **Make sure he can't take her. I <u>won't</u> lose mate!** He snarled.

I inwardly sighed.

Did I want to keep her from her true mate, though? Slater had made his feelings about it clear, but what about how I felt, myself?

Wolves, by nature, were very possessive.

They didn't like to lose their belongings, territory, or mates, and even if the union had not been blessed by Selene, I had marked her. Therefore, she was mine.

We were covetous, possessive creatures, and she was mine.

So, for my wolf, losing his mate—especially a formally marked and half-bonded, pre-copulated mate—it would be equivalent to losing a limb. Perhaps worse.

We may be half-bonded, but she *was* still bonded to me, and Slater was just waiting for the age to come when we would get to copulate with Silver.

We had given oaths, both for marriage and for the pack. I had accepted her as my beta female, and she had accepted me as the beta male.

That meant, explicitly, that we were recognized as a couple in the pack law. We had vowed to one another before I had marked her, as well, and the mark tied us together.

The only thing left was for *her* to mark *me*, and for us to physically mate—to actually copulate. Our bond wasn't complete until that happened.

I wondered, however...was it selfish of me to want to keep her for myself, when I wasn't in love with her, and wasn't sure if I ever would be?

After what Crow had told me about her extensive training to "exist for the pack and for her mate..."

My heart had been so stricken by that knowledge.

If her true mate challenged me...would I even fight back? Would he be better for her?

What would happen if I let her go on purpose?

I couldn't divorce her without justifiable reason, but I could lose without really putting in the effort to fight him. I could let him take her.

It was stressful to think about the consequences of giving her up, after we'd basically begged Selene to bless the union and favor us despite not being true mates...and then she had rejected us, and we had gone against her will, anyway...but perhaps losing her was what was best, and that was actually Selene's will.

If he challenged me for her, he technically had just as much claim as I did. Moreso, perhaps, because he was the mate that Selene had chosen for her.

If he comes, we must fight back. I will not lose mate because my human doesn't care about her. I love her.

I was startled by the ending thought from my wolf.

He *loved* her?

Already?

. . .

This was quite serious, indeed.

It had only been a couple of days, and yet Slater had already attached himself to her completely, whereas *I* hadn't.

I knew that when we had marked her, we had only seen her submitting, and Slater had accepted that as her submission...but I knew the truth.

I tried to reason with him, but remained obstinate, refusing to accept that.

She had been forced. I wasn't rightfully her mate, not really.

He had attached himself to her entirely, because of her "submission," but my human mind couldn't register that as a real, honest submission because it wasn't *her*.

I didn't dislike her anymore, per say...but I didn't love her, either.

For me, I felt civil and respectful with her, and I thought that we were well on our way to forming a friendship...but *love*?

I wasn't there yet. I didn't know when, or even if, I would get to that point, either.

Would I *ever* come to *love* her?

I wasn't sure.

CHAPTER 12

Cloud...

The rest of the day had passed rather uneventfully, and by the end of that month, all of the renovations and expansion to our den had been completed.

In total, we had a master bedroom with a bathroom, two bedrooms for pups—one for females, one for males—and we had an extra room that acted as a bedroom for Crow. There was a nice bathroom for guests, as well.

The kitchen area and sitting room were a decent size, and we had all the furniture and supplies we needed to really get us going well.

Since that fateful first day of construction, Sparrow—Dove's true mate—had not returned.

The alpha had told me that he'd spoken to Sparrow on his own, learned that Sparrow was her true mate, and given him leave to not return to help so that it didn't cause conflicts of any sort.

Sparrow had told the alpha that he had wanted to challenge me, but because of the reasoning behind the marriage, the forging of the alliance...he didn't wish to go against the pack that way.

It turned out that nobody actually had to tell him that our union was not blessed by Selene.

Sparrow himself had admitted to hearing a voice—much like I had heard when I had been told to earn Dove's submission—that our union was not blessed and went against Selene's will.

He had wanted to use this as an excuse to challenge me, but he didn't want to go against the alpha—the one who had arranged our marriage in the first place.

We may have forged the union to help the packs, but the union wasn't blessed by Selene, but I knew that there was no way that a male that had admitted to wanting to get her for himself would leave me unchallenged for her.

It was only a matter of time, I was sure. I was positive that once she came of age at fourteen, he would issue the challenge.

He had admitted to the alpha that he had little control of his wolf's whims, however, and that if he was around Dove...he might lose control.

He intended to stay away from us whenever possible, to keep his wolf reigned in, but he wouldn't promise that he would be able to control the urges.

I appreciated and respected that. He wanted to challenge me, as did his wolf, but he respected the necessity of our union and wanted to help the pack, even if it meant that he was unhappy. I just hoped that he didn't ever get around her after she came of age.

I didn't actually want to face a challenger for her.

Admitting to a lack of control over one's wolf, though?

That in itself was a little worrying; to know that he had such little control of his wolf counterpart.

That suggested that either his wolf was too wild to reign in, or his wolf was stronger than what he himself could contain.

Shifters who struggled for control with the wolf inside typically didn't do well in authoritative positions within the pack, because their wolves battled them so hard for that control...and I realized why it was that Selene had thought to make him Dove's true mate.

His wolf was strong, unruly, and undisciplined.

A free spirit who didn't want to listen to his human counterpart.

Dove's wolf was much weaker, and shifting was painful for her, but her wolf was calm and collected now that she had gained some maturity.

Together, the two of them would have been a fairly well-balanced couple...as much as I hated to admit that.

Several months had gone by, now, and Dove was finally able to shift with little effort as long as I was touching her.

Bringing her back in connection with her wolf and the shifting process was painstaking, tiring work, but it was worth it.

Without my physical contact, I noticed that she was still struggling a lot, but even that wasn't as bad as it had once been.

I noticed, with great respect and growing affection, that Dove's usual routine was to wake just before dawn. She would have Crow escort her to the pack house, and she would get busy making coffee and putting together breakfast for the alpha, luna, beta pair, and the deltas who stayed at the pack house.

She would help direct chores with the omegas, and then, she would return back to the den and wake me up with breakfast and coffee after letting me sleep in for a couple of hours.

She would have a change of clothes and shoes already laid out for me to change into, and a hot shower running for me by the time I finished with breakfast so that I could get washed.

When I would finish showering and dressing, she would be finished with the dishes and putting leftovers away, before stoking the fire and bringing me a coat.

I would head out to the pack house and get to working on training and learning pack laws and other important things with the alpha heir and offensive gamma heir.

The Pack Hunter heir was always, strangely, absent, and avoided me...but I knew that the offensive gamma heir would deliver our plans and paper work to him after I had left.

It seemed that everyone had figured out who Sparrow was to Dove...and I was the outsider; but the outsider was the one whom won in this case.

After construction inside the den had been entirely completed, we did still, surprisingly, sleep in the same bed.

It had been awkward at first, but we both realized that our wolves were on good terms and that we needed to follow suit if we wanted to have a good life together.

Our affection for one another was, in any case, slowly growing on its own.

After a while, sleeping together didn't bother us or feel awkward at all.

I did my utmost to be sure that she remained content, at the very least.

I had only raised my voice at her once, and she had raised her voice at me first. Honest.

I, at Slater's insistence, had apologized first, before she had blushed and turned to look away, looking bashful as she said that she was the one who should be apologizing.

Since the unification of the packs, there had been a few quarrels inside the pack, and only one ambush from outside. We had lost an omega that day, but the pack warriors and the offensive gamma had fought them off and driven the intruders away.

The ambush had been made by a handful of rogue wolves; pack-less, wild-roaming wolf-shifters who had either lost their packs or been cast out, usually the latter. They were commonly criminals, and it was rare that they didn't attack packs as they were passing through if there were males among them.

After that attack, the increased security and protection had certainly been gossiped about and the information had made its way to other packs in the state, letting them know that we were no longer sitting ducks that were divided on top of the pond.

No, now we had vision and structure, and force behind our territory.

Starting a battle with us used to mean we would lose several omegas, possibly a couple of deltas, and in one of the last severe attacks, the gamma himself had been killed.

Deaths of high ranked members of the pack were not to be taken lightly in any circumstance...losing the omegas and deltas was already hard enough.

As a pack, with a pack link mind for communication purposes, we felt those losses in our wolf forms and those bonds being severed was painful and traumatic, omega or not.

In other news...

It was only a few days until my birthday, now, and I could feel the changes coming.

Slater was becoming restless, impatient, and seemed to be wanting to come out and run more often lately.

The fourteenth birthday—the second awakening—was the one in which your wolf became of age to mate and start your adult life.

I could feel him pacing back and forth in my mind whenever we got close to Dove, and even I had to admit that I was growing more attracted to her each passing day.

Whether that be because of his influence in my mind or not, I couldn't say.

She was beautiful, in any case.

Today, for example, was a peculiarly difficult day...at least on my end.

She was wearing a pretty wrap dress, with her long hair pulled up and swept into a messy bun.

Her marking was on proud display as she watered her small bed of flowers by the entrance of the den, and I watched her with rapt attention.

The mark had faded from its angry red and purple, and only the teeth markings in a fleshy, tan-pink remained. It looked like any serious scar that had healed well.

Her legs peeked out as she walked, and the wind blew and lifted her long bangs.

Slater began to pant in my mind as my belly muscles tightened and loosened unconsciously in my body, and I stood abruptly when I had the urge to throw her to her knees and mount her through his blood pumping hard in my veins.

"Cloud?" She asked, concerned.

I shook my head, holding my hand palm-out to stop her. "I will return later," I told her. "Get inside and stay there until Crow arrives," I said, and I took off with the sound of her calling me in the distance.

'You will drive me mad! And you know that I don't like leaving her there on her own.' I rolled my eyes at Slater.

I thought of Silver's wolf, and I could feel my blood pumping hard again, panting out into the cooling evening air.

The human mind thinks too much, Slater's voice carried his thoughts to me, gruff and frustrated at me. **As soon as I hit my heat, she will be lucky if I do not take her. I won't be able to stop if I start.**

'You **will** stop if she asks you to,' I snarled at him in my mind, and I felt him pause.

I had never scolded him directly that way...not even once.

He didn't seem to want to reply for a while, before I finally heard the small, soft thought from him. **If she asked me to, I would stop**.

'Good,' I said, breathing a sigh of relief.

I didn't need a rapist for a wolf.

She wouldn't want to stop, though, he sneered in his thoughts. **It would be too good for her.**

I rolled my eyes at him.

Of course, the cocky and confident beta male thinks that he would be able to make her want him even before her heat hits.

'I know you are fixing to enter into your first ever heat, Slater, but Dove still has months to go before she goes into hers.'

He whined in my mind, but I took a deep breath and let myself shift into his form.

He stretched, shaking out his fur and bristling when we caught scent of another male.

I whipped around to snap at the male, and barely caught myself before I bit into Crow, who startled and jumped back, currently in his human form.

"Is everything alright?" Crow asked as he stepped up to me. "You have been acting strange," he asked me aloud.

"My heat is approaching," I told him through the mind link. "I go into heat in four more days."

"Ahh," he said, giving a nod. "That explains it. I will be going into my heat in another two months."

I remembered that he had a Year's Fall birthday.

"*As it gets close, your wolf goes haywire, ready to pounce. I'm having a hard time not straight jumping her,*" I laughed. "*I don't want to take her in the midst of my heat when she has yet to enter her own.*"

He gave a tight nod. "I'll go watch over her while you take a break for a while. Return whenever you feel better, I'll wait as long as you need."

"*Thank you, Crow,*" I said, sincere. Then I turned, taking off into the forest.

Four days passed in the blink of an eye...most of which, I spent in the forest and away from my mate.

Slater was getting harder to maintain around her.

At this point, I was even sleeping over at Crow's little home nearby, while he stayed at the den with Dove.

He usually stayed in our den, but with my heat so close, he had been staying in his own little den, so that he wouldn't be too close by if Dove and I did happen to end up getting...intimate.

Finally, the day of my birth had arrived, and it took all of my willpower to control the frenzied surge of lust that burned through my body as my wolf had his second awakening.

I hadn't seen Dove in over a day, and Slater was clawing at my skin beneath the surface to get free so that he could go to her.

He had reached his adulthood, and he wanted to show off to Silver.

• • •

I caught her scent, suddenly, and I gasped and snarled before a long, deep groan had me falling to my knees.

Everything spun as suddenly, I was dizzy, and fighting through the mental fog, I felt a surge of gratefulness when I saw Crow at the edge of the clearing of the forest that I was in.

Much to my horror...he was walking with my female, who was much farther ahead than him.

She must have wanted to walk alone, and he was just her escort to protect her.

"Get...get her out of here," I ground out through my teeth loudly, and he startled, looking to me and immediately noting my condition.

He stepped back, toward the den—the direction where Dove was headed—and Slater took it as a personal challenge against him.

I was having a hard time holding him back.

"Slater, he—" I groaned loud as I felt the bones popping and breaking so fast that it felt like I had suddenly been blown to pieces.

I sobbed against the waves of pain accumulating inside me.

"Get her away from here! Fast! Go! I won't be able to stop him! Protect her!" I snarled, and thankfully, he didn't say a word as he quickly turned and bolted for her.

I was already in wolf form before they could get more than a few yards back into the forest, however, and I could feel Slater's claws digging into the earthen floor as he tore after them, snarling.

That poor girl...

She shrieked in fear as Crow pulled her out of the way when Slater snapped in her direction, attempting to grab her by the coat.

Crow couldn't shift as fast as I could, so he held out his arm to shield me off while he pushed Dove behind him in a defensive manner...and Slater was having none of that.

"*Out of my way, gamma*," Slater snarled at him via mind link.

"Beta Heir, you are not okay right now! Cloud told me to protect—"

"*Don't speak of that fool! I will not hurt my female*," Slater's tone deepened. He raised his hackles, muscles binding tightly as he crouched and prepared to lunge at Crow.

Just as the muscles began to loosen to spring, Dove jumped out, arms spread wide. "No!" She cried; eyes clenched tightly closed, trusting me not to hurt her. "Please, don't hurt him! Don't hurt my gamma!" She sobbed, and to my stunned appreciation...Slater absolutely froze.

"Dove, you can't—" Crow tried, but she stopped him.

"*Leave*, Crow!" She insisted, forcing herself to stand fast even though she trembled. "Please..."

He glanced between the two of us even as I paced in a predatory circle around her, and I could feel Slater's patience wearing thin quickly as he licked his chops and panted, his girth thickening and pulsing in its furry casing.

I'd experienced a couple of erections in my human state, but never had I felt the wolf-form equivalent.

Crow gave me a once-over before giving Dove another cautionary glance.

"Dove—"

"Crow...this is an order from your beta heiress. I would rather he do..." she swallowed thickly. "I would rather he do whatever he is going to do to me, than to see you get hurt by trying to stop him. We both know you would only delay the inevitable. So, please. I love you too much to watch you get hurt. You're family."

● ● ●

He hesitated. "Yes...my beta heiress. Call me, if you need me. I will come...even if he kills me."

Then, he turned, and quickly left the area.

Dominant pleasure seared through Slater's mind.

"**Submit**," Slater ordered her, tone thick and heady.

His eyes were burning as they blazed, half-lidded. Heavy, lust-induced huffs pushed out of his snout into the open air, chest puffing in and out.

He was so overwhelmed, so ready to mount, I wasn't entirely secure in the thought that he would listen if she did ask him to stop. He had promised that he would, but with how lost he was in the lust...I couldn't take that at face value.

I'd always trusted my wolf implicitly, but this might call for more cautionary detailing.

"**Submit, or I will make you submit, little mate,**" he snarled at her, running out of patience for her.

I cringed.

I saw her flinch and quiver, and I felt like garbage. I knew that she didn't want this.

She deserved a *true* mate, a gentle mate; a mate she *instinctively desired* to submit to.

Not a mate who would threaten force if she didn't obey.

Guilt flared in my human mind, even as the animal continued to pace and circle her, running out of tolerance.

Calmly and quietly—like the good, good girl she had become over the years through forceful and intensive training—she slowly and calmly got down onto her knees, before finally taking a deep, shaky breath and baring her neck to him.

Her face was hidden by her hair, but her body trembling hard enough to let me know enough of what her face would look like.

She was afraid.

The scent of her fear was thick and it sickened me. I didn't want to put her in this position.

I could smell the most minute scent of urine, and that made Slater pause...because she was so terrified that she was literally struggling not to piss herself.

That seemed to snap him---very minimally, but still— out of the hazed fog he was in.

The only reason she submitted now was because she was already marked, and because if she didn't, Slater could use his dominance through the mark on her neck to force her to bow and bare to him.

It was similar to an alpha's command, but it was something only males of high rank could pull on their mates...because usually, their mates were the only ones not intimidated by them and on close-to equal footing as them.

This didn't sit well with me, though.

We didn't need to scare her or scar her for life.

"I s-submit," she stammered. "J-just p-please...please don't hurt me or m-my gamma..."

Slater was over her in an instant; he sniffed and licked at his mark on her, his tongue giving her entire collarbone attention, and she trembled as the sparks from our bond surely made their way through her.

They were making their way through me, and though I was struggling against the pleasure, I forced myself to have some sense.

I need to scent mark her, at least, Slater thought. ***How can I do that without m-mating her...since she is not in her heat...?***

'Are you...directly asking me a question...?'

● ● ●

You know more how to do this...calm behavior. I am too worked up to think. I do this for mate's sake, not you.

I chuckled, rolling my eyes. 'Of course, that would be the only reason you would speak to me directly this way. She has a way of breaking through your barriers,' I laughed. 'Now...what do you mean, exactly, by scent mark...?'

I need my seed on her somehow, on or in, I just—I need release with her, I need it, his voice whined pitifully as he began to dry hump over her body, and she trembled harder.

This time, she had a harder time restraining her body, and a bit more urine trickled out onto the ground through her dress.

I sighed, shaking my head. 'I will talk to her,' I said. 'But you will have to give me enough control to reach her. Loosen your control, just a bit. I promise, I won't shove you back inside...yet.'

I could sense the reluctance, but he finally gave in.

"Dove," I spoke through the mind link to her directly. "Slater...he says he needs release with you. He doesn't have to mate you, but he needs his...he needs..." I groaned. "He needs his cum to touch you, in some form. I am mortified to even say this, but I...don't want him to force you, and he doesn't want to force or scare you in any way. Do I have your permission for this?"

Her body shook, but she gave a timid nod. "I-i-If it h-helps..."

I let out a breath of relief, before I turned my thoughts back to Slater. 'You have permission to do what you have to. But you only have my permission to release onto her body externally through self-manipulation,' I told him.

What does that mean? He growled, impatient.

'You can't have her touch you, and you can't go into her body in any way. You have my permission to dry hump over her and brush against her skin until it is relieved.'

That's all? He whined.

'*She has given permission for that much, at least. Do not push this,*' I pleaded. '*Please. If you push it farther, it will hurt your connection to her.*'

He huffed, but he agreed. "**Mate**," he spoke, and she startled, looking over her shoulder at him. "***I won't hurt mate. Please, trust***," he said, his voice oddly...sweet.

Then, much to my eternal mortification...he began to lower and line his privates against the curve of her back, and he dry humped her.

I felt the tingles through my own shaft, the multitudinous magical sparks dancing over our flesh, groaning internally as his privates brushed against her back over and over.

The pleasure began to get intense as he huffed out gruffly and thickly, and I could feel it in my own body beneath his surface.

Finally, after an embarrassingly short experience—though still too long, for what it was—he released all over her back.

His smell did, indeed, began to envelope her.

He hadn't been playing about the scent thing. She smelled completely like him, now.

She shuddered as he came down from his high, but I quickly took the reins from him—without his protest—and shifted back to human form.

She gaped up at me, a look of horror on her face. "W-wait...is...is that it...?"

I didn't know what she meant at first, but I just went ahead and threw on the pair of clothes that I'd had in my back pack earlier that had been discarded nearby, and I took her into my arms.

"Dove," I said, soft, as she began to sob. I could feel a whirlpool of confusion in her emotions. "Dove, talk to me," I murmured.

● ● ●

"I...I was scared, but...I feel so...hot," she whispered.

I chuckled. "I know," I said.

"To be so...desired," she said, her voice soft. "I...I feel conflicted."

I gave a nod. "And you have every right to."

"But I...I am not...mad, or disgusted, or anything."

I smiled. "I'm so embarrassed that I want to crawl under a rock for a few years, but...I am glad that you feel that way." I took off my tunic, and I held it out for her. "Here, honey. Change out of that, and put this on," I said.

Without bothering to wait for me to turn around, she peeled off the tunic she had on and pulled mine on in its place.

Despite that most of his release had happened on her tunic, I did have to take her tunic from her and wipe the remaining bit off of the back of her bare arm.

She looked up at me. "Does...does he feel better...?" She asked.

I gave a tight nod. "Yes. Thank you...thank you, Dove, for being so cooperative and understanding."

"I remember...I remember reading about the heat," she whispered. "My father, embarrassingly enough, insisted when we found out that you and I would be entering an arranged marriage. He told me that you would hit your heat first, and what I should expect. He told me that your heat might...be rough."

For a moment, I didn't know how to respond, but I was so thankful for my father-in-law. He had already prepared her for the worst, and she had already resigned herself to accept it.

My heart, and Slater's swelled with warm, fuzzy feelings that I wasn't accustomed to.

You would be accustomed if you were just on board with me, human, Slater said smugly.

"So, you were already ready for the worst," I whispered to her, ignoring my wolf.

She gave a nod. "I am thankful it wasn't as bad as I expected."

I sighed. "You shouldn't have had to."

"Maybe, but..."

"But...?"

"You've been kind to me...Slater has been good to me. The least I can do is be understanding. Besides," she said, a small smile on her face. "I will enter my heat soon enough. I will understand for myself how it feels, soon."

My face heated, and I stood on shaky legs and helped her to her feet and then...then, I led her back to the den.

CHAPTER 13

Dove...

Things had...changed, since Cloud's second awakening.

For one thing, he wanted for me to smell like him anytime either one of us was leaving the den. I had tried to leave one time without putting something of his on me or letting him scent mark me, and he had nearly chased me out the den.

He had become very possessive, and I sensed Slater struggling beneath the surface.

Still, aside from wanting me to smell like him, wear his clothes, and never leave the den without him...

Nothing particularly *bad* had happened. He hadn't taken things too far.

In fact, we hadn't had another incident like the one at the awakening, either.

As the seasons changed, the weather got cold, and the holidays approached, however...Cloud seemed anxious about being around other wolves.

A wolf-shifter's heat typically lasted for about a month, before it finally eased off.

• • •

They would remain overly sexual and easily stimulated into mating for the remainder of their time, but only the awakening into their heat was any kind of dangerous or anything of that nature.

Cloud was more attached to me than he once was.

I could feel that he was putting more effort into being good to me—and not just at Slater's insistence.

He rubbed my shoulders, brushed my hair, massaged my feet, held my hand, and even cooked for me after hunting...

When we were sleeping, he would be sure that if I kicked the blankets away from myself, he would fix them and curl around me to ensure that I was warm.

All in all, I was actually...very pleased with him as a partner...even if I was still hurt that he wasn't my true mate, and we hadn't even gotten the moon mother's blessing.

It was as if I had married against my parents' will; running off and eloping when they rejected me wanting to marry him and coming back to surprise them, only to find out that they resented me for it.

I tried desperately not to let it bother me. This was just the way that things would be.

I *wanted* a true mate...my true mate.

I had seen him, realized who he was, and had been rather pleased and...to be honest, flattered that he'd been the male who would have chosen me.

I had always liked Sparrow.

He smelled so good, and he was always kind to me.

A very, *very* distant relative to our family, not close enough to really share blood at all. A cousin's husband's nephew.

I sighed, trying to shake him from my mind and also keep my spirits up.

It was late into the month, almost the holiday of the Folias Harvest Festival for the humans, when our stockpile of meat attracted someone who we didn't expect.

It was almost two in the morning, when we heard the door of the den crash open.

I felt my wolf leap inside of me, snarling and upset, and I opened my eyes and rubbed the sleep away to see Cloud already out of bed and shifting, rushing out of our bedroom.

I heard a lot of snarling and at the sudden crash, I looked out to see three wolves jumping all over Cloud.

He was fighting valiantly, but he was *only fourteen*. He wasn't even a full adult, yet.

"*Crow! Crow, we're being attacked!*" I cried in the mind-link.

I heard his sleepy voice jolt with force. "*I'm on my way, hold on!*" He growled, and thankfully, he was shifted and out of his bedroom, charging into the living room to assist immediately.

I tried to force myself to shift as I watched the fight unfold.

Since Cloud and I had married, I hadn't shifted without his physical contact, and never had I shifted in a dire situation.

Silver was, strangely, afraid to respond.

'*Please!*' I begged her. '*I know you're scared, but we have to help! Our den is under attack! Please, Silver!*' I pleaded, desperate.

She was absolutely silent.

No response.

Why was she not responding?

She wouldn't even send a thought my way? When our mate and gamma were struggling to defend our den from rogues?

In a moment of fearful, furious terror, I scolded her. *'You're just useless! First, I lose my connection to you because you're upset over the arranged marriage, because you're a drama queen and can't cope...but oh, wait, I was already struggling before then! You have never liked coming out, and shifting has always been horrible. Now, our mate is in trouble and you can't even help? Why are you even here?!'*

Immediately, the beginning stages of my shift totally halted, and I completely lost the feeling of my wolf.

She receded so deeply into my mind that I could no longer sense her presence...*at all.*

W...what the—?

"Cloud!" I cried, trying to figure out some way to help...but in my inexperience and naivete, I wasn't thinking about that drawing the intruders' attention...directly to *myself.*

One rushed me as they all snarled in my direction, and I felt myself thrown against the wall.

"Shift!" Cloud shouted, but I couldn't.

I sobbed, unable to respond when a fist knocked into my gut and knocked the wind out of me.

"*Shit!*" Cloud cursed, but the other two kept him from coming to my aid. "Crow!"

Thankfully, my gamma was rushing to help me just as my father rushed into the den, and it was only a few moments before the three rogues were lying, bound and tied, in the floor.

"What brought you here?!" My father shouted.

"W-we were just hungry," one stuttered. "We smelled the food, and this den was out away from the others..."

"We weren't trying to hurt anyone! We just wanted food," another said. "He's the one who jumped on us!" He said, pointing out Cloud.

"Who wouldn't defend their den?!" Cloud snarled. "You're fools!"

"That also doesn't explain why you'd attack my daughter!" My father snarled.

They froze, looking over to me.

"No one should have touched my mate!" Cloud snarled. "You broke into my den and tried to steal, then you attacked my mate!"

They glanced at each other, before looking to my father. "So, what happens now?" The third asked.

"Now...you go to the alpha," he said, and as he and a couple of deltas who had arrived as backup led the three out, I collapsed.

"Dove," Cloud said, soft, taking me into his arms as he came to kneel before me.

"Cloud, I...Cloud, I did something terrible...I, I drove her away," I cried.

"What...?" He asked, surprised.

"I scolded her so harshly," I whimpered, digging my face into his shoulder. "She was *refusing* the shift, and I got angry and scared and scolded her. I hurt her feelings. I wasn't trying to, I just...I just got so upset, in the heat of the moment. I feel so worthless and helpless with my struggles with her. It isn't fair. Do you...do you think she's gone for good? I can't sense her at all."

He hesitated for a moment, his eyes brightening as he called Slater forward a bit.

"Slater still senses her...but she is very weak," he said, sad. "When we hurt our wolves, it affects their power inside of us. Doubting her led her to be scared and not want to come out to help, and then scolding her...you have to be careful," he said.

• • •
164

I cried softly, and he took my face in his hands.

I looked up at him with pleading eyes. "What can I do?"

He shook his head, and I watched as he pulled away and slowly began to shift.

Soon, Slater was lying there in the floor.

As he whimpered and whined, giving some small yips and grunts here and there, I could feel Silver being pulled forward.

I let myself fall, letting her take over without even needing to see me switch with her, and I felt my body shift.

I watched as she lay there whimpering into his fur, and he licked her face and her shoulder as she whined and cried into his. He whimpered with her, letting her nuzzle into him and seek his warmth, and he curled his larger frame around hers, letting her curl into a ball as she shook.

He continued to lick on her, letting out a deep, comforting rumble from his center.

I felt tears run down my face as I realized that she loved him.

She didn't want to shift for *me*; didn't want to help me even when I was in danger...didn't want to hunt or fight...

The second that *he* called her forward, however, she came out with no problems and no excruciating pain.

Perhaps *I* really had been the problem all along...and that only served to further disconnect me from the moon and our Moon Mother.

I truly had been done so wrong in this life.

How would I ever be able to move forward?

Nivis's End, 1945 ILY

For the past three months since the rogue attack on our den, I had remained in my wolf form.

I had taken a back seat, and I remained in that condition. After all, learning that I was the issue all along, well...

That made me just not even want to exist anymore.

I could feel myself sleeping more and more often, too, and I realized that she was enjoying being out without my thought interference, or my feelings, or my input...because any time that I *did* let my thoughts drift to her...I could feel her shoving me down, and I felt myself falling asleep.

She didn't want for me to be her human.

I knew that she didn't.

What shifter was at odds with their animal? That wasn't even a *thing*...

Heck, three times she had let Slater be all over her and hadn't hindered him at all when he'd dry humped her in wolf form.

I noticed that Cloud grew increasingly concerned and tried to communicate with me via pack link, but I had remained silent because she had forced me back down.

As long as she was in charge of my body and she refused to let me out, there was nothing I could do.

All communication was left between Slater and Silver, and that consisted of majority nonverbal methods.

● ● ●

I knew that soon enough, it would be time for my heat...though, admittedly, I wasn't sure if I could even come out for that.

I hadn't shifted back even once since the attack at the den.

Would Silver even let me back out?

Would she handle it on her own? Would she remain in charge of my body for the remainer of my life?

She did seem to be enjoying the freedom and the time with Slater, and she certainly didn't let me get thoughts in edgewise.

What if she kept me trapped down forever...?

Finally, after what felt like forever with little question about me voiced...I finally felt that I was missed early one morning, when Cloud decided to actually ask about me, directly, for the first time.

I opened my eyes, woken as I felt Cloud brushing a comb through my fur.

"When will *my* Dove return?" He wondered, soft.

He was looking at the wall, at a photo of him and I from a few days after we married. It had been a random snap-shot that someone had gotten on their camera, but it was the only photo that we had of the two of us. In the photo, I was looking off at Crow, who was talking to me, but Cloud was looking at me...a look of calm peacefulness on his face.

Silver glanced up at him, an ear perking up in question.

"I *have* loved this time with Silver, that is true, and Slater has been happy to be with her by her side...but I miss Dove, too. Slater gets time with his mate, but I am quite lonely without my counterpart to be around. We grew close in the time we were together. I miss her."

I felt my heart tug painfully...

Cloud...*missed me?*

I could only hear Silver's whimpers as she curled up to him, and he sighed, giving her a kiss on her snout.

"I'm sorry, but I do." He sighed. "When will you let her come back?"

I could feel her snarling internally at me, and shoving me down even further.

I fell asleep, feeling the force of her hatred for me being her human pushing me forcefully into unconsciousness.

I wasn't sure when—or if—I would ever wake up, and I wished that I hadn't been born a shifter at all.

I'd never heard of a wolf hating their human counterpart this way.

Rain's Fall, 1945 ILY

It was officially my birthday when I finally awoke again, spurred by the heat...and I only knew it was my birthday because of the outrageous heat that was searing me and making me feel like I couldn't breathe.

My wolf had pushed me down into unconsciousness for months...?

I assumed that the only reason she wasn't doing so now was because the heat was making her too distracted to keep me down, but I actually hated to be woken up during this.

I felt like I was on fire.

Had Cloud felt this way, too? It felt like my entire abdomen was tense and burning. *Coiling.*

It was intense.

I was just waking up, and yet I *could* feel Silver wavering even now. Her control was loosening.

She didn't seem to realize that I was awake.

After that one morning that Cloud had addressed it, Slater had been spending less time on the outside and giving Cloud more control. It seemed that they were trying to wait Silver out, to get her to see that she needed to let me come back forward.

She was wavering, struggling to maintain her form without reverting to mine. That was how it usually felt before she gave back control.

I could smell him enter the den before I saw him. He was in the living quarters, and I could smell him through the shut bedroom door.

His scent was so tantalizing to me right now, and I could hardly contain myself. More rather, Silver could hardly contain herself, in any case.

I gasped out as I felt my blood pumping, heart pounding, and when Cloud came into the room from outside...

There was no control.

Silver was immediately in front of Cloud, sniffing and licking and nipping him, and he chuckled.

"It's time, isn't it?" He said, husky. "Yes, you have entered your heat," he said thickly, his eyes blazing as he scented the air. "Heat has arrived, indeed," he practically growled out.

She gave a growling response, crawling around on her belly in front of him. Whining and pining for him, I tried to gain some control back from her, but she wasn't having it.

She shoved me down, forcing me away like I was a fly that was disturbing her.

How embarrassing...

He laughed as he shifted, and the moment that *Slater* was released, I could hardly keep up.

Silver may as well have just won the lottery.

She responded in a very dramatic, over-the-top fashion, like the drama queen that she was.

They circled each other like crazy, looking one another up and down, before he licked her mark.

She panted heavily, brushing against him, and rubbing along his body almost like a cat would, before she flopped to her side and gave a roll.

What was this, a dog show?

• • •

I suppose wolves had their own methods for instigating interest?

We hadn't ever really discussed that much in class or in my family. They said that our wolves would instinctively know what to do.

She put her chest to the ground and raised her rear, shoving it into his direction, and he snarled out a bark as he climbed above her.

'Wait, wait, wait, what—'

He mounted her easily, and I shuddered and cried out in pain in my mind at the sharp, sudden invasion of my body.

Had I...just lost my virginity as a wolf?

I didn't know why, but I'd always hoped I would lose it in my human form.

Was that strange?

I felt my cheeks heat up, knowing that this wasn't as special as what I had hoped for. I didn't know what I expected, considering that heat made wolves go crazy...

She snarled as he bit into his mark on her neck, re-marking her and to hold her in place as he thrust and mounted himself deeper, forcing himself into her over and over.

I couldn't imagine what it felt like in human form, but this form...it wasn't entirely good or bad.

It just...was?

She let out a sudden bark-like snarl as a sharp, stabbing pain rushed through our abdomen. What...?

What was that?

It took about twenty minutes for us to become unstuck, and I collapsed to the floor.

Was this it? Was this all there was to this?

● ● ●

Our wolves had taken care of everything, but I had hoped that there would be more to it than that.

Was this what intimacy was...?

He nudged his head beneath my chest with a whine, and lifted up so that I was somewhat lifted.

Then, he helped me to bed and nudged me on, and I felt myself fall into a deep sleep.

CHAPTER 14

Dove...

When I awoke again, I was in my human form.

I reached up to push my hair out of my face before I realized that I had hands!

Hands, and hair, and fingers!

I sat up, and I saw Cloud sitting on the edge of the bed, watching me with an almost...wary expression.

"Cloud...?" I asked.

"You've returned," he smiled softly. "I am glad to see you back," he said.

"Is...that good or bad?" I asked, laughing.

He scoffed out a laugh, brushing my hair out of my face. "I am happy to see you. But I'm worried you'll be upset."

"Upset...?"

"Because we knotted."

I startled, sitting up too quickly, but I wavered and almost fell over. He caught me, even as I gaped up at him in shocked horror. "W-what? What did you say?"

He looked away. "When Slater and Silver mated...they knotted."

174

I gaped at him.

Knotting was something that most canine species—wolf-shifters, included—did to *ensure pregnancy*.

He leaned forward, and my eyes widened as he got right in my face.

"Though, I am not bothered. If you were to come to me, pupped...I would not mind."

I flushed, my pulse racing in me as my blood rushed.

"Cloud..."

He leaned further, where his lips were about to touch mine. "May I kiss you?" He asked, stunning me. "I've missed you a lot over the last several months that Silver had you locked away, and I was scared I'd never see you again. I am so...so happy to see you," he murmured, blushing lightly.

I barely nodded, before his lips were against my own, and I gasped into his mouth.

I felt his arms wrap around me, and our kiss got deeper.

I realized, with shock, that I was naked.

"Cloud—" I said, pulling away. "I...I'm alright with it, I'm fine that they mated...but I am not ready for that in this form, with you, quite yet. May I...have some more time?"

He gave me an endearing expression and a nod. "But, I would like to kiss you...often," he said.

I gave a nod to him, too. "I can handle that," I said, blushing.

Veras's Height, 1945 ILY

Nausea reared its ugly head, and I groaned as I turned over, wishing to stay in bed.

I had, indeed, become pregnant from my heat.

My family had been overjoyed, but I wasn't sure how I had felt about it.

Though, I wasn't angry at Cloud. He had simply responded to my heat, as any male would have responded to his mate's heat.

I was, however, angry at Silver.

She had kept me locked away for months, and then, she had gotten knocked up during our heat before she had finally let me have control back...?

She really did hate me.

Cloud...was on edge around me, walking on egg-shells. He didn't want to upset me in anyway, or pressure me.

I tried to assure him that he was fine, but he was trying to stay calm and respectful.

He reacted much better than I would have hoped...especially considering that I still wanted another male, besides him.

We had gotten much closer, yes. I even viewed him as a friend...but that true mate aspect was still hanging over my head.

I just didn't believe he could love me the way that a true mate could, and my instincts told me that I needed my true mate.

I felt, in my heart, that being with Cloud was a betrayal to my true mate, and I felt guilty and sad.

Soon, though, I was feeling too ill to function properly due to my pregnancy, and finally, the pack enlisted a delta female to help out with my pregnancy and around the den.

Though, something was eerie since she had arrived days ago.

She made me uncomfortable, and though I noticed that Cloud tried to steer clear of her, she didn't seem to get the message.

Why did she seem so familiar to me?

Silver still wasn't talking to me or letting her thoughts drift to me. We were still disconnected, so I couldn't ask her even if I wanted to.

Being disconnected to her so severely, with another female in the den that acted so strangely, made me feel incredibly uneasy.

It was late into the morning one day, when I got out of bed and grabbed my large glass for water.

Being pregnant made me incredibly thirsty, and Cloud insisted that it was important for me to stay properly hydrated.

It was when I came out to the kitchen, I dropped and shattered my empty water glass to see that same delta female, lip-locked with Cloud.

His hands gripped her shoulders, pushing her away, but she gripped him with everything she had.

"But you're my *true mate*!" She whimpered as he finally got her pushed back. "Can't you leave that girl and choose me? You've done all you need to do; you mated her and now have a pup coming, so you aren't forced to—"

"I'm not forced to stay with her anyway," he snarled at her. "I *chose* to stay with her because...I care for her. Maybe I even love her. I, Cloud Stone, beta heir of the Terra-Forest-Stone pack, reject yo—"

"*No!*" She shrieked. She turned as I gasped, glaring at me. "You! *You* caused this! You took my mate from me!" She sobbed.

I walked closer with my hands raised, trying to get her to calm down.

Silver's hackles were raised, but she still wasn't making any move to come out or let her thoughts to come to me, so I knew she wouldn't step forward to help me.

As I stepped closer, trying to help Cloud to deal with her, the girl backed away.

I wasn't sure what I could do, but it didn't matter because she leapt across the countertop and punched me in the face as hard as she could manage.

In my current state, I didn't see it coming and I didn't even stand a chance.

I spun on my heel, knocked so hard from her force, and fell forward directly to my belly because my socks slipped on the slippery, slick new linoleum of the kitchen floor.

*I noted, with sour conviction, that Cloud had been right—linoleum **had** been a bad idea.*

I fell, fell, fell...directly on my belly...directly on the large, shattered drinking glass that I had dropped.

The pain was sharp, and I gasped as I felt the glass slide deep into my abdomen, my arm, even a shard into my neck.

Shifter or not, I would have to be rushed to the physician.

Wolves healed quickly, but I was pregnant. All of my shifter power was being pulled to the baby in my womb, doing all that it could to protect that small new life there, and so in turn, I could feel the internal damage.

I could feel the shards shattering and spreading.

I would require *surgery*...all because I slipped and fell onto glass?

Another way for Silver to slight me, it would seem, because this was an extreme injury for something so small, in terms of wolf-shifters.

"No!" Cloud's cry ripped out of him, and he rushed forward.

He jerked the girl back and threw her against the wall, startling her, before he rushed to turn me to my back on a clean spot of floor and began working over me. I could hear the muffled sound of his voice instructing our omega servant, and I could hear him speaking through the pack link.

Everything was going in and out, and my vision was getting fuzzy and dark.

Crow rushed in, followed soon by the healer and even the shaman arrived.

Then, my father and the alpha...

I felt my eyes close as I drifted into the darkness, with my final thought being on my unborn pup.

The next time that I opened my eyes, which would be several days, two surgeries and hours of fearful waiting at my side from multiple pack members later, I would learn that the pup—so newly conceived, so weak, so new—hadn't been able to survive.

They had put my life first.

I'd needed to have so much glass removed from my body, the splinters and shards difficult to pinpoint. I'd also lost a good bit of blood.

Were I any normal human, I likely would have lost my life.

Instead, I lost my pup.

Lost before I'd even been into the third month.

"...Gone...?" I whispered.

Cloud sat beside me, holding my hand, a look of agony on his face.

"I'm...so sorry," he choked out. "But at least...you're okay," he said. "I had to think about you first."

It was, ironically, the first time that anyone had ever put me first. The first time that anyone had ever even said those words to me.

Cloud had held me all night in his arms in the hospital building's bed, silently mourning the loss with me.

He ceaselessly kissed my cheeks, forehead, hair...anything he could reach.

No words spoken.

My wolf was strangely still in my mind.

I could feel her emotions; she felt guilty, as if it were her fault.

I tried my best to reassure her that I didn't feel that way, that it wasn't her fault, but she knew the truth. I did feel a little bit that it was her fault.

She had refused to come forward, and hadn't even put her power into healing me.

She had left me on my own to deal with the injury, and I hadn't been strong enough to heal and protect my pup.

She did have some responsibility for that.

So, she just lay down in my mind and sat still, whimpering and crying softly.

There was no comfort to be had...for either of us, or for Cloud and Slater.

Cloud did, in the end, formally reject his true mate.

Not only that, but after the horribly painful, public rejection, the girl had then been sentenced to death for attacking the beta female and killing the beta heir's unborn pup.

That, in itself, was a grave offense in our culture that resulted in execution, as pups were what our people strove for the most, in order to survive and thrive as a society.

Slater, *himself*, had carried out the execution, in retribution for the attack on me, to avenge our lost pup.

It baffled my mind; it completely destroyed all of my preconceptions from before.

He had chosen me, and chosen our pup, over his true mate.

Had the roles been reversed, I wasn't sure that I could have made that same choice...but since he had, my feelings had changed quite a lot.

I couldn't believe he had even killed her.

He had killed his true mate, for justice. To avenge the pup between the two of us.

To avenge me, and our loss.

Yet, it hadn't made either of us, nor our wolves, feel any better.

I was simply relieved that she couldn't retaliate against us any further.

Thankfully, her family felt the same way we did.

The loss of a pup was a horrible thing in these times of uncertainty and war among our kind.

The whole pack mourned with us.

CHAPTER 15

Cloud...

I dressed in armor, heading out to war.

I glanced to my mate, who sat on the edge of her rocking chair, watching me with sad eyes.

Her eyes were always a bit sad, since we had lost our pup, but she had at least started speaking again after the third month after the loss.

I was so upset, even still, that I'd let that girl be assigned to serve us during the pregnancy. When they had originally asked me about her serving us, I hadn't even realized who she was.

I was already mated and expecting a pup with my mate. I hadn't been thinking about my true mate. Not even a little bit.

When she had arrived, and I had realized who she was, I had been uncomfortable with it, but Dove never said anything, and all of the other delta females were busy...

I wasn't comfortable leaving Dove alone with just Crow while she was pregnant.

It was my fault.

• • •

184

I felt so guilty, riddled with grief at the knowledge that I could have prevented this. I could have a pup. I could be a father.

I had known her true identity, but protectiveness and love for my mate had blinded me. I hadn't used my brain, and I felt responsible.

The pup was lucky it hadn't been saddled with me as a father.

I obviously wasn't ready.

War had arrived to our pack, shortly afterward, and I took that as another sign that this...may just be for the better.

Another pack was warring with us over territory boundaries and expansion, and I was called upon to go and battle. I was strong, young, fierce...and I was smart.

Though, I questioned how smart I really was, lately.

Dove hadn't been the same since the loss of the pup...or, since the conception of the pup in the first place, if we were being completely honest.

She was still conflicted, even now.

She had been made to submit to me because Silver had been in control, and we'd bred...because of her heat.

I had knotted her without consent, and that was because Slater had just acted on his own, without my consent.

It hadn't been a choice either of us had made.

It had strictly been our wolves, and because of the heat, and a pup had come from the union. A pup that I'd put in her, and now...

Now, I was responsible for the loss of.

Though she put on a brave face and tried to act normal around me, I could sense that she was still disconnected—more so than ever—from her wolf, and that she was still in mourning.

Many females in the pack were pregnant now, what with our age-group from the school hitting their awakenings and heats and finding their true mates. Many new pups would have arrived by the time I return from war.

...Our pup would not be among those, sadly.

I looked forward to war, if I was being honest.

I needed to take out some of this guilt and rage and mourning in the form of killing and aggression.

I needed to fight something, someone, somewhere.

It shouldn't be difficult, but Crow would be staying behind with my female while I left, and I wasn't comfortable about leaving her here without me.

Veras's End, 1947 ILY

It was the end of the war, and I was tired.

It had taken much longer than I had thought.

Sleeping in the field had made me wary and alert, paranoid, and on edge.

I was rarely rested.

The leader of this enemy pack, however, had surrendered after they had experienced overwhelming losses, and so we had, officially, won the war.

Now, I could return back home.

There had been a few losses on our side; a few deltas and quite a few omegas, but we'd had a lot of pregnant females at home when we had left, and the loss somehow didn't seem quite as severe, knowing that there was a new generation waiting for us.

It was early morning, and we were all preparing to set out for home.

Oddly, I'd had a strange feeling, that day, when the sun had gotten to its highest point.

I felt...eerie, in almost the same way that I had when Dove had been attacked.

That was the last time that I had felt this gut-wrenching, stomach-clenching, heart-sinking feeling.

Pain continued to radiate throughout my entire core.

I had no idea what was happening, and it was unlike anything I had ever experienced.

Slater was howling in my mind, snarling and barking between the howls of pain and misery...but he wouldn't talk to me.

At least, not for quite a while.

I wasn't sure if he even knew what was happening, or not. If he did, I wish he would tell me.

I noticed a couple of our wolves glancing at me, concerned.

Several had suspicions, but nobody asked me about it.

I knew, though.

Something was wrong.

Slater wouldn't stop pacing, snarling beneath his breath, howling in pain...

It surely had to do with our mate. There was no other explanation.

Was Dove alright?

What was going on?

It was when Crow, hours away from the pack, had arrived to me, there in the battlefield's aftermath location...that I knew something *was* terribly, *terribly* wrong.

For him to come out this far, away from his beta female...

Something horrible was happening.

"She's gone!" He'd cried to me, falling to his knees. "I stepped behind a tree to relieve myself, not sensing anything bad in the area, and when I came back, she was *gone!* I couldn't find her! Her scent cut off at the river, scent blocker had been sprayed, and—"

He didn't even get a chance to continue.

It was in that moment that I understood the depth of the situation, and the realization of what was going on hit me all at once.

Somehow...I just knew.

Dove was with her true mate.

To this day, she still hadn't given her heart over to me.

She hadn't marked me, in return.

That meant that Sparrow could still challenge me for her and take her.

If she wanted, she could give herself to him, even now.

The pain that had radiated inside of me...it *had* to be infidelity.

I'd read about it before; I had known the rumors about what it felt like, but to experience it first hand was excruciating.

I, in my shifted form, ran with all my might back to the pack.

Slater wasn't even slightly concerned at how tired and ragged that I was.

Slater didn't care how far it was, or the fact that we hadn't rested.

All that he knew was that his mate was in trouble, and he was going to get to her...period.

It was hours of running, and my legs felt like jelly. I could barely hold myself up.

Still, I drove myself forward.

She'd been taken.

She had to have been taken...and I could only hope that she had fought him.

I *had* to hope that the burning of my bond to her wasn't her choosing and her doing. That she wasn't *choosing* to cheat on me...

After a few hours, I had finally reached our territory.

The familiar smell was a minimal comfort for me, but I couldn't linger on it.

I had to get to her, and I had to get to her now.

I could feel in our bond that she wasn't far from me...

She wasn't at the den.

In fact, they were close to the borders...but *why*?

I caught wind of her scent, but the scent that I caught *with* her confirmed it.

Sparrow had taken her.

I heard raised voices as I got a bit closer, and Slater told me to wait.

'Why wait?!' I cried in my mind.

'Just wait. Trust me.'

I felt it deep in my belly.

He made me halt, as I listened to his instincts.

"I know that you're my true mate, Sparrow...and I want to be with my true mate. I do, really. But I'm already marked. A marking cannot be taken back, and we already mated, too. We might have an unconventional relationship, but I care about him. So, I'm trying to accept my relationship to him, and I can't just leave—"

"He's at *war*!" He said, exasperated. "*I* am your true mate!"

"Sparrow—"

"I am a powerful Pack Hunter Heir, and I would have never allowed another female to come into our den and make you lose our pup the way that Beta Heir Cloud did! He isn't good enough for you! He isn't good enough to father your pups...Please, Dove...*please*, give me a chance. I know that I can make you happy—"

"I'm *sorry*, Sparrow. I trust Cloud. He's already doing so much to try to be good to me and build this bond with me. I may want to be with my true mate, but Cloud and I...well, we're in a *good* place. I care for him—"

"You belong with *me*!" He cried, refusing to hear it.

I watched with raising hackles as he pulled her into a kiss, and though she gasped and kissed him back, making the bond in our blood sear and scald me with pain...her hands gripped his shoulders and pushed him away.

"That isn't fair, Sparrow. You can't kiss me that way, you can't—"

"*I* am your true mate. I also know that the Moon Mother didn't bless your union with Cloud!" He shouted, towering over her. "I know that I can challenge him for you, and if I win, the pack laws would take *my* side because you haven't marked him in return. I love you, Dove. You're the one meant for me! I'm meant for you! Don't throw that away for another male just because he's a beta!"

She looked like he'd slapped her. "Excuse me?"

"I know the beta is a better position than the Pack Hunter, but I'm almost as powerful as he is, if not more so. Pack Hunters have to be powerful, to uphold the laws. I could be better for you. Don't let titles dictate this!"

"I'm not," she said, tone soft. "This has nothing to do with titles, honest. I don't hate Cloud. Sure, we were awkward at first, but we've become good friends, and I'm...I have feelings for him. They are growing, still, and he might not be my true mate, but I *want* to build with Cloud."

"So, you just don't even want to try?"

"I, Dove Terra Stone, beta female heiress, *reject* you—"

"Dove—"

"*No!*" She shouted, putting authority into her tone. "You came into my home, knocked me unconscious and dragged me out! You took me by *force*. Then, you started kissing and touching me before I could even *give* consent, because you think you *own* me! You didn't even have the decency to challenge my mate first—"

"*I* am your mate!" He shouted.

She shook her head. "No. There is order to these things. You did things the wrong way, and I don't want this. You are acting like I am your property, and I am not property!"

"Dove—"

"No," she sighed. "I reject you, Sparrow, Pack Hunter heir and delta of the Terra-Forest-Stone pack, as my true mate. I hereby refuse submission to you. I refuse the gift of our true mate bond."

"No!" He sobbed, crying and falling to his knees.

I could feel the pain rushing through my mate as she struggled to remain standing, the breaking of the true mate bond hurting her deeply.

I could feel Silver slip away from her, drowning in the newly added, self-inflicted pain that her human had just given her, and Slater could hear her howling in her mind.

She collapsed, sobbing, even as Sparrow began snarling at her, turning. His eyes began to glow, and he was starting to turn feral.

"How could you? How could you choose him over your true mate? Over *me?!*"

I shifted to my human form, ready to step out to retrieve her.

He looked up at her with desperate eyes, reaching for her. "Mate, please, I—we can fix it. We can fix it! If you just take it back, if you mark me, then we—"

"***Get. Away. From. My. Mate***," I snarled, Slater putting his own dramatically powerful force into the tone.

His eyes whirled to find me, face full of shock. "C-Cloud—"

"Get *away* from her!" I shouted. "She is *mine*. You failed to challenge me before you took her by *force*, and thus you *forfeited* your right to claim her by challenge. She's right; there *is* an order to things according to pack laws. You might want to brush up on those laws, you know, if you expect to uphold them as Pack Hunter." I shook my head. "She is marked and refused you, rejected you. Now, get away from her."

He struggled to stand, and he looked over at us as I came and took her into my arms.

"You *weren't* her true mate," he said, upset.

"It doesn't matter. I would have accepted your challenge, had you issued it properly and fought me for her. But according to Pack Law, you broke the law and violated that right when you took her by force. She then rejected you. Forcing a wolf after being rejected is also another law that you are breaking."

He snarled at me, pacing because he knew that I was right, and he had messed up.

"...This wasn't what I had intended. I had intended to tell her that I would be challenging you...but then, I was overcome by her scent, and her presence, and I just...acted without thinking. She was supposed to be mine."

"Yes...but you lost your chance. Now, leave."

He glared at us for a while longer, watching with agonized eyes as Dove turned into my side, looking away from him.

I thought that he was going to leave...but then, he shifted, and I forced the shift a little too fast.

I was in the middle of shifting when he jumped on me, snapping at my throat and trying to grab me, not letting up.

"No!" Dove cried, pacing to the side.

I knew that she and Silver weren't on good terms, so I knew that she wouldn't be able to shift, and I knew that she was still weak from the injuries she sustained the year before.

I was on my own.

Slater finally made it through, and I shoved my way away from Sparrow.

His wolf was the same color as his hair, eyes blazing as he tried to approach Dove, a snarl coming out of him.

He stepped another step closer to her, trying to get her situated behind him, and it pushed Slater over the edge.

No matter how tired we were, we leapt over-top of this delta, getting him on the ground easily and snarling into his face as we pinned him.

Sparrow tried to push me off, to fight back, and I was ready to rip his throat out...but one look from Dove, shaking her head in the negative with that sad expression...

I huffed, letting him up.

He shifted back to human form, and I followed suit.

Tears ran down his face. "But she was *mine*," he said, soft.

"It is over, Sparrow. She doesn't belong to you."

"She used to," he said, sad.

"You're right, in a way. She did belong with you." I told him. "But I love her, and I will do all I can to take good care of her. It is too late. I'm sorry, truly. But I promise, I will keep her safe and provide for her."

He huffed, turning. "Then that is all I can ask for."

"I truly hope you can find a mate who can give you what you deserve...can be the mate you can love and have," Dove said, sad. "I wish the best for you."

He looked at her, glancing at her before looking to me.

Then he turned again.

With that, he walked into the forest...and she and I clung to one another as she gasped into my chest, happy that I had returned and happy that I had confessed my love for her.

The last she had heard, I "might even" love her...but for me to admit it, in earnest, that I loved her...?

Oh, how far we had come.

We made our way back to the den in silence, this den where so much had happened.

I led her to bed, neither of us saying a word, and I lay her down on our bed.

It smelled of her, so bereft of my scent for so long...and it drove Slater wild in my mind.

Love mate first, sleep after, I heard his thoughts drift in.

I laughed, rolling my eyes at him internally.

Outwardly, I lightly chuckled, pressing my lips to her skin, kissing her neck, her mark, her chest...

Our clothes were shed somewhere along the way.

I groaned with wanton desire as I swirled my tongue over her breasts, getting her nipples hard for me and flicking the peaks.

I left suck marks and bite marks all along her ribs and sides, her hips...

I nibbled along her hips, nipping, and once I had her mewling for me,

I pressed little nips and kisses along her thighs and down to her feet, sucking on a couple of her toes before I kissed back up her legs on the inside.

I spread her wide for me, licking my chops before I set to licking her.

I flattened my tongue, using the entire surface area to create extra friction.

I pressed fingers into her heat, curving and twisting and thrusting them in her heated core.

She gasped and mewed, gripping the sheets and her hair, anything she could reach.

Her fingers gripped in my hair, and pulled me with force until my tongue was pressing into her.

I curled and swept my tongue, ravishing her.

I could have lost her that day, but she had confessed her love for me and rejected the mate that had been born for her...so I wanted to cherish her.

I felt her body tensing, the muscles tightening and pulsing, before it sprung out like a spring coiled too tightly.

She cried and pulled, but I held her steady as my mouth continued working on her, sweeping into her and gathering her taste of her cum on my tongue as her pussy squeezed my tongue and fingers tighter in rhythmic pulses.

She rode my face, riding her high out before she started to relax, and I climbed my way up her body.

It didn't take any further encouragement for my hard-on to be ready, and I slipped it into her slick heat without issue.

She gasped and quenched up her face, and the smell of blood hit the air.

How...?

Wolf lost virginity, human did not.

* * *

The explanation made me glad, and I was thankful that I was getting a separate experience with her myself to give something so special to each other.

I groaned, breathing heavily as I moved within her.

I didn't have high stamina yet, and I was quite tired, so I felt my release coming much earlier than I would have liked...but we had plenty of time.

I didn't want to rush her.

We reached that high together, and I couldn't even stay awake to learn the result.

Sleep took me, but I heard Dove snickering at me before she cuddled into me, joining me in my nap.

I would realize later that we hadn't used any form of protection, and I hadn't pulled out of her body.

In fact, I slept incased inside of her body safely, all night long.

I was completely unaware if I had knotted her or not.

We would find out soon enough, I supposed.

I wouldn't be upset if I had, though. Perhaps another pup might heal us both.

The following morning, she would ride me all morning long in the bathtub.

She would ride me until she had squeezed every last drop out of my cum out of my body, and all throughout the next day...and the next...we would not leave the cozy safety and warmth of our den.

CHAPTER 16

Dove...

After that night—the night I had rejected Sparrow—things had finally reached the best place for me and Cloud.

Though I was still to be punished for my "infidelity" to Cloud, for willingly kissing Sparrow back before rejecting him...things had turned upside down when we told the pack that Cloud and I had just mated.

Thankfully, they decided to wait to see if I had been pupped or not to delve out a punishment.

Surely enough, just over a month later, we'd discovered that I was pregnant.

I had conceived him that fateful Solaris's Gifts day, back three years ago. Nine months later, I had given birth in Rain's Fall of 1948 ILY, to a son who had my silvery hair and my emerald green eyes.

However, for my infidelity, *for kissing Sparrow back*, for putting Cloud through the pain of infidelity because I had kissed Sparrow a few times, to be honest...and I had let him touch me more than I cared to remember because I had been so, so lost in the feelings of those mate-bond-sparks, so overwhelmed by his scent and the true mate bond tugging at me...

Well, I had been punished.

They waited until I had given birth to my pup, but then I had been punished.

I'd been made to wear a silver shackle on my ankle.

Silver drastically weakened and slowly poisoned wolves, if left on the skin for long periods of time, and for my already very weak wolf and my very thin connection to her...it may as well have been a dose of coma-inducing drugs to our system.

The alpha had decided to leave this shackle on me for an entire *year*.

At least I hadn't had to *inject* any silver.

Silver, if injected, could potentially be fatal if it was more than a few drops.

Many wolves who committed crimes were made to inject a dop of silver a day for multiple day or weeks, depending on the crime.

Enemies or prisoners who were tortured were tortured by slicing them open with silver.

They even took to pushing it into cuts, before letting their wolves heal for a few days and then doing it again.

I couldn't be angry that I had been punished.

I had, after all, really entertained Sparrow far more than I should have. I should never have let him take me as far as he did, or do as much as he had. Cloud had suffered unimaginably and I paid the price for it...but then, so did my wolf.

She was barely functioning, now.

Now, I may as well be human, with a very weak wolf.

Disconnected from the moon because I found out my true mate wouldn't be my mate in the end.

Disconnected from the Moon Mother because I mated someone other than my true mate without her blessing.

Disconnected from my wolf because I had cursed her.

Now, weakened from long exposure to silver on my skin for cheating on Cloud.

I had deserved every bit of it.

I looked down at my pup, playing with Cloud now.

"Now, let's stay with daddy," I told the pup, trying to toddle away from his father with haste.

The pup just laughed, ignoring me, but his father caught up to him quickly.

It was already his second birthday, and we had invited most of the pack to join us in the celebration.

There were lots of excited pups at this party, enjoying playing with our toddler.

As I watched them all playing, chasing after Cloud and tackling him as he made a big dramatic show of being taken down by the children...I knew that I was ready for our next pup.

Maybe a girl this time?

A girl that looked like her father...yeah.

I knew we would be all too thrilled to try, I thought with a smile.

Year's Fall, 1954 ILY

I took a deep breath, looking down at my clean sheets.

I could sense that I was several weeks late for my cycle.

I'd been supposed to have it at the end of Folias's Blessing, and it was now the end of Year's Fall, almost Blizzard's Reign...

I had gone this very morning to the pack doctor, and he had confirmed...I was pregnant.

I looked at my sheets now; clean, and free of blood that I would have expected from my menstrual cycle...

According to the doctor, I was about a month along, now.

I was due in late Solaris's Reign.

I was surprised that I'd managed to get pregnant again, to be honest. We had been trying ever since my punishment had been over—when our son was a year old—but I hadn't conceived.

The long exposure to silver on my skin had so drastically weakened my wolf that it seemed conception was no longer an option for us.

I had all but given up, crying and upset that I couldn't have any more pups.

Cloud had assured me that we could adopt, or go with a surrogate. That he would be happy, even with just our one son, that I didn't need to feel pressured. That he was there for me no matter what happened...

I just felt cursed.

Now, joy rushed through me at the prospect of another pup in our lives.

I had waited so long, longer than any other wolves I had known.

Even Sparrow had moved on; he had found a good delta female to mate, mated her, and had a pup recently, whom they had named Sage.

Nausea rushed through me, and I groaned as I clenched my chest with my hands, taking deep and slow breaths...before I ultimately ran and lost my breakfast into the toilet.

"Dove?" Crow asked, knocking on the bathroom door. "Are you alright?"

I finished my business, cleaning up after myself and stepping out. "I'm okay...I just...have big news," I smiled at him.

His eyes widened, and a broad smile lit his face. His own mate was pregnant, and so he must have recognized the signs right away.

"Really?" He asked, excited. I gave a nod, and he pulled me into a gentle hug. "I am so happy for you."

I gave a nod. "Yes, I am thrilled. Where is Cloud? Is he still in a meeting with the alpha heir?"

He smiled. "Yes, though they should be finishing up. Does he—"

"He doesn't know, and I want you to keep it quiet until I tell him. I will announce it tonight. We're having a family meal for the new year, anyway," I smiled at him.

He nodded. "Of course," he smiled. "The omegas are prepping everything for the dinner tonight. It is still just the major families, isn't it?"

"Yes, nothing too large. Just a small celebration. It happened to be a perfect time for us to announce something like this," I smiled.

He pulled me into another hug. "I am sure that he will be happy."

"I am, too. We've been trying for a long time, now."

We had been trying to have another baby since Quill turned one, and it just hadn't happened yet.

He was now four, and it felt like it just wasn't happening.

Crow gave me a hug, rubbing circles into my back.

How many times had he done this, while whispering comforting words into my ear as I cried over the discovery of my menstrual cycles after hoping for so long that I was pregnant?

Every single month had been the same.

Every time I would wake to my bleeding, I would cry, and Crow would comfort me.

As my gamma, my safety, protection, and comfort were his top priority, and for that, I was thankful.

Being the Beta Female Heiress, all of my concern had to be poured into the Luna Heiress, and I had to take care of the pack with her.

I had nobody on my side beyond my mate and my gamma.

I took a moment to compose myself and pick out something nice to wear for the dinner that evening, before I spent the remainder of the afternoon directing the omegas and setting things up around the den for visitors, making sure everything was perfect.

Once I had about an hour left, I made sure that I took a good shower and dressed in a very pretty purple dress, long-sleeved and elegant looking.

● ● ●

Then I was pulling my hair into a braid over my left shoulder and putting in small, pretty amethyst earrings.

I startled when I felt Cloud step up behind me, pulling me into his grasp.

"You look *lovely*," he said softly, voice a murmur of heat into my ear as he tongued my mate mark.

I groaned, turning to face him. "We don't have time," I smiled up at him.

He pouted, but he took his own turn in the shower.

While he was washing, our families arrived, and I got everyone sat at the dining table and waited for food to be served.

Cloud arrived a few minutes later, dressed sharply and looking handsome.

When food had been served and we were all sitting there, I took a moment to stand and tap my fork to my glass.

"Attention, please," I said, glancing around at our guests before locking and holding my gaze with Cloud's. "I have some exciting news. After getting it confirmed by the doctor this morning…I learned that we are expecting our second pup," I said.

Cloud leapt from his seat with a happy exclamation, rushing to me and taking me into his arms, pressing happy kisses all over my face as he laughed and hugged me.

"I am so happy by this news!" He said, smiling down at me before glancing to our son. "Do you hear that, my boy? You are going to be a big brother," he said.

Quill looked at me in surprise, before his eyes trailed down to my belly. "My brother is in there?" He asked.

Cloud and I paused, looking at each other before we both chuckled.

I glanced back at my oldest pup. "Are you saying you want a brother?"

"It has to be a brother," he said, huffing. "You wouldn't give a strong beta male child like me a sister," he said.

Cloud burst out laughing even as I scowled. "And who told you that?" I asked him.

"Ebony Stone, and Blossom Stone."

Those two rascals, I rolled my eyes.

They were former Alpha—turned Defensive Gamma—Sierra Stone's son, Ebony, and Blossom, a niece that he was raising because her parents had died.

"You know that strong couples don't *only* produce males," I told him. "You could very well get a sister. After all, *my* father is a Beta, and he *only* had a daughter—*me*."

He looked at me with a confused expression. "So...it really *could* be a sister...?"

I nodded. "Yes. You are the future Beta Heir, because your father and I are the beta heir couple...but you will be the heir for the beta title when you come of age. If you have a brother, he could be eligible to become beta if you don't do your job right, or if something happened to you. But a sister...she would depend on you to love her and take care of her, as the beta. She would be your biggest supporter and fan, and you would be her biggest protector."

"But I..." His bottom lip wobbled a bit. "I thought I'd get a brother."

"You might still get one," I laughed. "But you might get a sister. Either way, we are just happy if the baby is healthy and happy. Can you promise me that no matter which it is, you'll love and protect the baby either way?" I asked.

He huffed, but looked at my belly. "Yes, mommy...I promise."

"Good boy," I smiled at him.

Solaris's Reign, 1955 ILY

I was resting in the pack hospital's nursery room, holding my tiny bundle in my arms as Cloud sat in a rocking chair next to me, watching me with a blissful expression on his face.

Against what our son, our little Quill who looked so much like me, had wanted...I *had* given birth to a girl this time around.

The labor had been strenuous and difficult, and I had almost died during the birth.

Because of the danger level of my pregnancies and childbirth, the doctor had taken out my reproductive organs during the cesarean-section birth I'd had with our daughter...a result of a labor that led to an emergency.

It had been scary, but I had been endlessly thankful that we'd both made it through it safely.

Thank goodness for modern medicine.

She was stunning, I would admit it. She looked so much like her father.

She had his peppery, dark silver hair, and his pale green eyes with just the barest hint of jade around the pupils and little lines of emerald around the outside of the iris.

She had my darker tan skin, though.

She was quite an eater, and nearly suckled me dry of my milk it seemed like.

A big eater, for such a tiny little wolf.

There was a gentle knock on the door, and I looked up to see my parents and Cloud's parents step into the room, our son peaking his head in with them.

"Can we meet her?" My mother asked.

I laughed softly, pulling her off my breast and fixing my tunic before I wiped her pouty little lips.

"Of course," I smiled. I glanced to my oldest. "Would you like to meet your sister?"

He let out a breath he'd been holding, stepping over like he was tip-toeing until he reached my side. I held the baby so that he could look at her.

"Hi, sissy," he said, soft. "I'm your big brother, Quill. It is nice to meet you. I will protect you forever." I saw when he looked up at me. "She looks like you, mommy," he said.

"Me?" I questioned, wondering if he had even seen his father.

"Yeah...she's pretty, just like you."

My heart swelled so much, so quickly, that I thought I'd burst.

This little boy and his baby sister held my heart even more than their father did, and that was really something.

I hadn't expected to find such a happy life through an arranged marriage.

I hadn't thought that we'd be so close, or so inseparable, but we truly had grown to love each other.

Now, we'd given each other pups, and I didn't think that we could have been any closer.

"What is her name?" He asked, looking at me.

"I named you," I said. "So, I am letting your father name her."

I glanced to Cloud, who looked out the window and took a deep breath before looking back to me.

• • •

"Have I ever told you that your skin's tone reminds me of my favorite trees?" He asked me.

I cocked my head. "No," I said after a moment of contemplating the question.

He shook his head. "I thought not. Your tan skin has the barest hint of this tone, and it is striking against your light silver hair and your bright, emerald green eyes. And so, like my favorite tree and like yours and her skin tone...I will name her 'Cedar.'"

My heart thumped wildly because he was right; our skin *did* hold the barest hint of cedar under tones.

"Quill and Cedar Stone," I whispered.

Then, I let my family pass her around, celebrating her.

I did worry about her future, as I watched them smiling and cooing at her.

She had been born very weak.

Because of the prolonged silver poisoning I had experienced for a year, she was a weak pup with not a lot of energy.

She required much more feeding than even Quill had, but she was still so tired and weak and pitiful. She was a little underweight, and her skin tone was the same as mine, but paler.

She didn't look very healthy.

I had the most awful feeling over her future. I felt that she wouldn't be able to attract a powerful male, if she remained this weakened.

What kind of life could she be looking at living?

Folias's Blessing, 1961 ILY

It was utter chaos, as we tried to pack whatever we could carry and escape while we could.

Humans had discovered our presence here, deep in the forest, and had started hunting us.

Six omegas had been hunted, killed, and skinned; their skins left hanging in the forest as a warning.

What with this new threat on one side, and the threat of territorial fights with the other packs in the area, we decided as a pack that it was best if we left.

With the clearance of the Aurora-Peak Pack—the royal pack of our kind, located in the Northern Kingdom—we had decided to move to a place in that territory that they owned.

It may cause more territory disputes, but they had agreed to help us smooth things over.

We had eighteen pups in the pack, and so it was increasingly dangerous for us and crucial to the survival of our people for us to move.

Those facts changed things.

However, we hadn't made it far into our plan to move before war had arrived in our pack.

Our dens were on fire, the humans were hunting us, and it was all we could do to get out with what we could carry and our pups without getting killed.

Severe pain speared us, snapping like a rubber-band on our hearts, as we felt the bond break with our alpha.

"*Alpha Falcon has been killed!*" The news was announced by my father via pack link. "*Negotiations fell through! Alpha title passes to his son, Finch Terra! I, the Beta and the Gammas will try to help buy time for the rest of you to escape. In case anything happens, we remind you to look to your betas and gammas for leadership with the new alpha. We love you all,*" he said.

Tears ran down my face as I lifted my six-year-old.

She was still so weak, so timid and tiny and slight. She was skittish and quiet, but was a submissive, obedient child.

Her brother was absolutely wild over her, hardly letting her out of his sight because he felt the need to protect her so fiercely.

He spoiled her almost as much as we did.

Her dark, peppery-grey silver hair and her bright, light pale green eyes reminded me of her father, who shifted for me.

He let me lift our six-year-old to his back before he took what he could carry into his mouth and began trotting toward the mountains.

Quill, our thirteen-year-old, took a deep breath, letting his wolf, Nickle, take over and had them shift.

He stood as a decent-sized, pretty, long-haired silver wolf, like me.

I shifted despite that the process took entirely too long and was entirely too painful, lifting what I could carry as well, and I followed after him.

It was going to be a long journey, and our pack was in mourning...but hopefully, things would get better from here.

I was a weakened beta female, the daughter of a powerful beta couple that were true mates, love made right away. I had been made to give up my dream of being with my true mate, but I had found love even in an arrangement I hadn't wanted.

Things were looking on the upside even in the world of chaos around us.

I truly believed that things could get better.

This was my story, and...

We could always hope for a brighter future.

To be continued in Part 2

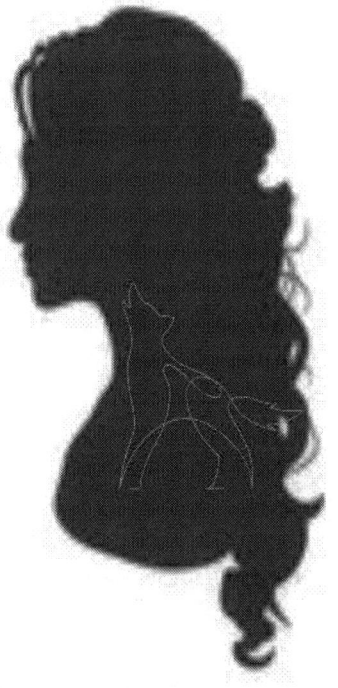

PART 2

Mother

CHAPTER 1

Cedar Stone...

Veras's Height, 1962 Imperial Lunar Year

It was in the Veras before I turned seven-years-old, when my pack managed to hit the Northern Kingdom's border.

We were searching for a new home, or so my big brother Quill told me.

Our pack had been attacked, and we got permission from the Royal pack in the Northern Kingdom to move to some land they owned in that territory.

The land was called "Mackenzie Mountains," and it was going to be cold compared to our old home...but we would build good strong dens.

During the journey, we had encountered and disputed with several other packs, but with the order we had from the Royal pack on paper helped to protect us from attacks.

We did face attacks from rogues along the way, but we needed to get to our new home.

I peeked my eyes open from my place on mama's back, looking up to see what had stopped us.

The alpha of our pack, along with my daddy, stood there conversing with a much older man, and a man around my pawpaw's age.

They glanced at one another as they looked over the paper that my father presented.

"It is signed by the Head Alpha, alright," the older man said, a bit of a mean tone. "But that territory is directly bordering my own, and we have a lot of males in our pack. Our extended families joined the pack, rather than joining new packs or making branch packs in the area. We have four gamma-level males, and six beta-ranked. We cannot afford to have other high-ranked males in the area, what with our lacking females. You must adhere to the boundary and strictly stay on your line."

"We can agree to that," our alpha, Alpha Finch, said, his voice soft. "We just needed to find refuge from the humans. I am newly appointed as the alpha of our pack, so we aren't looking for trouble."

The other man nodded. "We understand."

My father extended a hand. "It is nice to meet you. I am Beta Cloud Stone. We are the Terra-Forest-Stone pack, from the East."

"We are the Glacial-Stone pack," the older man said, shaking my daddy's hand. "Tread carefully. Our pack is quite large and is the only pack in this part of the country...for a reason."

I felt the hairs on my arms stand up, the air thick and cold, but we simply faced a new direction and continued to walk on our way.

<u>Solaris's Reign, 1962 ILY</u>

My grandmother stood by, watching with anticipation as the bones broke and my body burned like fire.

Whimpers left my throat, but I tried not to be too loud.

The neighboring pack didn't take kindly to our noise, and had often made noise-complaints about us.

As my young instincts had once told me, and as I had feared...they weren't friendly.

The one person who had accidentally stepped onto their territory had been killed...a young delta female.

Our pack had been outraged, but they simply said that it was her fault for not knowing the boundary line before going and urinating on the tree beside of where they had killed her.

It had been a rough several months for my pack after that.

It had been only nine months since our pack had been attacked and we had been forced to relocate.

It was my wolf's awakening, now that I was seven-years-old and my wolf was one, and my grandmother had taken me into the forest to complete my first shift.

I had been sad that my mother couldn't join me, but she didn't have a good connection to her wolf, so participating in my shift could actually make things worse.

I cried and sobbed as I shifted, but once I stood on all fours and I felt the wind brushing through my fur...I had never felt more right.

"What a pretty long-haired, dark peppery-grey your wolf is!" My grandmother gushed. "I wish your mother could have been here, but I needed to be sure that your shift was successful."

I felt sad as I was reminded of the reason that my mother had *not* chosen to join me for my first shift.

My mother hadn't shifted in a long, long time.

She was disconnected from her wolf, and it took quite a bit of pain and time for her to shift, if she was able to do it at all. Often times, her wolf refused to cooperate at all.

My father tried to help her, but her wolf was...difficult.

According to my big brother, mother and her wolf were disconnected, and she, herself, was disconnected from the Moon Mother.

I wasn't sure, at the time, what that meant...but I knew that it was a very, very bad thing for our kind.

I was weak and slender, petite...I was small for my age.

Brother told me that mother had been punished with silver poisoning for a crime she committed, and struggled to get pregnant with me for a long time.

She almost lost me during birthing me, and *I* was weak because *she* was weak.

I had to always be protected and looked out for.

My brother didn't like to leave me alone, and I couldn't wait until I got older so I could have a little freedom.

I shook out my fur, struggling to stand, before we went back to my family's den.

Father, mother, mother's Defensive gamma, and my big brother were waiting there for me, as well as my grandfather, the former beta.

They were all shifted, aside from my mother.

● ● ●

She stood there in her human form, which made me a bit sad.

I had only seen her wolf a couple of times in my life, and she had such a beautiful wolf that I loved to see...but she didn't shift often.

"Oh, she's beautiful," I heard my mother speak in the pack link.

I saw my father come over to me, his wolf giving mine a lick on the nose and a happy yip, dipping his belly to the ground and butt up in a playful manner, and my wolf jumped on his back and gripped the fur on his shoulder.

My brother stepped over to me next, wagging his tail at me. His wolf looked a lot more like our mother's.

"What are you going to name her?" He asked me, cocking his head at me.

...We named our wolves?

I hadn't known that was how it worked. I thought that they just...had their own names already...

If we named our own wolves, I would want to pick a nice name for mine, so I thought about that.

My wolf looked a lot like father's wolf, but she had long fur. She had the same dark grey, peppery-silver—

Wait, that was it!

"Pepper," I smiled in the pack link.

My wolf yipped and wagged her butt hard, happy with the name.

"I think she likes it," my father said, barking out a laugh. *"How was the shift?"* He asked my grandmother.

*"Nothing out of the ordinary, just like with Quill and Nickle. She did great. It **was**...a little slow...and she seemed to be in a great deal of pain, of course, because she is so petite and delicate...but overall, not as bad as I had feared. She should be alright."*

● ● ●

"*Good,*" grandfather said, relaxing.

"*The pain she felt was the typical for first shifts, so I don't think she will have her mother's problem...at least, I hope not.*"

"*That's good,*" my father said, relieved.

My mom stirred a bit, uncomfortable. She rubbed her arms, looking away.

She felt guilty, knowing that we wanted her to shift and be comfortable but knowing, also, that it wasn't that simple.

My family and I left to trot around the woods near the den for a while, letting my wolf get a good feel for the outside world for the first time.

She was still only one, so she would get worn out and tired quickly and wouldn't have much stamina for a while.

After I started to get tired, my grandmother took me to the side and helped me through the shift to return to my human form, and then we re-dressed, before going back to the den.

I stretched and yawned, before I retired early for the night and took a good, long sleep that night.

I silently thanked the Moon Mother for giving me a proper, successful first shift.

Folias's Blessing, 1964 ILY

I was nine, the first time that I saw *him*.

I had been on the edge of the territory, playing with the Defensive Gamma Crow's son, Violet Terra, when we caught a sudden strange scent, and he perked up.

I liked this scent, for some reason.

It didn't smell familiar to me, but it *did*, all in one weird smell.

It smelled...it smelled like home, for me.

I wanted to follow it.

"Hey, do you smell that? That isn't someone from our pack—"

"What are you doing on my land?" I heard a voice say, and I gaped over the line between the trees to see a boy who was...*stunning*.

He had pale skin and dark, silky, inky black hair...but his eyes were a bright, stunning shade of magenta-lavender.

"We're not on your land," Violet growled out. He pointed to the small X's that were notched into the trees that he stood by. "We know the boundary."

Granted, we *were* only a few feet away, and thus a bit *too close*, but we certainly were not over the line.

"We're expanding the territory," he said, huffing at us. "Hasn't my father met with the alpha of your pack about it yet?"

I glanced to Violet. "They are in a meeting, but we haven't heard any news, yet..."

"I wasn't speaking to you!" He said, crossing his arms. "Let the boys talk. Boys are leaders of the pack."

"Excuse me?" Violet said, gaping at him. "You have it wrong. Her rank is higher than mine."

"Oh? What rank is she, then?"

"I'm the beta's daughter," I said, soft, and his eyes widened a bit.

"My rank is still higher than yours," he grumbled. "I'm the Gamma's son."

"That rank is *not* higher!" Violet shouted, pointing at him wildly. "Where did you get that idea?"

"Have you smelled how weak she smells?" He asked in a scoff. "What kind of beta's daughter smells that weak? And what kind of male does the beta's daughters usually get *mated* to?" He asked calmly, smirking at me. "Many beta's daughters end up having gammas or deltas for mates. She might get lucky, and have a Pack Hunter as a mate, but even then, it's rare for a as weak-smelling as her to get anything higher than a delta. No higher-ranked male goes for a female so pathetic. If she was a powerful, strong beta female, perhaps she'd have better luck, but I'm still struggling to believe she is even related to a beta—let alone being a beta's daughter."

I knew he was right about that...my wolf wasn't very powerful.

Unlike mother, I didn't have any issues with shifting, but I was weak...

I was perfectly connected to my wolf and to the Moon Mother...however, because of the weakness of my mother's wolf, my wolf was also much weaker than an average beta's daughter would be.

There was no way that a beta or alpha ranked male would choose me as a true mate.

They would avoid me.

• • •

This male, unfortunately, was correct; I'd be lucky to have a gamma or delta, at my power level.

"Who I end up mating is none of your business," I told him calmly. "Besides, it doesn't change that my parents and my older brother are higher ranked than you are. You don't have the right to talk down to me."

He shrugged. "Either way, my father is meeting with your alpha and beta to let them know that we bought part of this land from the Head Alpha, which means that our territory is expanding. So, you are, in fact, on our land...and that means that you're in trouble," he said, snide.

"You can't just say we're in trouble because we were over a new boundary line that we hadn't even been informed of yet!" Violet snarled.

Just a few minutes later, black wolves came into the clearing where we were, and Violet and I grasped each other's hands, him coming to stand in front of me to block their path in an effort to protect me.

One of the black wolves snarled at us, and I trembled, clutching my friend. He was the Defensive Gamma heir for the future beta female...and I had dragged him into danger.

I was not the future beta female. I was the beta heir's sister.

I didn't have rights to the defensive gamma heir.

I felt guilty.

I had brought him out here, because there had been only one single Cedar Tree out in this part of the forest, and it had beautiful roses blooming all around it in a very bright, peculiar shade of magenta.

It was my favorite place, and now, the Glacial Jewel pack was taking it away.

"What is going on here?!" I heard my father shout as he rushed into the clearing, my mother and Violet's parents with him.

Our alpha stepped out as well.

"You are the beta?" The boy asked, glaring at my father. When my father nodded, he continued. "Your daughter favors you." He huffed. "I had a hard time believing them when she said she was the beta's daughter, but sure enough, she does look a lot like you. But, back to business. These two are on our new land, and I was informing them that they were trespassing. They should be punished," he said, his tone cold.

"*Punished*?" My mother asked, appalled. "My daughter and my Defensive Gamma's son play here all of the time. The land was only *just* purchased, and we were only just made aware of it *less than an hour ago*. We haven't even had time to tell the children, let alone mark the new boundary lines! How dare you be so rude and demand punishment when nothing has been intentionally done wrong?" My mother asked.

He scoffed. "And how dare someone as weak as you speak back to me?" He said.

"I am the beta female!" My mother snarled, shooting him a frightening glare.

"Oh, I see. So, she's weak because of you. I can barely even sense your wolf. And even more obviously, your daughter learned her *audacity* from you," he commented snidely.

"Excuse me?" My mother glared at him.

"*Women* in our pack do not hold authority to talk to ranked men this way," a man who looked a lot like the boy said as he approached the scene, going and patting the boy on the shoulder. "My son has simply been raised in a predominantly male-driven, male run pack."

My father huffed. "In our pack, *women* are treated as a high commodity because they *are* so severely outnumbered. They hold a special place, because they give us our pups and take our heats. Male-driven packs that shove women down should learn a thing or two from this. We treat our women as the *Moon Mother* would wish us to. "

• • •

The man shrugged. "Either way, he knows that women do not hold the same status that we do. Your daughter may very well mate a gamma or delta, but she will still hold lower rank than that of my Offensive Gamma Heir son."

My brother stepped forward. "I am the Beta Heir of my pack, and if I have to, I will hold her position higher. She might be a little weaker, but she is the daughter and sister of betas. She deserves respect."

"She deserves *nothing* from me because she has *earned* nothing from me," the man said, shaking his head. "The only reason I have made this trip is to inform you of the territory changes. My alpha sent me here. You are an enemy pack that we are trying to avoid war with because of explicit orders from the Head Alpha. Keep your pack members— particularly weak, pitiful, omega-power-leveled beta daughters—off of our land in the future."

With that, the black wolves turned and walked away, and I looked to my father.

"Did they *really* buy this land?" I asked, my tone timid.

He looked at me and gave me a tight nod. "Yes...they are encroaching on the territory by an entire mile."

"A *mile*?" Violet asked, stunned. "But that only leaves us with—"

"Four miles across," Defensive Gamma Crow said, soft. "Barely enough to survive, and *definitely not* enough to feed us properly."

"They can't do this!" Violet cried.

The alpha shook his head. "Unfortunately, they can. They went and bought the property themselves from the Head Alpha. They paid quite a hefty price for it, too. We were outbid for it."

"Will they...continue buying more of our land?" I asked, afraid.

My father looked away. "More than likely," he said. "They are probably slowly trying to buy us out. Their pack is almost three-times the size of our pack, so we don't have another choice. We *have* to cooperate."

"Will we have to move again?" Violet asked.

"It is possible...but finding land that isn't being bid on already, or isn't already owned, is tough. Many packs are facing hunting problems with humans right now, so land is hard to come by. Unowned land is almost unheard of. That was why we went through the Head Alpha to begin with...but it seems that he isn't too worried about our little pack compared to such a large, powerful pack," Alpha Finch explained. "Being a newer alpha, I just took whatever deal I could get, our situation desperate enough to earn us this small area. But we might have to leave anyway." He turned to my father. "We need to start scouting for new land, finding out who owns what, and trying to find something unoccupied."

CHAPTER 2

Cedar...

There had been quite the learning curve on our part, when it had come to the new territory lines.

The Glacial Jewel pack had no pity for us and spared none any time one of us stepped over that line.

They had multiple warriors guarding the boundary, and when one of us stepped over...even if only for a *moment*, even if only by *accident*...they were killed.

They were a cruel pack who made no exceptions.

Still, things had gotten a little more back to normal.

We had about forty pack members—most of them around my age or my brother's age.

My brother, thankfully, had found his mate and had been made the official beta male and beta female pair.

Strangely, though, in all of our pack meetings and gatherings...I had not once found a smell that I was attracted to.

In our society, at school, we had regular weekly school meetings that brought together all of the children of the same age group so that we could all talk and have snacks and see what we thought of one another.

● ● ●

I was eleven, now, and so it was only going to be three more years until I found my mate...but there was still the major issue of *smell*.

I hadn't found any male who attracted me, and no male had hung around me, more, either, as would have been the norm and expected at our ages as we got closer to our second awakenings.

In fact, all of the males in my grade had females that they were drawn to and gravitated towards, and *I* was the *only* single wolf left in the entire school in my age group without a single person who my wolf drew closer to.

The next closest in age that was single was only an eight-year-old omega boy, so I didn't think he counted for me.

He wasn't drawn to my scent, either.

All of the older kids in higher grades, like my brother, had all found their mates at this point.

Was I just...mate-less?

My mother and father were growing increasingly concerned and upset about this, because they both desperately wanted for me to have a true mate.

My parents, as it turned out, were *not* true mates, which had surprised my brother and I to learn. They seemed so natural with one another, that we never would have suspected that they were in an arranged marriage.

They had been arranged partners, to unify their brother packs.

They'd both had to formally reject their true mates, and losing the ability to have a true mate was exactly what had caused my mother to become disconnected from the Moon Mother, Selene.

That was exactly why my wolf was so weak.

It was of utmost importance for us young wolves to mate and reproduce, because our numbers were so few, now.

That, and without an ally pack to find me a match from in the area, we couldn't use me to unite packs, either.

The closest ally packs were further north than the borders of the Northern Kingdom, and we had an enemy pack blocking our way.

We'd have to take extra time to go around them and weeks—*possibly months*, on foot—to reach an ally pack in Acadia, that kingdom was called.

It was an all-around bad situation.

As I was getting closer to the age of my second awakening, my heat...my parents grew terrified of what it would mean if I were to not have a mate at all.

I remembered my mother's fearful, bitter question to my father the other night that had stayed and lingered in my mind.

"What if she is mate-less because we forced a mating between us, and I became disconnected from the moon? What if Selene is punishing her, and punishing us through her...?"

Folias's Blessing, 1967 ILY

Things had been...a bit off, lately.

For over a month, now, I had felt as if someone were...*watching* me. I may be paranoid; I spent quite a bit of time alone, after all.

Still, I felt that I couldn't be imagining things.

I smelled something really, really good around me every time that I was out in the forest.

It smelled of Cedar and fresh mowed grass, with a dash of something...almost like flowers...?

I couldn't explain it, and I was afraid to talk to my parents about it.

What if they thought I was crazy? Or worse...what if they thought that I was in danger, and decided to keep me cooped up at the den?

I certainly didn't want that.

I was twelve, and I still hadn't found a male who drew me in our pack. No male had been drawn by me, either, and my parents grew further and further worried over the issue. Even my brother was growing quite concerned.

Still, I felt like I had someone out there.

I caught myself following the smell often, this *amazing* smell, but I didn't know why.

It was one day, when I was sitting beneath a beautiful pine in the unusually warm weather for Folias's Blessing in the Northern Kingdom, when I felt that prickle on my flesh again.

I was in and out of a nap, enjoying the heat, but when I caught that smell again…so close, so *good*…I couldn't resist it.

I turned, and I caught sight of a beautiful, stunning, large black wolf.

His fangs were bared at me, fur bristled, but *oddly*…I didn't feel any danger.

I could only smell his amazing scent, feel like my body heated up so much at his hungry, dark expression…and those *eyes!*

Those bright, gem-like eyes.

He was borderline snarling at me, but he panted heavy and fast, his belly tensing repeatedly as he almost…almost dry-humped empty air, staring at me with those bright eyes.

"…You…smell so…*good*…" I whispered. "I've never smelled something so amazing in my life. It is *divine*…"

A throaty, thick whine that heated me to the core pulled out of his throat, and Pepper jumped up in my mind, whining and clawing at me in return.

I felt the blood drain from my face when I suddenly realized what was actually happening.

This…this was my true mate…

Tears welled in my eyes at what this meant.

An enemy wolf from a pack full of *monstrous beasts*…was my true mate.

That would explain why no male had been drawn to me, why no male drew me in. It would also explain why this male was snarling at me, but I didn't actually feel any danger.

We stayed that way for what seemed like a long, long time.

We just stared at one another.

• • •

Slowly, almost hypnotized, I got down onto my hands and knees before him, looking to the ground, and turned my head, baring my neck for him.

This could be really dangerous, Pepper thought. **But if this is mate, mate won't hurt us. Mate will not be able to hurt us.**

The thought *did* reassure me.

Though she was weaker than average wolves of my rank, she was very intelligent. My parents had taught me well.

The wolf paused for a moment, going quiet, before he trotted over to me, glancing around carefully before he began to sniff me.

I startled slightly as he nosed my face, my back, even nuzzled his snout beneath me and between my legs to scent at my core, and I trembled as he let out a low, thick rumble.

I glanced up at him and he snarled, and I quickly tucked my head back down.

A pleased sounding moan came out of him, before he nuzzled his snout into the junction of my neck and shoulder, where a mating mark would go.

I flinched, pulling away, but he followed me, not letting me escape.

He whined, really digging his nose in, and panting hard, nicking the spot with his teeth.

A gasp escaped me and I whimpered, feeling my core tighten. He huffed heavily, growling at me in a freshly angered way, before he began to hump the open air again.

All the while, he whined and snarled into my throat, but he didn't hurt me.

I held my position firmly, my heart pounding as my true mate—whomever he may be, but the smell was vaguely familiar to me in an odd way—humped away at the open air.

Finally, a long, drawn-out whine and a grunt before a thick growl came out of him, and I saw white streams spurt out of him beneath his belly and onto the ground.

He'd not humped me directly, nor had his ejaculate touched me, but it was obvious that my true mate was in the middle of his first heat, his second awakening.

How long had he been in this state?

The heat didn't cool down for us until we managed to get a release with our true mates, I had learned.

So, how long had my true mate been waiting for me?

For as long as I had smelled his scent?

Had he been fighting it?

Judging from the unhappy, hateful snarls coming out of him, and the irate pacing back and forth, I would assume that he had fought it since I had started sensing him back in Moon's Dance.

I heard my brother calling for me and I startled, looking around wildly.

The wolf held his spot, looking at me before looking toward the approaching voice.

He looked resigned, huffing, and looking away to his territory.

"Go," I whispered, and he startled, looking at me with wide, bright eyes. "*Quickly*, before he finds you! My brother is the beta. He will report it if he finds you on our land, please…I don't want any more land disputes," I pleaded. "I know women don't mean much to your pack, but I…I don't want anything bad to happen to your pack, especially…not *you*."

He looked surprised, but as my brother continued to call for me with his voice sounding louder and closer…the male looked me over one last time before giving a frustrated sound, turning, and taking off into the forest and out of sight.

About two minutes later, my brother and his mate popped out of the woods and into my space.

● ● ●

"Cedar, where have you been? It's getting late, you should have been home hours—" He froze, scenting the area, and my nerves sky-rocketed. "Who was just here? Did you see a male here?" He asked, tone cold.

"No," I said, keeping my heartrate calm. "I smelled something weird, and I came out here to investigate. I didn't find anyone."

He held my gaze for a long time, before he puffed out a breath and took me into his arms. "You know that shouldn't be this far out, and you certainly shouldn't follow *this* scent again, Cedar," he said, tone firm. "This is a bad, bad scent for a female to follow. This is a male's ejaculate," he told me. "And from the smell, he isn't from our pack. This is very dangerous and reckless of you. You need to promise me that you won't follow this again, you hear me? Or else, I won't let you out of my sight again, and I'll make sure mom and dad keep guards with you at all times. Understood?" He asked, tone leaving no room for argument.

I gave a nod. "Yes, brother."

"Yes, what?"

"I promise not to follow this smell again," I said, only promising in my mind not to follow the smell of my mate's *cum*.

I wasn't promising not to follow his actual smell again...

Quill took a breath of relief, and pulled me toward the pack. "Good girl. Now, come on, dinner is done. Mom made an amazing roast tonight for us, because Jasmine and I have some news," he said, too cheerful.

I smiled, nodding without paying much attention.

That night, I would find out that I was to be an aunt, because my brother and his true mate were expecting their first pup.

Meanwhile, I was wondering if my true mate and I would ever get to see each other again...

A lot had happened on that warm Folias's Blessing afternoon.

Solaris's Reign, 1969 ILY

It had been almost two years since I had actually *seen* my true mate, but I knew that he kept an eye on me whenever I was close to the boundary lines.

I could feel his bright, gem-like gaze on me.

I could smell his scent in the air.

I could feel his energy pulsing from the forest, rapt attention on me.

He didn't approach me, but I almost never went a single day where I didn't sense him sometime during the day.

I found myself dressing up more often, going out to my favorite spot and brushing out my hair, wearing beautiful dresses and all the pink jewels I could find.

I wasn't sure why, exactly, but I just...wanted to.

His eyes would follow me all over the forest, and though I caught glimpses of his bright eyes through the trees, his black fur...he didn't approach.

He must be angry that I was his true mate, but all I could think was that I wanted his approval.

*I wanted for him to look at me, look for me...**want** me...*

Strangely, no more disputes between the packs had happened since I had met him, and I could only hope that it was because of me.

At least, I liked to flatter myself by thinking so, though it was true enough that nothing bad had happened since I'd come across him.

● ● ●

It seemed too good to be true, but I had noticed that two omegas had mentioned having been hunting too close to the line, and one had tripped with her heavy kill on her shoulder...but she wasn't killed when she leaned over to pick it up and bring it home.

If it really was because of me, why was he halting hostilities for me?

Why was he going this far for me?

He hadn't approached me again, but I could smell him and feel his eyes on me at most times, so I had to think that he was watching out for me and making sure that our pack was at least a *little* safer than before.

Thinking such a thing made me want to give my all to him.

*He seemed to actually...**care** for me.*

For example, one day, a few weeks ago, I had been lying out in the forest, sunbathing, and my stomach had been growling.

We had noticed a lack of prey lately, and we were having to ration ourselves.

Unfortunately, my brother's child was especially hungry even after eating, and I had given my ration over, trying to be a good aunt.

I lay there with my belly growling, and I moaned softly.

"There's nothing for it. I'm too hungry to hunt...but I have to be a good aunt. Giving my ration over is nothing bad." I sighed. "I just wish I wasn't so hungry..."

I had drifted off, and when I had woken up a little while later to a huge thud, I had sat up and found a large buck just over the edge of the boundary, just a few yards away from me.

It was absolutely *covered* in his scent, dead on the ground...

● ● ●
238

I had looked up and around when I found it, and I saw his magenta eyes blazing through the trees.

The magenta swirled around with red and lavender in a hypnotizing way, and I had to shake myself to come back to reality.

He had **hunted** for me...

Provided.

Was he...wooing me? I had to wonder.

He pulled back his shoulders and gave me a tight nod when I lifted the buck, pulling it away as he boasted over his kill for me.

It felt like...I was taming this wild wolf that I didn't know.

The only issue was that my parents and my brother were beginning to get a bit...suspicious.

My mother and the luna had called me to talk to me about it, and have me examined by the physician to prove my innocence; that had been a very invasive and embarrassing experience, to say the least.

Once they had proven that I was still a virgin, and they believed me that I wasn't meeting a male secretly to mate outside of my true mate—a white lie in a truth, sort of, considering that I was trying to meet a male but he actually was my true mate—they finally agreed that I could continue on as I was, without guards.

That didn't end the suspicion, though.

My father sat me down and talked to me one evening.

"Are you sure that there isn't something that you wish to talk about, Cedar?" He had asked me. "I'm a bit worried for you. You have been acting...oddly, lately. Are you sure you don't know who your true mate is?"

I shook my head.

He hesitated. "Let's say that I believe you for now, then."

Back to the present, my birthday was a week away, now, and I was coming to my second awakening. My heat.

I was turning fourteen.

Would he approach me again?

The school all gathered for the Mating Ritual the Friday before my birthday—a week before I would turn fourteen—and we all found our respective pairs.

Or, at least, everyone else did.

The crowds in the stands, brought in for this monumental moment in our pack—the forging of the new mate couples—were shocked and surprised...some upset...when I stood there without a partner.

The head operator of the school pulled my parents aside, telling them that I had never shown interest in *any* of the males of our pack—as if it were somehow my fault.

My mother had looked bitter and angry, but my father had looked confused and sad. My brother looked at me with pity.

If only they knew the truth...

To them, I was just mate-less.

In ninety-eight percent of cases, a wolf didn't find their true mate outside of their pack. In rare cases, they were found in *allied* packs...but an *enemy pack?*

It was unheard of, and in the one recorded case of it happening—only once in all of our thousands of years of history— it had definitely not led to good things...for *either* pack.

I hated to leave my family in further disappointment.

I knew that they were already worried by how weak Pepper was, and they constantly worked to protect and provide for me because I was so weak...

● ● ●

They had been waiting to hand my care over to a loving mate.

To not draw any male, though? *At all?*

That was almost a death sentence.

My brother took me into his arms, promising that I could stay with his family, that he didn't mind me being part of their beta family and working to take care of me, too, but I felt guilty for it.

He didn't need an extra mouth to feed, with a toddler at home and another pup now on the way.

I would just be a hinderance to his family.

No, I needed to start a family of my own. I wanted a family of my own.

I doubted seriously, however, that my true mate would be approved of, or that I would be approved of by his pack. It would be beyond a miracle if our parents agreed.

I didn't even know his rank, or his name.

I only had a general idea of his birthday.

What was I supposed to do? Walk into his pack and beg for them to let me mate him?

How had we even become true mates?

Typically, a male and female would pick one another's smell around the time of their first awakening, and continue to be drawn to their scent throughout their life.

When had I ever met a male around my age in their pack?

There were two occasions.

Firstly, had been that dispute when they bought up some of our land, the Gamma Heir that had been so mean to me and Violet.

Second, there had been a delta that had been learning how to be a warrior on one of their trips to the pack to discuss a couple of omegas that they had killed.

He had looked a little older than me, but not by much. He was learning his future position as a pack warrior, guarding his delegation.

So, it was one of those two. It had to be.

There had been no other males my age that I had come across, right?

When we got home, my mother stayed very quiet.

Our family—*myself*, particularly—had been the center of whispers the entire trip back to the den.

I had gotten used to it, over the years, but this was the first time it was so...in our faces.

I had been literally the *only* wolf my age without a partner.

Out of eleven of us at my age level, the only one without a partner.

Nobody expected that for a beta's daughter.

The only one without anyone drawn in, even in other age groups. What was I to do?

I knew the truth, but they didn't...and that just made things all the worse for me.

I knew that I had a true mate. I wasn't hopeless, or mate-less, or any of the other mean slurs people whispered my way.

I wasn't a punishment or a curse from the Moon Mother...

My father didn't have a lot to say, but he had held me in his arms and stroked my hair, promising that I would find love someday.

Surely, I wouldn't be cursed to stay alone.

● ● ●

Lone wolves *always* ended up expelled from packs, because it was in a wolf's very nature, the basest of our core desires, to be social pack animals.

That was why we had packs in the first place.

I could only hope that I could become mated to someone, *anyone*...preferably my true mate...before they declared me a lone wolf and banished me.

I wouldn't survive out in the wild on my own.

Before that would happen, they would likely mate me to a random male who was unmated, which happened sometimes. Sometimes, a mating didn't work out, or one partner died, or something like that.

I did know of one other person in the pack my age who was single, but as far as I knew, he'd had a true mate. I wasn't sure if they had rejected one another or not, but I never saw him with a female...and that was the Pack Hunter heir, Sage Onyx.

CHAPTER 3

North Frost...

*Of course, it would have to be **this** female.*

Of *all* the females in the world, it would *have* to be *this* one from our neighboring enemy pack. It pissed me off.

The small, dainty, pitiful beta's daughter from the small, fragile, dwindling Terra-Forest-Stone pack.

They were weak, expendable, more mouths in the area to feed when we had over three-times their number.

They were prey.

We were in the area first.

How dare they come in here and encroach on our land, our feed, our lives?

*Now, **this**?*

This pretty, dainty little pup of a girl was my true mate?

I had turned fourteen and had my second awakening, my heat, almost two years ago.

I'd turned fourteen in Moon's Dance, and I was livid when, during the ritual celebration where the mate

● ● ●
245

groupings were decided and the entire school was gathered together to witness it, I was the *only male* in the school who hadn't found a female.

My parents were pretty damned livid, too.

How could *their* son—the son of the Offensive Gamma of the Glacial Jewel pack, the largest pack in the Northern Kingdom—not have a true mate?

Of course, we could forge an alliance.

Use me for a political marriage...but, come on, was I *defective?*

No wolves in history had ever *not* had a true mate *somewhere,* at *some* point in time. No wolf had ever been truly mate-less.

If you couldn't find one, that meant that they were in a different pack, a different part of the world...or, they were simply already dead.

There had been a case, about sixty years ago, where a male had come across the scent of his true mate in a graveyard.

Dug her up, found her rotting corpse, discovered she'd died of sickness a few years earlier.

I was running that day, burning up some tension and stress as Coal—my bulky, angry, grumpy, super short-tempered wolf—shook out his fur and just let me tag along for a good ride.

Suddenly, out of nowhere, I'd caught it; the faint, beautiful scent of cedar trees and roses, with a hint of sage.

I followed the tantalizing scent immediately, ready and rearing to meet my female and put her in her place; scent mark her, mate her, mark her, the works.

How had I missed this scent at school?

I hadn't even realized where I was going until I caught sight of the X's marking the boundary line, and I froze in my place.

No.

Hell. **No.**

This couldn't be happening to me.

Was this a joke?

I glanced at the guards, noticing how I was riding the boundary, but they didn't say anything. They knew better, unless I actually crossed the line.

I did, however, keep moving. I followed the scent as it moved from a distance, hoping that the female was, at least, powerful.

The scent seemed...a little familiar to me.

I'd smelled it a couple of times, but it had never pleased me to this degree.

Who had it been?

I'd seen so many of their females now, it was hard to keep up.

What I had *not* expected to see, was exactly what I saw, and I hoped against all hope that my senses were just stupid and I was totally wrong.

If I'd felt joked and insulted before, this took the icing on the cake, and I was pacing in my wolf's mind.

Shit.

Shit, shit, shit!

Damn it all.

This could not be happening to me, me of all wolves.

I even pitied her, too, as much as I hated myself for it.

No female from an enemy pack should have to be my true mate. It would never work between the two of us.

The best I could hope for would be to have my way with her, and I wouldn't mind, but let's be honest...she was going to get hurt.

Females were especially weak in the knees for their true mates.

Made every excuse for them, turned traitor for them...

I could have her eating out of my paws...but did I want that?

I didn't want this girl to be my true mate.

Anybody but this girl.

He didn't mind, of course. To Coal, Cedar Stone looked like a delectable, delicious, wrapped-up candy bar, all pristine and ready to rip that wrapper off of her and feast. Figuratively and literally.

I saw her puttering around, pilfering with some doo-dad device and fiddling with it. She seemed a bit nervous.

"Cedar," I heard a voice say, and I glanced to the male approaching.

Coal almost began to snarl and jump in, before I recognized him as Quill—Cedar's older brother.

"Yes," she said, her voice tired.

"You know mom didn't mean that."

She stopped her pilfering. "She did, Quill. And she's right. Mom is right, I'm just...a *curse*. Mom and dad were an arranged marriage, and it went against the Moon Mother Selene. Selene was angry that they rejected her gift of true mates, and angrier that they mated against her wishes after she rejected their union and refused to bless them...and so she cursed me to not have a true mate at all, I guess." She shrugged, sniffling a bit as she went back to her tinker project. "All so that I could punish you all even more. So, I can at least prove my usefulness by fixing something."

Tears streamed down her face, eyes puffy.

I was impressed with her attitude, oddly.

She was obviously sad and down, but she was putting her hands to work.

By the looks of the small machine that she was working on, she was quite good, too.

He sighed, sitting next to her. "You know mother doesn't really think that way. She's just...worried for you. After all, I've mated and moved to my own den, now. You still haven't found any scent you like, and no boys have approached you. Mom and dad want for you to have a true mate to love you, because...they didn't get that. They love each other now, sure, but they didn't at first. They disliked one another at first."

"I remember the story," she said, soft. "I just...they promised that we would get to marry for love, unlike they did. But now, I feel like maybe mom is right...maybe I'm just a dud."

"She didn't mean it—"

"Yes, she did, Quill. I am a dud. But that's okay. I'm fine with marrying outside of love, Quill. As long as I don't become a lone wolf, I don't care."

"I would never let them deem you as a lone wolf," he said, adamant. "You can live with me, and I will protect you forever," he said.

She smiled, and pushed at his shoulder. "Thank you, big brother."

"You're welcome, little sister," he said, pressing a kiss to her forehead. "Now, don't stay out here much longer. I don't like you out here and not having a guard with you."

"I'm just a weak daughter of a former beta, Quill. Nobody is going to bother me," she laughed.

She was right about that.

If it wasn't for Coal fawning all over her, and that she had managed to impress me with her "keep moving forward" attitude, and how *pretty* she was—

Fuck, I was getting off topic.

Over the next few days—*weeks*, if I was being *honest*—I had started looking for her often. Making excuses all the while, but I wanted to make sure that she was safe...and I—or, Coal, more rather—grew more and more impressed with her.

She often worked with her hands, or was working verbally on hard arithmetic equations, and I had to admit that she *was* very intelligent.

She might not be *physically* strong, despite her position as the daughter of a powerful beta male, but she was sharp as a tack in her knowledge.

She was sweet, and I grew to quite enjoy watching her.

It was going into Folias's Blessing, when I noticed how hard it was for Coal to control himself as I watched her.

My heat was coming to a high.

I knew that by the shifter's nature, we would remain in our heat until we had a release with our true mate, of some kind, and Coal was forcibly clawing at me on the inside.

Every day that I saw her, in those pretty sundresses or wrap dresses...her growing curves, the soft subtle beauty of her body blossoming...

She was becoming a woman.

If I remembered correctly from the reports, she was almost two years younger than me.

If my heat was this difficult to control, how hard would it be to control Coal when it came time for her to enter *her* heat?

Truly, the best thing that I could do, at this moment, was go up and reject her formally.

I knew, though...

I knew, in my deepest thoughts, that there was no way that Coal would let me walk up to her and *not* take her.

● ● ●

One day, not long after that, she'd been alone, and I could feel Coal about to be driven mad.

His eyes, normally a bright magenta burgundy shade, blazed crimson like blood.

He was much harder to control that day, when I found her laying nearby the line.

It just so happened that the guards were switching shifts, and I crossed the line quickly and quietly.

Surprisingly, she didn't seem afraid or alarmed.

I saw her scenting the air, curious and happy to see that she had a true mate after all.

Like me, she had been thought to be mate-less. To have a true mate confirmed…it helped revive her spirits.

I could see it dawn on her face when she had realized who I was, the blood draining from her face like she'd just met a ghost.

She basically had.

I was from the enemy pack; the pack that was picking off her pack's members like flies.

There was no way that she couldn't be upset by this.

Understanding and shock, fear, hurt, curiosity…her face was a myriad of different emotions, and I watched them all cross her pretty face.

Then, shocking me beyond all belief, because after realizing who I was, I would have expected her to run from me, but hardly able to believe my own eyes…she got on her hands and knees, still in her human form, and submitted to me.

Submitting to me…?

Why?

She knew who I was, so, why?

Was she saying that it didn't matter?

Was she trying to appease my wolf to not harm her by offering herself up to him?

She was brave, I had to give her credit on that.

Somehow, she had instinctively known exactly what to do...and it *did* appease me.

Whereas I had felt angry and betrayed by Moon Mother Selene, I now felt calm and contemplative.

What did I want to do with my little female?

Would I take her?

If I took her during my heat, I knew I would knot inside of her.

It was the design of the heat, to take your mate for the first time and ensure she's pupped for you.

I knew that I absolutely couldn't allow myself to get inside her body right now, no matter how livid and furious Coal got with me for it later...but I *needed* release, and I needed it now.

I had been absolutely mortified beyond belief when Coal had started humping. He literally dry humped empty air—not even *her*, but straight *empty space*—and had released his cum in streams all over the ground next to her.

Fury.

Unbridled fury that *this* was *my* female, and I was stuck knowing that it would never work out.

We were from enemy packs.

This couldn't happen.

We'd be labeled traitors...put on probation in our own packs, if we weren't labeled rogues and expelled from our packs entirely...

I had been utterly shocked when, against my expectations of her turning me in to her brother as he grew closer, searching for her, she hurried me along to run, telling me she didn't want trouble.

• • •

She wanted me to be safe…

That had done something to me.

That had made not just Coal want her more…but now, *I* wanted her.

I couldn't want her! I just couldn't, but…

I **did**.

When I had returned to my family den, my parents had been confused and a bit perturbed to learn that my heat had passed after a month of suffering.

They both knew that it wouldn't just *go away.*

I had to find a mate and release with her at my *side*, at least, to get the heat to subside minutely.

They were suspicious, and my father had questioned me, but I insisted that I had found a random female and simply dry-humped her until I released onto the ground.

He had been a bit frustrated and embarrassed with me, but had accepted the answer and let it go without any further fuss.

I couldn't get a girl pregnant outside of an official coupling leading to being mates, was his only comment on the subject.

I knew that, but he always tried to remind me to be careful.

I couldn't go just giving our bloodline to any random bitch.

The months continued to pass with me watching her, keeping an eye on her.

I'd stopped reporting every single toe I saw crossing the line of our boundary as I had used to do.

Yes, as I thought about it now, *that was a bit extreme.*

There had been multiple wolves that had simply gotten a toe or arm over the line but jumped right back over, realizing the mistake, and had pleaded for their lives for the mess up when I'd reported to the guards and had them slaughtered.

I wasn't a good person; I would be the first to admit it.

I was cold, ruthless, not caring about any outside of my own pack...just as my father had taught me to be.

I was the nephew of the alpha, nephew of the beta, and son of the offensive gamma. I came from one of the most powerful bloodlines there were, and I was cocky about it. I knew it.

This girl, I could admit, also came from admirable bloodlines.

After I had met her, I had learned all about her, which, in hindsight, should have been my first clue about us being true mates. I had never shown such interest in anyone else before then.

That was a bit of a red-flag.

Her father was the former beta, her cousins were the alpha and gamma. Her brother was the new beta.

Despite how weak her pack was now, they had once been a large, considerable pack in the Eastern Kingdom in their hay-day, before the hunting had begun.

They had originally numbered to over two hundred, but now were under forty.

The hunts, the trip to the Northern Kingdom, and war with our pack had not been kind to their people.

I went close to the boundary line every day—thanking my lucky stars that this was, in fact, my usual routine—and I would watch her.

One day I had returned to the pack, and I was met by my cousin, Amethyst.

I didn't like dealing with her.

She always clung to me, acting like I was *hers*, when I didn't want to be anywhere near her.

She was my Beta uncle's daughter, and she annoyed the piss out of me...but he ordered me to let her play with me, and I didn't have much choice.

"Where do you go every day?" She asked me, tugging on my arm.

I huffed, tugging my arm away roughly. "It isn't your business. I just make sure those pests don't come over the boundary."

"Are you sad that you don't have a mate?" She asked, looking up at me with...*too* much interest.

"I have one, somewhere. Just not in this pack."

"I could be—"

"No," I told her. "I am not interested in a mate. I would prefer to remain as I am."

She didn't respond to that, but she pouted at me and had a look of determination on her face that made my skin crawl.

Later that same day, I had seen a male in Cedar's pack present a rabbit to his mate, and she had blushed and accepted it, giving him kisses and affection and praise...

Would Cedar be that happy to receive a tiny little rabbit?

...*What if I got her something even better than that?*

As it turned out, I found her lying in the forest with her stomach growling so loudly that I could hear it from yards away.

I heard her whispering about giving her rations to a child—that she had to be a good aunt—and my stomach clenched with discomfort.

Our pack had been starving them out for a long time—we had been doing excessive hunting in the area, and I had heard rumors that the pack was now on rations.

Any males lucky enough to actually catch a rabbit and present it to his mate was blessed, indeed, and had quite a lot of skill.

Perhaps I could prove to her that I cared about her if I provided—something that was instinctive in the male mate.

I rushed out into the forest—probably a little too enthusiastic—and stalked down a stag that I killed and took to the borderline.

I glanced around, making sure nobody was around, before I dropped it over on her side of the line, and poured my pheromones all over it, to let her know that it was from me.

I watched as she sat up, hearing the body thump, and drawn by my scent, she came to the body.

She was surprised by the sudden hunt I'd left for her. She glanced out into the forest line, and I confirmed it was for her, and sure enough...

She blushed.

I watched with amused, rapt attention as she attempted to drag it off toward a small nearby den, and I barked out a small chuckle as she struggled.

The stag was quite sizeable compared to her, and so it was hilarious to watch her try to get it away by herself.

I wanted to show her how strong I was, lift it with one arm like I had in order to bring it here, take it to her home den and tell her family that I was claiming her...but I shoved the instinct down.

I couldn't claim her.

I didn't want another male to have her, but I couldn't claim her myself.

What a shit situation.

● ● ●

It was during the last week of Solaris's Reign a few weeks later, back to the present, when I caught her scent yet again...only *this* time, from farther away, and stronger.

Her heat, Coal's eyes blazed, and it took me planting my feet and gripping the tree I was sitting beside of for him not to fly off the handle and shift.

'*No, Coal,*' I told him.

Mate is in heat, he snarled at me. **I want mate, mate is ready! True mate, true mate is just by—**

'*She is from an enemy pack, and yes, she is in heat. Are you planning to use protection? Are you doing the right thing by going and giving in to something that can't happen?*'

He began snarling at me all the harder, clawing beneath the surface, and I whimpered as he got extra close to ripping out of me.

When a wolf fights their human in this way, it is actually physically painful and can even damage the human.

The wolves inside of us each of had their own minds and wills of their own.

'**Only one stopping me from having mate is my human**,' he snarled. '**Wait until your control slips...I will get mate and you won't get in my way. You'll be glad I did.**'

My wolf was powerful, and he was a pretty, inky black with thick, thick long fur and beautiful bright, scarlet magenta eyes.

I kept him well groomed, and he knew just how sexy he was.

I was going on sixteen, and my true mate had just entered her heat. Keeping this strong, beautiful gamma male under control was difficult.

CHAPTER 4

North...

She was out hunting, but what exactly it was that she was hunting for, I wasn't sure.

From the heavy, husky thickness of her scent, the heat from her body practically *beckoning* to me...perhaps it was *me* that she was hunting.

Her heat hadn't ended yet, I could smell it on her. I could smell arousal thick in the air.

I had left her three more kills since the first, and she was growing increasingly wanton whenever she sensed me around her.

She would rub against the trees, whining, whimpering...sauntering around in those sinful as fuck dresses she wore, cleavage peeking out and her scent positively murdering me.

It took all my will power not to let go of my control.

On this day, she had worn a loose, breezy red sundress, and I was *here* for it.

We were both in our human forms, today, and I had tried all I could to resist her scent...but after seeing her in that dress, I had lost out to Coal and his impulses.

● ● ●

I'd tracked her down with ease, facing her and following her.

"So, you are here," her voice was thick and heavy with want, and I felt a lump form in my throat. "I thought you would be."

She'd caught my scent, it seemed.

Thankfully, I had led her beyond her territory line, and beyond *our* territory line as well, meaning that we were in free land.

There were no laws holding us back, here.

Hell...I had even found a place to mate her nearby.

"I know you smell it...you *feel* it," she whined, running a hand along her collar bone, facing my direction.

She was still unable to see me, but her thick, luscious dark silver hair was cut shorter than I remembered.

It hung around her neck, thick and wild and bouncy curls. It suited her heart-shaped face, her dark skin tone that was rich with life. Her pale green eyes, shining brightly in my direction.

"I want you," she whined, seductively grounding her hips around in a sexy circle. "I want mate," I heard her wolf's voice push through, whispered...but I heard.

Fuck it.

I strode out to her, and she gasped, her face losing some of its confidence as I made it up to her, taking her face in my hands.

Up close, I could see the jade and emerald beams in her irises.

She was gorgeous. I could admit that to myself.

"N-no...of all people..."

I nodded. "Yes. I felt...much the same way."

"It...was you," she whispered, eyes full of fear for a moment, though the tones of lust swirling in her gaze were still there.

"It was me," I said. "And it was you," I ground out, forcing my hips forward and rolling them into her, letting my hard-on poke and prod into her. "What does that make you want to do about it?"

She hesitated, looking down at my erection before her eyes clouded over again, looking up at me through thick, sultry lashes. "Mate," she said, soft. "I hadn't thought it would be you, but..."

"...But?"

"You are powerful," she said, still a bit off. "How could I attract someone so...*perfect*...?"

*Then and there, I was **fucking gone**.*

I crashed my lips to hers, all caution and care out the window.

I'd waited for two months while she was still in her heat, and I'd avoided her scent like the plague until it was wafting over to me over at my den, even.

Somehow carried through the air, miles away, just to torture me.

My deft hands made quick work of her sundress, and she was bare before me.

I stripped my tunic and unbuttoned my pants, pushing them down so my cock, heavy with my lust, could hang low and heady in her direction.

I pulled her with me, slamming her back into a tree with a snarl, and she said not a word as I forced me way up and into her tight, perfect, blissful heat.

She gasped out and tried to cry with her voice, but I took her shout into my mouth and worked over her, in and out, over and over again. Thick juice and a little bit of blood from her hymen coated me, and that only served to stoke me further.

I'd made her bleed. I'd taken her virtue, claiming her with my body. Her body belonged to me.

I pumped her like a piston, but it just wasn't enough.

"Shift," I ground through my teeth. "Let me see *her*," I commanded against her lips. "Never have I seen *your* wolf. I want to see my true mate's other self," I told her.

She flushed, but as I set her to her feet, she closed her eyes and breathed.

I watched, mesmerized, as she began to shift and take form.

After a minute or so—a surprising and impressively short shift time—there stood a beautiful dark, smoky grey wolf with peppery fur standing in her place.

She looked worth a million dollars.

The shine of her thick, heavy, long-furred coat. It was obviously well-brushed and bathed often. Her nails were trimmed and proper, tidy, and filed down to soft points.

Her fur was trimmed, paws shaped out, the works.

She was high maintenance, but that meant she had high standards for herself and I loved it.

She was stunning.

I finished stripping, shedding my clothes as I shifted, and she gaped at me when I was finished.

She was only about half the size of my wolf.

"**What is your name**," I directed the thoughts at her, growling and rumbling and yipping. "*I am Coal.*"

"**Pepper**," she spoke, timid, and before I even had to take the dominant position, she did something that wrecked me; she bore her neck for me, submitting, and bowed her head before she turned around, pushing her ass at me.

I didn't need to be told twice, my wolf and I thought at the same time.

• • •

Coal mounted her, and we had the best sex I could imagine...

I lapped at her center like the rabid dog I was, nibbled her paws, my wolf uttering obscenely sweet nothings to her and calling her endearments all night long...

Shit. He was already attached.

How could I call him off of her? How could I get him to see that this...whatever the hell it was, it wasn't happening?

How could I convince him?

At the very least, I made sure he didn't knot in her, and I didn't release into her in my human form, either. I knew better.

If I just held control enough to make sure it stayed like this, maybe this arrangement wouldn't be so bad?

I could only hope.

Fear and apprehension rode within me for quite some time after that.

My father had already decided on a political marriage for me—a union with the beta's daughter.

She found my scent to be the most amazing she could find among our pack. She was highly attracted to me, and the two males who had wanted her, well...she *didn't* want them.

She was my uncle's daughter, and that just didn't appeal to me.

She cared not.

Outraged, I had backed her against the wall, snarling in her face and threatening her...and *she had kissed me*, baring her breasts, and trying to seduce me that way.

I wasn't seduced...

Each night, I sat in silence with my family and ate without a word as they talked about the arranged marriage, the perks that would come from it.

I would become beta one day...even though now, it seemed for naught.

I didn't care about it like I would have, at one point in time.

All I wanted was my female, and I knew with a stomach-sinking feeling that I was getting too attached.

During the nights, I was waiting until the dead of night, before making sure everyone in the den was asleep.

Then, I was dressing all in black and I was sneaking out and meeting Cedar by our special spot—a den in a neutral land spot, after passing a blind spot in the territory line, between some *cedar* trees...I know, right?

Perfect.

Each time I met her, she looked so perfect.

I would meet her at the spot, and I would greet her with some quirky, smirky douche-bag line that would make her chuckle.

"Well, look who I found," "Well, look who we have here," "It's time we take our nightly trip to pound-town,"—I'd even cringed at that one.

Today's line was, "Fancy meeting you here, pretty thing," and she had giggled like usual, before she threw herself at me, and we found ourselves on the floor together, kissing and biting and sucking...

Completely taken with one another.

• • •

I loved fucking her for all the love in the world until just before dawn, before we would run off to our respective lives.

I had to admit, I was...getting a bit attached.

Way, way, way too damn attached...but I couldn't seem to stop.

However, what with this political marriage now in the works—marrying the pack's beta's daughter to me to make me the beta heir because the beta hadn't had a son—I couldn't think about a true mate.

I would have to reject her...but...

When?

How could I just give up on what I found?

Blizzard's Reign, 1970 ILY

It had been a week since I had seen her, due to the holidays, but I had been sure to leave her some turkeys killed and ready for her to pick up from a large, strapped down cooler I had left at our sanctuary.

When I had returned days later, I had found them gone, and a thank you note with the letter -C- signed at the end.

Now, on the third day of the new year, I was about to head out when my father stopped me.

"What have you been doing?" He asked me, arms crossed.

"I've been fucking a random omega," I told him, shrugging. "Don't worry, I've been using protection and I haven't been releasing into her. I know better. No getting girls pregnant."

He cocked his head to the side, contemplative. "Do be careful, son," he said.

"I will, father."

He nodded, and stepped out of my way as I rushed out the door.

I did, as a precautionary tale, hang out in a random part of the forest for a while before going to my sanctuary.

I made sure I hadn't been followed, though I didn't think my father cared that much.

I made sure, one last time, that nobody else was around, before I stepped into the neutral land and rushed to our den.

● ● ●

I found her there, waiting, lying on the bed of blankets there.

...Looking at me with those sensual eyes of hers.

I made my way over to her, and she lay on her back as she took me over her, kissing each other and pulling one another closer by the hair, anything we could grab.

I had pulled out my stiff shaft, slipping up her sundress and sliding home into her body in one fluid movement.

She gasped out, pulling me into a kiss and sucking me deeper into her body.

She was everything as she pulled me in, lulled me into her arms and made me want to stay here in her body.

"North," she called to me like a siren. "North, North, *North!*" She gasped as I slid home into her again and again.

It was a seemingly endless cycle, and one I would never want to end.

It was the only thing that I wanted to do lately, it seemed.

Nivis's End, 1970 ILY

"Yes, yes, yes," she whimpered as I pounded into her from behind, my arms on either side of hers as I lay on top of her back.

Her legs were shut tight between my thighs, my cock shoved through her ass cheeks and stuffed into her tight pussy through that magical glory center.

"Fuck, yes," I snarled, nipping her shoulder. "Cedar..."

"North...N-North, I—" She began to spasm beneath me as I felt her tighten and clench, her orgasm ripping through her as I clamped down on her shoulder blade with my teeth. "Y...y-yessss," she whispered. "F-fuck me, North...!"

"Yes," I groaned, licking her around the reddened bite print. "Take my cock like a good girl," I said, lewd.

She knew I liked to hear her curse for me.

I liked making her act like a bad little bitch.

It was so against her usual behavior, that it only made me have a stronger hard-on for her to watch her lose herself because of me.

She continued to whimper, before I spun her over to her back and throwing her legs open, slamming into her, and making her cry out as I used brute force on her tiny body.

This was my fourteenth time seeing her *just this month,* and every day had been like this.

I didn't want to leave her...but I needed to reject her, soon.

● ● ●

Every time I returned to the pack, Amethyst would immediately find me and cling to me before giving me a sour look, snarling as she glared at me.

She knew what I was doing, but she was still trying to force a union with me.

I had caught her trying to follow me a few times to my meeting spot, but so far, I had managed to get her off my trail.

I didn't care for being followed and spied on, especially when I was so enjoying plowing my true mate and bringing her to deliciously endless orgasms.

"Oh," my mate moaned, her pussy beginning to relax around me as her high subsided. "You are so *good*..."

"So are you," I murmured, licking a trail of sweat on her temple.

I could tell from her expression that she had the desire to say something more, but she clamped her mouth and didn't say it.

I tongued the clavicle of her collarbone, up her throat and to the tip of her chin.

I crawled down her body and lapped her center with my tongue, shoving fingers into her pussy as I stirred her clit around and ate her for all she was worth.

I wanted this female, as she mewled and took me in, eating up everything I did to her.

I crawled up her body once I had gotten her off again, coming to straddle her face and shoving myself into her mouth until I felt my cock hit the back of her throat, and then down.

I throat-fucked her for a while, feeling immense pleasure as I watched tears squeeze out of her eyes.

Then, I groaned as I spurted my shoots of cum down her throat and she choked around me as she tried to keep up.

● ● ●

I made sure she swallowed it all, and I wanted to fucking brand her with my mark.

I wanted to mark her so badly. I wanted her to bear my pups and start a life—

Fuck.

I wanted to own her, for her to be mine...and I even wanted to be her's.

I was fucked.

Screwed.

Ruined.

Shit out of luck.

CHAPTER 5

North...

"Do you think that our packs will *ever* be able to get along?" She asked me after one particularly amazing sex session, stroking my chest absentmindedly as we lay in our little haven together.

I had grown to love this den—small, just big enough to mate in—right on the border of the land. It was technically on neutral territory, so I could meet her here as much as I wanted.

I was seeing her for the first time in a few days, but we usually met every day.

I wasn't sure what had changed...or *when*...but now, she and I would always cuddle together after our sex sessions, warming one another and enjoying our company with one another.

I had to admit that I had grown to care for her more than I had ever anticipated, and it bothered me more than I wanted for it to.

Now we were starting to have conversations?

This had to end, soon.

• • •

Mate is mine, Coal grumbled in his thoughts. *I don't want to reject her*.

'We don't have a choice,' I told him. *'Alpha commands are a bitch.'*

"I don't know, but I don't think we can," I finally answered her.

"I wish that we could," she said, looking up at me.

Too sweet...too loving...

Too damned trusting, Coal snarled at me. *Considering that you plan to reject her and take my true mate from me. Fucking fool human mind.*

I was going to have to rip her heart out, because I was officially to be mated and wed to the beta's daughter by Solaris's Reign. I only had a few months left.

Amethyst was coming into her heat, then, and they wanted to wait until then.

I sighed. "I just don't see it happening," I told her.

"North...?" She asked, looking up at me.

"Cedar?" I replied.

She curled into me, nuzzling my neck with her face. "I...I love you," she said, and I absolutely froze.

That was the first that either of us had said it.

We had started this, the first time, back in Folias's Blessing *three years ago*.

We'd completely given to one another two years later.

Now, as I looked down at her and thought of all the time that I had spent watching over her, looking at her, thinking of her...

I loved her, too.

I didn't say the words...but her saying that had just destroyed me.

● ● ●

I rolled us over, still naked, and I worked my muscular frame down her body.

She gasped out, perky breasts bouncing with the sharpness of her breath as I dove my tongue into her, in and out, swirling around her clit and sucking her lips between my teeth and giving them little nibbles.

She mewled the most delicious sound, and then, I couldn't get enough of my face between her legs, making her come for me.

I took her all night long, and later...

I was so lost in our heated passion that I didn't think to pull out of her to release until I was coming undone inside of her tight body, and the only thing I could think was, "*Oh, fuck.*"

I was disturbingly aroused at the mental image of her, round for me—round with my pup, bore from my seed.

It made me hard inside of her all over again.

Rain's Fall, 1970 ILY

When I had arrived to the den today, she had been spit-roasting a rabbit for me, and I enjoyed a good meal with her...though, my mind had to pause and think this over.

This was starting to seem too...domestic.

She was feeding me, now?

I pushed it out of my mind as I took her body with mine, ignoring the irking feelings that we were too close. She was just enjoying me the way I was surely just enjoying her, right?

When I rejected her, she'd move on, right? I was sure she would.

I'd move on, too.

The rest of our meetings this month would go this way, and I would continue trying to convince myself that this was all *just physical*...even though that Coal and I both knew, deep down, that Cedar and Pepper were much more than just a physical release for us.

She refreshed our very soul, and sooner rather than later...she wasn't the only one would end up getting hurt.

We were both in too deep, now...and I realized that I had made a terrible mistake by not ending things before they ever started.

Veras's Height, 1970 ILY

"Father," I said, quiet.

It was dark out as my father sat by a small firepit, a little fire starting to die out into the night as it ran out of wood to burn. It was late, and mother had already gone to bed for the night.

"What is it?" He asked.

"I…I need to speak with you."

He looked at me with a neutral expression, and I could feel in his spirit that he seemed to already suspect this.

"It is about the female you've been seeing…isn't it?"

I looked away…way too damn guilty. A small nod. "Yes."

He sat up from lounging on his outdoor lounger, and put his elbows on his knees, hands clasping as he rested his chin on them. He was giving me his full attention, which was rare for my war-minded Offensive Gamma father.

"Speak," he said, tone still neutral. *Cautionary.*

"I met my true mate," I told him.

He didn't look surprised, the way that I had expected that he would. "I had suspected," he confirmed.

This shocked me. "You…you *knew*? How?"

He looked away, before he leveled me with an amused expression. "Son…*no other female* can put an end to one's heat other than your *marked* mate…or your *true* mate."

"…What?"

● ● ●

"Since you have no *marked* mate—at least, not to my knowledge, and if you did, it would be a serious break of trust—you had to have found your true mate female. I have come to presume that she must be rogue, as I have gone through every *inch* of our territory and have not found a single female around your age with your scent on her. That can only mean that she isn't from our pack at all."

I looked away. "I underestimated you," I said, giving a small chuckle.

"You weren't entirely aware," he conceded. "Many males don't realize that only mates can end the heat, at your age. But once you get to my age, you've seen multiple generations hit their heats and seen that only their mate—whichever type that may be—can bring the endless burn of the heat to completion. As soon as you came home *relieved* that one instance, and I could smell the lingering scent of a female on you, I knew."

I really *had* underestimated him. "You don't seem angry..."

"That will depend on your answer to my next question," he said, leveling me with a serious expression again. "I already assume you have mated this female...and you have assured me yourself that you have been careful, *but*..."

"...'But?'"

"Have you *marked* this female?"

"No," I said, skipping the part that I'd released into her body...because when he'd originally confronted me about that, it was true that I hadn't.

At this point, however, that was no longer the case.

"Good," he said, standing and patting me on the back.

"Huh?" I asked, confused.

"I am not opposed to you enjoying the female meant for you; but end it now. You get married in just a few months, and I will *not* have you keeping a mistress. This changes things. You have to reject her, so that we don't have to beg for Selene to bless the union."

"But, father—"

"I will *not* have a rogue for a daughter-in-law," he snarled. "If she were from one of the allied packs, there would have been signs when they were here for negotiations and meetings."

"I don't want to marry Amethyst, father, I want my true—"

A hard slap stopped me, and I fell to my knees from the force.

I glared up at him.

"You will marry whomever the alpha commands you to marry, because you are an Offensive Gamma Heir. You will not be disgraced by having a rogue for a—"

"She's *not* a rogue!" I shouted as he went to hit me again, and he froze, his hand mid-air.

"*...I beg your pardon?*"

I huffed out a deep breath. "She's...she's...from the neighboring pack."

"*Fuck!*" My father raged, picking up his bottle of vodka and slinging it to shatter against the wall of our stone fence around the back yard of our den. "Fuck it all, *no*. No, no! This is *not* acceptable, this...what rank is she? What family is she from? What kind of lineage is she from?"

I really hesitated here, because there was no way that he would approve of this...but when I hesitated, he moved to strike me again.

"She...is the daughter of former Beta Cloud Stone, the sister of Beta Quill Stone."

He paused in his tirade. "The beta's daughter..." He glared in the direction of their pack, before his cold red eyes met mine again. "That *is* an impressive female for a gamma male," he conceded.

I almost, for an instant, thought for a moment that he was actually okay with it…until he spoke again.

"But you will still reject her, because that is almost…worse than a rogue. Beta's daughter or not, she is from the *enemy* pack, and—"

"But what if we could fix the problems by uniting *us* through marriage? She's already my true mate, so—"

I didn't get to speak again, because he had forced me to my knees again with a strong blow to the back of my head.

My ears rung, my head pounding as Coal started to have enough.

I was on the verge of shifting, but I kept my head because my father was already snarling as he held his body over mine.

"**You. Will. Reject. Her**. End of discussion. If you reject her, I will pretend that we never had this conversation, and your little weak ass, pathetic true mate, as pitiful as I remember her being…she and her family will remain *safe*."

Is he threatening mate? Coal snarled, digging his claws into me deep on the inside to try to claw his way out of me. **Nobody threatens mate, not even father,** he said.

When I didn't respond, he gave me a tight nod. "Now that we've cleared that up," he said. He turned. "Let me know when you've completed the deed. I won't mention this to the alpha or beta if you handle it quietly, on your own."

I couldn't move until he had gone inside…but the moment that he was gone, I felt my shoulders tremble.

That hadn't gone as *badly* as I had imagined…but it wasn't *good*, either…and now?

Now, I really had no choice. It was this, or father get the alpha involved.

● ● ●

All I wanted, in that moment, was to see the one person who I shouldn't.

• • •

CHAPTER 6

North...

It was just going into the month, and it had been a week since the conversation with my father.

He had been keeping an eye on me, and he glared at me when the alpha asked if I was excited for the wedding in Solaris's Reign...and I hadn't been able to jump with a response.

"Have you rejected her yet?" My father had asked.

"I haven't seen her since our talk," I had told him.

"Go and see her...and I promise, I won't even follow you," he smirked t me. "Go be a good boy and reject her."

Fearful rage burned through me, but I knew that he could have very well waited and tracked my scent later if he'd really wanted to. He could have killed her if he wanted.

We wouldn't be in her pack's territory.

I made my way to the boundary line, and when I had waited for a few hours, I finally caught her scent.

I took a breath of relief, excited that I would get to see her, but upset at the prospect of what I would have to do.

Then...oh, ho, *then*...I saw her.

● ● ●

She appeared before me in the most stunning white, marble-printed sundress.

Her hair was down, but there was a braid around the crown of her head like a halo, silvery and shiny in the light but dark grey undertones.

She had light makeup on, with a shimmery coral gloss on her lips and beige and coral tones on her eyelids. Thin, light brown eyeliner lined her bright green eyes and her silvery, dark grey eyelashes were thickened with a dark brown mascara.

She looked stunning.

Her cedar-toned tan skin was glowing, and she lit up when she saw me.

"*North,*" she said, *way too happy* to see me, and after the last week I'd had...I *broke.*

For the first time in my life, I broke in front of another person.

Tears burned my eyes as I looked at the one creature in my life that didn't *expect* me to be strong, obedient, and perfect all the time.

The one who let me be comfortable, the one I wanted to be strong for.

The one who didn't pressure me, and who let me feel like I didn't have to be cruel.

Like I could be more than just my rank in a pack in the middle of nowhere.

Coal and I, in that moment, shattered.

One last time. One last time, I would give myself over to her completely.

I took her into my arms, and we stumbled back into our little den together.

That night, I didn't worry about anything. I didn't stop myself from leaving bite marks on her, even biting into her flesh.

It was only a mate mark if I marked her in my wolf form, so biting into her flesh in my human form was just an enjoyable experience.

She trembled beneath me, cupping my face in her hands as tears spilled down my cheeks...but she didn't ask. She didn't pry.

She let me be emotional, and kissed my tears away as I gave myself over to the pleasure that she brought out of me.

When I released into her body, I didn't even care.

I wanted it to be everything in that moment.

That was exactly what I got as she clasped over my length, even as I emptied my load into her.

I couldn't imagine anywhere I'd rather be.

Solaris's Gifts, 1970 ILY

It had been about a month and a half since I had seen her.

I had told her that I was busy around the pack lately—which wasn't a lie, honestly—and that I wouldn't be able to meet her as often.

I knew, though, that *this* was my last chance to see her before the wedding.

My father had asked me about the rejection after I'd returned, but after smelling my love-making—yes, I was actually referring to that session as love-making because of how loving and intense it was—he assumed that I had not gone through with it.

I couldn't lie to him.

I told him that I would, absolutely, reject her the next time that I saw her.

I told him that I had been so irritated by everything going on that I just had to fuck out my frustrations.

I'd seen him breed out stress enough times to know that when he was angry or frustrated, he often fucked my mother...or *whoever*, really.

He sighed, but insisted that if I didn't formally reject her the next time that I saw her...he would officially go to the alpha and bring war to her pack.

I made sure that nobody was following me, before I began the trip to the den.

Surprisingly, she was there, and...I could smell something...off.

Something…off…?

Something was wrong with her scent. Was someone else with her?

I rushed forward, worried.

Had we been discovered? *Was she in danger?*

When I came rushing into the den, however, I found only my true mate…but she was…*different.*

When she turned to face me, glowing and beaming at me, I gaped at her in sheer horror.

She was changing.

Mate is pupped, Coal informed me, his chest puffing out inside me in a boastful way. **Mate belongs to me. She carries my pup in her**, he declared proudly. **Soon, Pepper will be round for us, bringing us a pup from that beautiful body of her's. I can't wait to try her milk. I want mate's milk for pup, I want her to feed me, too,** he spoke with sickeningly aroused interest, lust dripping from his tone in my head as the image of him sucking from her teats in wolf form rushed into my mind.

Somehow, I was—*alarmingly*—not put off by the image.

If anything, it made me proud to think of.

This wasn't something to be proud of. This wasn't good, it wasn't good at all.

Formally rejecting her now could cause serious harm, to her or the child or *both*…but I had no choice.

I had no options here.

She hadn't even needed to say a word. It had been a month and a half since I'd seen her, and I specifically remembered releasing my cum into her body…*multiple* times.

She was pupped, and I couldn't deny the overwhelming scent of our child emanating from her body.

● ● ●

It was mine.

Though, of course, it was mine. I was the only male she'd been mating with.

Fuck.

I was engaged to the beta's daughter of my own pack. I was being put into an arranged marriage to promote me to the next rank up...and my true mate, from our enemy pack, was now pupped by me.

I was getting married the following month, for fuck's sake!

I couldn't draw this out anymore...but one last goodbye was in order, wasn't it...?

I took her face in both of my hands, leaning down to kiss her—when out of fucking nowhere, I was tackled to the ground.

I leapt up from the ground, snarling as I shifted quickly, and I realized that I was in the presence of her alpha.

Shit.

They had followed us here.

The alpha, the luna, Cedar and I all stood there at a crossroads.

Things were about to take a turn for the unchangeable.

Nothing would be the same after this, and I had goosebumps all over.

"Stay away from her," he growled at me, but I snarled at him, baring my fangs, and letting loose a long string of rumbling. The luna took a defensive stance, trying to defend her alpha.

"Please! Please, don't fight!" Cedar begged, even as her brother popped out of the bushes.

"Get away from here, Cedar, now. This whole thing," he said, pointing between her and me. "*This* is *over*. You don't even care that you've ruined her future, do you? Now, *no* male in his right mind would enter an arranged marriage with her! How dare you force her—"

"*I wasn't forced!*" She shouted at her brother, even as I shifted back to my human form and put my clothes back on from my backpack. "He's...he is my true mate! I...I *love* him, brother. Alpha Finch, please...please, can't we—"

"No," Finch said, glaring at me. "They have killed too many of us. Too many pack members, *dead*, just for almost nothing. They hunt us on the boundary for *sport*. They are evil. You will reject him, and you will return home with us where your parents can care for you. For goodness' sake, Cedar, he was playing you! He probably intended to drag you along until you got attached and close, and then reject you. He doesn't love you; he's using you!"

Everything that he said filled me with rage, because he didn't know. He didn't know what she meant to me; he didn't know how I loved her.

"No!" She cried, looking to me. "Please, North...please, take me with you. Show my pack that we can be united, instead of enemies."

She was pleading with me...but I said nothing.

There was nothing that I *could* say, because it was too late.

I had people above me who expected things from me, and I had to deliver. I was under orders.

When a long pause passed without my response, she began to panic, and I could hear her heart racing as the blood drained from her face. "You...you can't...you can't mean to—"

"He is a waste of your time, sister," the beta spit out, rolling his eyes and gripping her arm. "It is time for you to come home."

"Quill—" She tried, but he kept going.

• • •

"We can forget this whole thing, and you can get back to your place in the pack. Surely, Moon Mother Selene didn't give you a true mate from another pack."

"Quill—"

"You have to be mistaken. A mate from an enemy pack? That's *nonsense*. That's against the nature of Selene's love. He is going to leave you! So, you should just reject him first."

"Cedar, please," I pleaded. "I...I care for you. I love you...but I have been alpha commanded to marry—"

"See?" The brother scoffed. "*He* won't turn traitor for *you*, sister...so don't turn traitor for *him*. We can even get rid of the pup, if you want—"

I snarled at them. "*Let her make up her own mind!*" I shouted. "She and I have something special. We are true mates, and I didn't just give her a pup out of some vile plan to hurt her, or plan to go against your pack. I just wanted to love her—"

"Get out of here, and *maybe* we won't think of dumping your bastard pup at your door; *if* her parents decide not to rip the disgusting, vile little beast out of her, that is," Alpha Finch grated out at me...and that fucking did it.

That was my breaking point.

I shifted yet again, snarling at them as Coal was ready to defend his pup and his mate. Fuck it all.

He and his mate got between Cedar and I, trying to block her from me.

Just as I went to leap at him, Dove Stone—Cedar's mother—jumped out of the woods.

"No!" She cried. "Cedar, you can't do this! You have to reject this boy!" She ran over like a fool and tried to get in the way, interceding.

She was trying to defend the alpha, the luna, and protect her children...

● ● ●

It was just too bad that Coal had no control, and no sympathy for anyone who got in his way, and I had already leapt.

CHAPTER 7

Cedar...

I cried out, startled, as my true mate jumped all over my mother.

I could see the flash of regret in his gaze—an *unintentional* casualty—but it didn't alter his course of action, either.

She was easily killed, before he turned his attention to the alpha.

I shrieked, terrified, as he began ripping him to pieces, crying in pain as the bond between alpha and pack broke.

"Get out of here!" My brother shouted, shoving me away. "Get away, and go get help! We can take him down if we—"

"No!" I shouted. "I won't fight him. I won't let him get hurt! He's—"

"You're a damned *traitor*, then, and I never thought you would betray us that way," he snarled at me, glaring at my true mate as he finished the job on our alpha and stalked toward us. "He just killed our *mother* and *alpha* in cold blood. You can't be serious, Cedar."

"Quill—"

• • •

"No!" He shouted.

"But...he's my true mate," I sobbed. "I love him, brother, I—"

"You are a traitor, and you two deserve each other."

I looked to my mate, trembling.

Blood coated his muzzle menacingly, and my brother turned tail and bolted away for help, rushing the luna away from the scene as she sobbed and cried over her lost mate.

"What have you done...?" I asked, soft, looking up at the wolf that towered over me, on my knees, where I had fallen to the ground. "Do you truly love me so little...?"

He huffed, turning away, before he shifted again. "I do love you...more than I have ever loved anything. That's why I couldn't listen to them talk about our pup that way...but I don't have a choice. My alpha has arranged me to marry someone else."

"W...what?"

"It is already decided. This," he said, pointing between us. "This is something amazing, a wonderful, liberating haven. My only true escape, but...it can never be, Cedar. I have no choice. You are the one I want. You are the one, the only one, who gives me peace...but it can't be between us. I've been alpha commanded already. I am not powerful enough to override that. I can't betray the alpha command."

"Can't...can't you tell your alpha that you have someone you love? Or your father? That you found a female—"

"I tried!" He exploded. "I tried, Cedar. He wasn't having it. He favors the female *chosen* for me. I am alpha-commanded to wed her next month. There is nothing that I can do." He turned, walking away, and sprinting into the forest.

Two weeks had passed by since the incident, and now, it was nearly the end of the month.

After the death of the alpha, and my mother, the closest heir left was my brother's oldest child, Oak Stone.

He became the Alpha Heir, while former Alpha, turned Defensive Gamma, Sierra Stone, took over as the interim alpha for the time being.

Our pack wrote to the Head Alpha in the royal kingdom, who had journeyed out by plane to come and settle our dispute, and he used a special ability to watch what happened in our minds via the pack link.

As a Lycan, he had the ability to do that.

He watched how the Glacial Jewel pack had been treating us all along, hunting for any excuses to pick us off, and he watched the situation with North and I.

The romance, the blossoming love and feelings...

He watched him murder my mother and the alpha, but kept in mind that he still wasn't even a full adult by law. He was only seventeen.

He and the Head Luna both decided that, to make this situation *fair*...

North's father, Easton Frost, would be offered up as tribute to maintain peace.

North and his mother had cried and held one another, watching me and my family with glaring eyes filled with hate.

War was officially outlawed between the two packs, with the agreement that North would marry the beta's daughter of his pack and become the beta heir, and I, the beta's daughter of my pack, would marry the Pack Hunter of my pack.

He was the only single male near my age in our pack, and so, that was the only choice I had left.

My son or daughter's fate would be decided later on.

After Offensive Gamma Easton Frost was hanged in front of the packs, and the Head Alpha made his proclamation that our packs were to stay on civil terms from that point on...North had come to me afterward.

He looked dead on his feet, bags under his eyes. His pale skin looked sallow.

He looked almost...ill.

"North—" I tried, but he cut me off with a hard look.

"I curse the day that I found out that you were my true mate."

I froze, my heart nearly stopping as the blood pounded in my veins, painfully.

I could barely hear him over it, but then again, his voice was all I could focus on, as he continued to deliver this fatal blow to me.

"I should have rejected you, from the very beginning," he said, eyes dead and void of emotion as he turned to look at his father's dangling corpse. He turned back to me. "I, North Frost, Offensive Gamma, son of Offensive Gamma Easton Frost and Lady Snow Storm, hereby reject you, Cedar Stone, daughter of Beta Cloud Stone and beta female Dove Terra Stone, sister of Beta Quill Stone and aunt to Alpha Heir Oak Stone, as my true mate. I reject the Moon Mother's 'gift,' henceforth...and I never wish to see you again. Please, accept my formal rejection and please, don't ever show your face in front of me again."

Tears burned my eyes and sobs ripped out from my chest and bubbled out of my throat, but I bared my neck for him...knowing that I would never get to wear his mark.

My true mate had rejected me.

Pepper crumbled in my mind, withering like a sandcastle that had gotten hit by waves.

I felt her weaken dramatically; she was too hurt to even cry. I barely felt her whimpers as she let them out silently.

She was completely broken.

I glanced to my father and the pack who watched us with distain filled expressions, before turning back to him.

My voice cracked when I finally spoke. "I, Cedar Stone, accept your formal rejection as my true mate, North Frost. I wish you well, and truly hope for your every happiness."

He turned without another word, walking off with the rest of his pack, even as I crumpled to the ground...utterly spent.

I had lost everything.

My once extremely overprotective big brother couldn't even bear to look at me anymore.

Since I had tried to protect my true mate, even *after* he murdered my mother and the alpha, he'd branded me a traitor and refused to look at me.

He refused to speak to me.

He had formally given up on me as his sister that night, told me to forget he'd ever even *been* my brother.

From promising that I could live with him and that he would take care of me forever, to renouncing me.

It didn't matter that it was in a female's core nature to love, protect, and excuse her true mate because she was his female. It didn't matter that we were wired that way.

● ● ●

My father...he looked at me with such disappointment, such hurt, that I *wished* he wouldn't look at me at all.

He didn't speak to me, whereas my brother said nothing but hateful, awful things.

I felt like I was being ripped apart.

The interim alpha stepped up to me, still on the ground, with the young Pack Hunter at his side.

His name was Sage Onyx, and coincidentally enough...his father, Sparrow, had been the true mate of my mother.

Now, he was the only single male in the pack because he had been a lone wolf—he had rejected his true mate to focus on training as the Pack Hunter. He was an extremely powerful, gamma-blooded male.

He was only accepting me because the alpha had ordered it.

"It is time," Interim Alpha Sierra said, motioning to me. "In lieu of what has happened, we will not ask Selene to bless this union, because your true mates have already been rejected. You may simply...proceed to marking," he said, stepping out of the way for Sage to step over to me.

We were doing this here, in the middle of the sacred circle where someone had just been hanged? His corpse was still swaying nearby, for heaven's sake...

The members of the other pack were still leaving, not bothering to stop and watch or pay any mind to us.

I was a traitor now, after all, and my pack couldn't bear to look at me.

It was obvious by looking at me what had happened.

I had chosen to breed with a male from the enemy pack. I was pupped by that very male, and he had slaughtered my mother—our beta female—and our alpha.

The male dangling nearby, dead, smelled like that male...obviously a blood relation.

The truth of it was obvious to anyone who looked.

I was a traitor, and I was pregnant with a wolf that was fathered by an enemy and a murderer.

Sage got in position above me, looking down at me with no expression.

At least he wasn't...*angry*...

He helped me to the right position, and I was instructed to shift.

Tears ran down my face, but I forced my body to shift.

It was still before the danger point, where I wouldn't be able to shift any more due to pregnancy, but it was a bit painful, especially considering all that my wolf had just been put through.

He shifted into a large, dark, smoky grey wolf with little shimmer. His fur was rough and thick, scratchy almost. He was a warrior, so it made sense.

His wolf's name, itself, was Smoke, for his dark smoky color.

He was quite large, as he came and stood over me.

I forced my wolf to submit, and she did so without any fight on her end whatsoever.

After her mate had rejected her, she had no fight in her left.

She would face this empty void the rest of her days, and I could already feel her wasting away inside of me.

I knew, within the next several years, that I would likely be dead. The decay in my wolf was thick.

She had been so in love...

* * *

Most wolves who were rejected by their true mates were rejected right away, and without any love and feelings involved.

However, that wasn't the case here.

North and I had been together for a few years, seeing each other, chasing each other. We had been intimate with one another so, so many times.

We had a pup between us, now.

There was no way that it wouldn't destroy my wolf.

I forced down my trembles and sobs as I felt Sage prepare to mark me, and I held back my sharp cry when his teeth broke the skin and grabbed hold, deep into the muscle tissue.

Forever branded by a male I didn't love, who didn't love me, and had just been brought to marry me out of nowhere with no real purpose but to keep us both tied to the pack.

Not lose us as lone wolves.

He stood, shifting back, and putting on his clothes again.

I felt an omega drape a dress over me, and I shifted, not caring who saw me naked, before I slid the dress on.

"I pronounce you male and mate," the alpha said, looking away. "You may go, now," he told us.

I followed my male without a word.

My father and brother looked on, mixed emotions on their faces, as they refused to look me in the eye, but they didn't stop me.

CHAPTER 8

Cedar...

When we reached his den on the very far outskirts of the territory—*terrifyingly* close to where I had been mating with North—he led me to the larger of two bedrooms inside, pointing to the bed.

"We sleep here," he said.

I didn't fight. I simply nodded.

It didn't matter if we slept together.

Who cared if he had his way with me?

I was as good as dead, anyway.

When I stood there with no response and no expression, he rubbed the back of his neck, a bit awkward.

"I, uh...I also bought a crib. It is in the other bedroom. It should suffice, but I didn't have much time to prepare when they told me that I was getting a pupped mate," he said, glancing at my belly.

I brought a protective hand over my belly, and he sighed, giving a single, half-hearted chuckle.

"I mean your pup no harm, I promise," he told me. "In fact, I care not if you and I ever mate at all, to be honest with you."

I hesitated, giving him a questioning look, I supposed, because he went on to explain.

"The bond is just to hold me to the pack. I was becoming feral, and all of my hard work and my endless hours of training would have been for nothing. They didn't want to lose me or my skill. I made high marks during testing."

I gave him a nod. "I remember your scores," I whispered...and I did.

As the daughter of the beta couple, it was my job to help learn how to help run the pack and learn the roles of different ranks for females here, so depending on who my mate was, I would be able to perform my role properly.

I remembered him from watching him train with the delta males, their testing with the Pack Hunters and gammas...

I had been so impressed at the time.

Now, he seemed like a joke compared to my true mate.

Even after the rejection, it seemed that Pepper and I had grown to love him too deeply.

I was thrashed by this, completely destroyed.

I still loved him and craved him, wanting him by my side, even after a formal rejection, and that didn't happen often.

I remembered those delicious tingles and sparks every time he touched me, and I knew that I might get a cheap imitation with my new mark-bonded mate, but it would never be able to compete with what I'd shared with North.

He smiled. "There is food and drink in the kitchen. Help yourself. I may not love you, and you may not love me, but we are mates. I am the male, and I provide for my mate as I should. You will not lack, here."

I had to admit, it was comforting to hear that.

"But what about your reputation...?" I asked. "I am the pack traitor. A shame to the pack."

He shrugged. "True mates...they are not defined by normal rules. I know you loved your male. He likely loved you, too. Who he was and where he came from wasn't up to you. It wasn't your fault, nor his. This pack worries too much about reputation and moral values, when we are sexual, possessive, sensual beings by nature."

Since I had been outed as having mated an enemy wolf, I had been ostracized and subjected to ridicule and mean glares. This male, however, had a very refreshing new perspective that I hadn't heard before...

It was deeply comforting to me.

I could deal with this male's attitude all day, and be content.

"Thank you," I said. "Um...how would you prefer me to address you?"

"What do you mean?"

"Should I call you by name? Pack Hunter? Or...mate," I whispered the last, barely audible. "I will admit, that last one...might never happen."

He shook his head. "Whichever it is that you are comfortable with. We will be together for the remainder of our lives. You will grow accustomed to my presence, and the same can be said for me." He gave me a nod. "There is a bathroom through there," he said, pointing to a door in his room. "And the closet," pointing at another door. "Your things are...already here. The alpha set all of this up before he went after you that day..."

"I see," I said, voice tight.

That meant that they had already planned to marry me to Sage, and had been planning this for quite some time...even before I had been discovered to be pregnant that fateful day, and they followed me to my safe-haven.

Marrying me off to the Pack Hunter had been the plan all along.

"Right," he said, awkward. He cleared his throat. "Well," he said. "Welcome home," he said.

Then he turned on his heel and left the room, leaving the door open behind him.

I sighed, before he startled me as the door jerked back open unexpectedly...though, he wasn't in the doorway...?

"You can shut the door if you like...I just didn't want you to think I was shutting you inside to keep you there," he said loudly from outside, and I had to give a light chuckle.

He was very awkward, socially.

He hadn't been socialized with other pups normally, because being the Pack Hunter heir meant that one day...you might have to kill those same wolves.

Bonds that were formed as pups were harder to conquer.

He had been homeschooled.

I glanced around the room, taking note of it.

It was somewhat bare; plain cream-colored walls with one solid black wall behind the bed, with only one family photo on the wall and a painting of a beautiful snow-covered forest with a beautiful snowy mountain range behind it, the sun peeking out just above the ridge.

It looked like a sunrise.

The comforter on the king-sized bed was a sage green, with grey sheets and pillowcase covered pillows on the bed.

A few throw pillows in different shades of green.

The bedframe and bedside tables were wood—what looked like it was oak, and the dresser and nightstands matched. he dresser matched.

There were various items on the dresser...a box of tissues, some hunting magazines, and a bottle of cologne...but on the left side of the dresser, closest to the wall of the inner part of the room, there was a glass vase of beautiful marigolds and mountain flowers in a pretty blue shade.

Marigolds were my favorite flower.

Roses had once been a close second, but now they reminded me of...someone who shall not be named.

I turned again, looking at the bed.

I looked at the side of the bed closest to the inner wall of the room, and noted that it looked particularly unslept-in. The other side had the barest hint of an impression of where his body must lay, and he was closest to the door.

I smiled despite a lack of real humor.

Most males chose the side of the room closest to the door, to protect their females from potential intruders, and it seemed that he had this same mindset.

I both hated and appreciated that he was a protective male.

I didn't want to be with anyone at all...

To be with a male who wanted to look out for and protect me?

It made me feel like puking.

I looked at what would be my nightstand—bare except for a small lamp, one that had a twin lamp on his own side.

There was, however, a note on the pillow, and I stepped over, taking it and unfolding it.

"Cedar,

I have always had a habit of sleeping closer to the door, so your side of the bed remains untouched.

I have never had females in this bed, if that matters to you.

Though I have slept with females outside of my den, but, I will no longer do so, now that we are mated, so you don't need to be concerned about any infidelity pains.

I left your side table and your half of the closet and dresser mostly empty...your father put most of your things in here, and I left them as is, because I was sure he would know your preferred tastes.

If you need anything and do not wish to venture into the pack, please let me know. I will go to the pack store and buy anything you want, if you ask me.

I bought new pillows for you, and this is an entirely new comforter and bedsheet set. I hope you like them? I've never shopped while thinking of a girl, so I might be lacking in that department, but I will do my best to learn.

You may decorate as you wish; I've never been bothered with it due to my position in the pack, but if you want to add some color or art, whichever...just let me know.

I make a decent wage as a Pack Hunter, you know, and the owners of the shops love me because I keep their wares safe from thieves. I usually get discounts on my purchases, perks of offering safety.

(Sorry if that sounds like bragging, it isn't intended that way.)

I usually leave for work at dawn, and return for lunch.

I do not expect for you to cook for me, just so you know.

I tend to keep something small set aside for myself, prepped and ready to eat when I arrive, so that is not necessary. I go back after lunch, and return around ten at night.

● ● ●

If you need for me to adjust my hours for anything to suit your needs, let me know.

We do still have another Pack Hunter and their Pack Hunter heir, so we work on shifts and can adjust our schedule to whatever we need.

I hope that you will be comfortable here...and I hope that you like marigolds.

Beta Heir Quill had mentioned, once, that they were your favorite, but that was a long time ago. That could have changed by now.

Welcome to my—our—home.

-Sage-"

I sighed at the note.

It was sweet of him, to think of me and consider me. He was already a good mate by doing things for me, even without formal education to learn those behaviors and traits.

Most Pack Hunters assigned the strongest of the deltas they could find to succeed them, if they chose to focus on training and reject their mates...and most Pack Hunters did.

Just as Sage had.

I set the note on the side table, and sat on the edge of the bed, testing it.

It was firm but soft, and very comfortable. The pillows were plump and full, and the plushy jade-green blanket on a nice oak rocking chair in the corner that I hadn't spotted before was soft enough I could curl up and fall asleep.

I stood and stretched, before I stepped over to the closet.

I opened it, and saw that most of my things from home had been brought here, and hung the way I would have hung them, surprisingly.

I hadn't realized father and brother had paid attention to my preferences.

I was even further shocked that they had actually been considerate enough to hang them in the closet neatly and tidily, after having branded me a traitor to the pack.

I stepped to the dresser, checking my side, and noted the neatly folded homey-clothes there.

I kept my nice clothes hung and pressed, but my home clothes and comfort wear stayed in the dresser, along with underwear.

Just out of curiosity, I peeked into Sage's side—and blushed profusely.

His underwear drawer was full of silky, tight, black and silver boxer-briefs. Thick black socks that I noted were extra-cushioned, for running.

The other drawers held regular t-shirts and V-necks in varying shades of greys, greens, navy, and a lot of white, too.

I stepped to the closet again, glancing inside...

Mostly button-ups that looked tailored, and sharp blazers. There were a few uniforms. Some nice, rich-looking blue-jeans that were dark-wash or almost black, some with grey tones.

Boots.

He was like me, it seemed. His nice clothes went in the closet to hang, and comfort clothes were for the dresser. I liked that.

It was...familiar. Comforting.

I didn't want to be comforted.

I wanted to be horribly miserable, and angry. I wanted to hate him, hate this place, hate everything in the world.

I had lost my chance at true love. I'd had my heart shattered, all while I was carrying a pup of a wolf who, as my brother had so eagerly rubbed in my face...hadn't been willing to turn traitor for me, as I had for him.

Love had ruined my life.

I shook the thoughts from my mind, focusing again on what I had been doing.

Then, I took the chance to glance into the bathroom.

It wasn't large—a simple single sink with a nice vanity and mirror attached, and a—thankfully—*clean*, tall toilet.

I felt my jaw almost drop, however, when I saw the large, beautiful, stone-tiled walk-in shower.

There was a bench seat, an overhead large, flat sprayer, and two rounder, detachable sprayers on the sides—one on each side.

There were two racks hanging on the wall; one filled with obviously masculine things, soaps, and razors, etc.

Then, there was one that was empty, ready for my things.

The bathroom itself was painted a war-toned green, with a solid black wall behind the tiled shower.

I looked to the sink and counter, and noticed a plug in scent releaser in the power outlet...one of the fancy new ones.

I laughed, genuinely.

That certainly looked brand-spanking-new.

I could tell, right away, that he'd gotten word that he was getting a mate out of nowhere, and he rushed out to the store to get things ready for me last minute so that I would be comfortable.

I had to admit that I was touched by the gesture, but that just served to make me even angrier.

The plushy, army green mats in front of the toilet and shower looked new, too.

Hanging on the wall beside the shower were two hooks—a black robe, and a delicate yellow plush one...mine, from home.

I looked beneath the bathroom cabinet to find a good stock of toilet paper, two rolls of paper-towels, some cleaning products, a toilet brush and plunger, and a basket...that I recognized, from home...to my mortification.

A basket filled with sanitary pads and tampons.

My face flamed.

I glanced on the wall beside the mirror over the sink, and realized that there was a small rack hanging there, too.

● ● ●

It was filled with tooth pastes, mouth-wash, hand-soap, and there was a cup holding two tooth brushes.

The bar on the bottom of the rack held a hand-towel, in a nice shade of gold.

Where were the towels...?

I was immediately overly emotional over this issue. Where were the darned towels?

It was so well-stocked, set up for *both* of us, of all the nerve! He was prepared for my living here, but where were the damn *towels*?!

I stormed out of bathroom in a crazy, questionable, *unnecessary* rage, and stormed through until I came back to the living area.

Sage looked up from his hunting magazine, alarmed and immediately on edge, when I stormed into the living space.

"Cedar? What's wro—" He started, standing quickly and looking around, as if expecting danger.

"Where are the towels?" I asked over him, overly aggressive and tears forming in my eyes.

What the hell was wrong with me...?

He paused for a long moment, a baffled, confused expression on his face. "...Towels?"

"Yes!" I exploded, *completely irrational.*

I knew that I was being irrational, but I was so angry...!

How could my family do this to me?

They just handed me off to Sage...

I imagined, deep in my heart, that they had prepared this a while ago—to hold him to the pack, and to give me a chance at being with a partner, as I had no true mate in our pack...

Only, then I had come up pregnant, and the rest was history.

They had likely told him, very quickly, to expect me much sooner, and to get ready for me to be dumped on him.

He looked at me, alarm still on his handsome face that I didn't fucking want to find handsome. I wished I could tear his face off so that I didn't have to look at it.

I wanted to destroy everything.

I wanted him to absolutely hate me so that he wouldn't be good to be, and I wouldn't feel so guilty about my situation and burdening him.

"The towels—"

"The damn towels, in the bathroom, where are they? I saw everything else! Even my *damn pads and tampons!* Even when I'm pregnant, and don't even fricking need them! I'm knocked up, remember?! I don't need those things, but, ohhh, they're there! But, no *towels*!?" I fumed.

He bit his thick bottom lip, shoulders shaking, trying not to laugh.

I pointed. "You're *laughing* at me?!" I raged, irate for really no reason.

A little butthurt that he was making fun of me, but no real reason.

He chuckled under his breath, and—without giving me any response—walked into the bedroom.

I followed him, following him into the bathroom.

He stepped inside and motioned me in, before he shut the bathroom door. He stepped aside, and I saw that the door—which opened into the room, against the wall to the right—blocked the view of a small linen-closet door.

He opened that door, and I saw about a dozen thick, fuzzy towels, hand-towels, and wash-clothes to match.

There were even extra robes, extra toilet paper, extra soaps...

To my utter doom, there were even fresh, *unopened* packs and boxes of pads and tampons that matched what had been brought from home.

He had gone out of his way to buy more.

He'd paid way, way too much attention to detail...

My face flamed with my embarrassment, and then...

Then, my tears began to fall.

He gave me a tender expression, a warm and gentle smile on his lips, coming and patting my shoulder.

"It's alright. It took me a while to notice the door at first, too. My father chose this den for me, bought it pre-made, and I moved in with the layout already like this. I had to learn it, too."

That was right...

Many wolves bought pre-made dens, sold by deltas and omegas to make extra money to buy nicer dens for themselves.

We were an evolving economy...

"I...I don't know what to say. I'm sorry," I said, looking to the floor.

He took my shoulders in his hands, and I looked up at him.

He was handsome enough, with his dark grey, smoky hair and skin darker, like mine. His eyes were a calm, warm army green with sparks of gold along the outsides of the iris. Very pretty, really.

Thick black lashes framed his eyes.

Sharp features...

He was handsome.

Perhaps not the stunning beauty that my...former true mate had been, but handsome, all the same.

Tears stung my eyes all over.

"Why don't you get a shower, and when you finish, supper should be finished too? We'll get you a good meal in you, get you something warm to drink, and get you tucked in bed, hm?"

Tears cascaded down my cheeks by this point.

"Why...why are you being so *kind*?"

"Huh? Why wouldn't I be?"

"I...I don't want you to be kind to me. I want you to hate me."

"Why?"

"...Ever since I mated with an enemy, I've been a traitor to the pack. They all hate me. My own father and brother won't speak to me. Why are you so kind to me? I even just snapped at you, but you didn't bat an eye..."

He smiled. "Because the Pack Hunters are also heavily disliked, shunned, ostracized, feared, and generally avoided like a plague. I understand that. I understand how it feels. You're pregnant, you've been abandoned, and you are emotional."

I blushed. "I—"

"You have every right to be emotional. What exactly did you do that was so wrong? You found your true mate outside of your pack. Again—who cares *where* he's from? *He was your true mate.*"

"But...he—"

"Am I defending his crimes? No, of course, not. But *you* didn't commit them." He gave me a soft hug. "We might not ever fall in love, Cedar, but I am your partner."

"What...?"

● ● ●

He smiled at me, warm. "I am your partner. I marked you. That means that I am your mate, now. I am your male, and you are my female. We are in this together, and I will stand by you."

My heart swelled with gratefulness, as he turned and walked out of the bathroom...leaving me with thoughts that felt like a plague, thoughts that I didn't want to think.

Now, I was even more upset...

CHAPTER 9

Cedar...

I was almost at the end of my fourth month of pregnancy, now, and I was well and truly showing already.

I had always been slight and petite, but now it was obvious that I was pupped.

After that incident in the bathroom, Sage had indeed had supper ready for me when I finished and he sat with me in a comfortable quiet as we listened to some light music over the stereo, and then he'd made me some warm tea and taken me to bed, tucking me in and telling me about his childhood to pass the time.

He hadn't poked and prodded, asked me questions, or tried to pry into my feelings or into my thoughts.

He kept conversation light.

He mentioned his love of photography, how he tried to do some in his spare time as a hobby.

We continued talking—well, he did almost all of the talking—until I had fallen into a blissful sleep, and he had stroked my hair for a while before going to his own side of the bed and going to sleep himself.

Since then, we had grown quite close—as friends.

● ● ●
317

He had told me that I was welcome to talk to him about things, if I wanted...but I didn't.

Somehow, I didn't want to risk that he would become annoyed with me, or agree with everyone else that I was just a dirty traitor, or get angry with hearing about another man...even though he wasn't really possessive of me.

I knew he was growing fond of me, though, because when he would find me cooking or cleaning, he would give me this oddly tender expression before he'd chuckle and tell me that I could be lazy and sit around and do nothing if I wanted to.

He would tell me that he'd handle the cooking and cleaning.

I needed to relax.

I was pregnant, and I had always had a weak constitution, so he felt that I needed to get plenty of extra rest.

We were growing so close to each other...and I loved it...but I hated it, too, and I hated myself for it.

I didn't want to ruin that by talking to him about an enemy wolf I'd bred with, but I also did want to ruin it and make it so he didn't want to be friendly toward me.

He would get mad, wouldn't he?

I thought he would, at least.

Maybe I was off base with that, but I couldn't expect him to always be so calm and level headed.

Wolves were fairly temperamental.

He did begin asking me other questions, however, such as: if I was excited about my pup.

What I thought the pup might be, what the pup might look like.

What I intended to do once the pup had arrived.

● ● ●

All questions in good curiosity that he had the right to ask, because I *was* living in *his* den, and he wasn't asking me overly personal questions like I'd sensed that he wanted to ask, but thankfully hadn't.

I thought now, to North's birthday, which had recently passed. That had been a particularly emotional, hard day for me.

I wondered if he thought of me, of the moment he had found me in the forest and began to watch me...

I had finally told Sage that I would prefer not to discuss my pup's father or my relationship with him, and after a while of having asked with no response or me shutting down...

Sage finally stopped asking about it, with the lingering comment in the air that if I decided I wanted to open up and talk about it...he would listen, and give me unbiased feedback.

Things changed a little after that.

He didn't get too personal with me, and I was thankful.

He kept conversations focused around general pack news, gossip, and general questions about me and my pup.

I eventually *did* have to start requesting things from him, much to his odd delight, and it made me vaguely uncomfortable.

He told me he'd been waiting for me to "need him," and once I had started showing...I'd needed him.

He'd heard tales of how the other wolves treated me, but the ones who gave me the worst of it were females, and they never did anything whenever Sage was with me.

Unfortunately, Sage couldn't always be with me.

I avoided going out all that I could, now. I was no longer welcome at pack-wide events, and Sage usually stayed home with me through them unless he was expecting trouble.

He'd been...rather pitied for "having" to be with me, per the alpha's command.

That was how everyone had come to justify and choose to view his relationship with me.

There was simply no way that any wolf in his *sane* mind would have *chosen* to be with a traitor, after all.

Especially not a traitor, who was pregnant with an enemy's pup on the way.

I'd had mud, cold coffees, food, trash, and anything in between thrown at me, had been cursed and called horrible names...

I was treated worse than any omega I'd ever seen.

I was treated as a criminal.

The doctors made sure to keep my general health taken care of, but refused to do ultrasounds or anything other than the basic necessities for my pregnancy.

I didn't even know the gender of my pup.

Was my baby a villain to them?

Would he or she resent me for having him or her? I was beginning to wonder.

I couldn't bear to kill the baby, though.

It was the last part of my true mate that I had, and I was still in mourning over him.

I couldn't bear to lose the one gift he'd left me...but I was absolutely terrified of what to expect as far as treatment of my pup went.

I could only pray that I took the worst brunt of the negativity of the pack...that my pup wouldn't be subjected to it just because of what I had done.

Year's Fall, 1970 ILY

I finished the last of the dishes from our Heaven's Gift Holiday meal, glancing at Sage as he said goodbye to his parents as they walked out of the door.

While they had been here, I had made sure that the meal was perfect. I had everything cleaned and pristine, and the food had been divine...and then I'd stayed out of the way.

I had gone and shut myself into my nursery, where I waited silently as a mouse, until it sounded like dishes were being placed into the kitchen sink.

I knew they didn't like me and didn't want to see me, so I had waited to eat until they were finished and were on their way out to come back out.

As I had waited, I'd looked around the nursery; the light, minty green walls. The oak crib, cata-cornered in the room with a waste basket beside of it for diapers, because Sage was overly thoughtful and had tried to purchase everything I'd need.

A well-cushioned, comfortable rocking chair cata-cornered across from the crib.

An oak dresser already filled and stocked with diapers and wipes, and a lot of neutral baby clothes, since we still didn't know what I was expecting.

Mostly greens, golds, greys...

He had gone out of his way for me, and my pup...and I wasn't sure how I felt about it, anymore.

It certainly made it sink in that I really was fixing to become a mother, that I had a pup on the way.

I had growing affection for Sage. I cared about him a lot, as a friend.

That romantic line, however, I just couldn't seem to cross it.

I almost...wanted to, honestly. I wanted to feel that way for him...but I was just broken at this point, I feared.

Since the rejection, my wolf had stayed eerily quiet. She didn't come forward, wanting to run. Sage had offered to run with me, if I felt in danger...but Pepper had stayed silent, laying in my mind, and just breathing. No life.

She was rotting away, barely even moving with her breath.

The look of concern in Sage's face was enough to let me know that he worried about the situation, and how abnormal it was. How sick my wolf truly was...

He began to plead with me to mark him in return. Even if we didn't mate, marking him would bring Pepper back to life, at least a little bit. Even if it was only a little, still, it would help her...but I wasn't sure that I wanted to.

I was so, so tired.

I also knew that there was no way that his family or that our pack would be okay with me finding happiness with Sage, in the end.

They would all condemn us.

During the Folias's Blessing Harvest Feast, when I'd tried to join the family for the meal, his father had glared at me, all hateful and angry.

Not only was I the child of his former true mate, whom he had loved, and the male who had been arranged to her and taken her from him...but I was the reason my mother had died.

That was the way the entire pack had seen the outcome of what happened.

My mother came to stop the fight, bring me back where I belonged, and jumped in the way to try to stop the attack because she felt we were in danger, to try to help the alpha...but neither her nor our alpha had been a match against North.

She had been killed because of my foolishness, because of my love, and so had the alpha.

Sage was the only wolf in the pack who didn't view it this way.

Sage's father had made snide comments all of Harvest Feast, and had eventually said that I had no place being at the table or being in the room with them at all, outside of cleaning and basically presenting myself as a servant.

So, for the Heaven's Gift holiday dinner, that was what I had done.

I had only allowed myself to play servant...

I'd had set aside a plate for myself for later while the group ate in the dining room, before I had started doing dishes and putting things away.

My family was, as they had been for the Harvest Feast, absent.

I couldn't expect or hope for them to willingly sit with me and have a meal, I supposed...

I missed my family.

My loving, caring, warm father...

My doting, overprotective older brother...

I still loved them. I wanted to see them, be part of my family.

So, once Sage's parents were gone and I was able to come out, I stepped into my bedroom and to the closet, pulling out a large bag of wrapped gifts I had purchased a while ago.

I had toys for my brother's pups, my nephews, and a nice new survival knife for him.

I had gotten my father a nice pair of hiking boots and a nice, expensive watch, both picked out courtesy of Sage, who was sure that my father would like those gifts because they were useful and nice.

I hoped he was right.

He had originally thought that I didn't need to do this—I didn't need to get them gifts, but...I wanted to.

This was my very first holiday season without my family, and it didn't sit right with me.

I had already lost my true mate. I had lost my mother.

Weren't those things enough of a punishment...?

I had even gotten my brother's mate something; a pretty amber necklace, with the stone in a beautiful steel encasing.

I stepped out with the bag, and Sage took it from me.

"You shouldn't lift heavy things," he scolded non-committedly, smiling at me. "Cedar, I'm sorry about—"

"It's fine," I told him. "I made sure not to come out this time, unless I was cleaning, just like your father had said before. Don't worry, I won't bring any more embarrassment or problems to you," I smiled up at him.

He looked at me with a sad, dejected expression, before he sighed and turned, carrying the bag out the door without a word.

Oh, no...

I had made him sad...*again*...

I followed after him, and we walked for about thirty minutes...to my father's den.

When we arrived, my father was actually already outside, grabbing more wood for the fire.

Two young pups ran around him and he laughed, trying to make sure he didn't step on them and turning it into a game...like he was a giant, holding an entire village on his shoulders, and they had to watch out so they didn't get squished.

My chest tightened as I wondered if my own pup would get an experience like this...

He noticed our arrival, and his face got sour right away.

"Beta Cloud," Sage said, greeting him.

My father nodded to Sage and shook his forearm— the familial greeting of our race. Then he'd looked at me— my belly, more accurately, because he refused to look me in the face.

The expression on his face...was very unpleasant.

"Your scent has changed again," he said, voice gruff and surly. "His disgusting bastard pup will take after him, with that scent," he said.

I startled, looking to Sage, and seeing him look away...a bit like a toddler caught with his hand in a cookie jar.

Oh...

I hadn't even realized the change...but my scent becoming more like North's during my pregnancy meant that the pup was taking more after his bloodline, and that was a *bad* thing for him or her in this pack.

I sighed, looking to the bag we'd brought. "I've come with gifts," I said, soft. "Please," I told him, and I pulled out the boxes meant for him.

He gave my general direction a weary expression, but Sage gave him a nod and an easy-going smile, so my father began to open the presents, even as I gave the pups their presents.

They squealed and peeled with excitement, jumping around and playing with their new prizes.

● ● ●

My heart soared as they were hugging me and thanking me, before they ran off into the house while my father worked meticulously on unwrapping his gifts carefully, as he always did.

He liked to collect the gift-paper, to use it later, because he hated going and buying wrapping paper.

As my brother and his mate came out of the den, pups in tow, father managed to get his gift open and looked at them.

"These are good boots, and I was needing a pair. Mine were wearing out," he said. He glanced at Sage. "I assume you picked this, because you know the struggle?" He smirked.

Sage nodded, a grin on his face. "Yes, good boots are always a must have to keep on hand. I figured you could always use some."

"You were right, thank you, Sage. You are very considerate," father smiled at him, looking proud. "My son surely never thought to gift me something so practical. He gave me bottles of <u>wine</u>!" He laughed, but my brother approaching us was not amused, even as he carried a bottle of wine in his hand as he approached.

Case in point.

My father pulled out the other gift, opening it and finding the nice, expensive watch there, and he glanced to me.

"If he chose the boots, did you choose this?" He asked.

I gave a nod. "Sage...gave some input, on what was practical, and the quality to look for. I picked it out, though.

He gave a tight nod. "It is a nice watch," he said, looking away. "You got the pups good toys, too."

My brother crossed his arms, rolling his eyes at the scene. "So, she's back in with some nice gifts? Father, I understand she's your child, but she's a trai—"

• • •

I rushed to hand him his and his mate's gifts, and they looked at me in surprise...before my brother's expression turned to rage.

"You think you can just come in here, on a special holiday—our *first* holiday without *my mother*—and with you, smelling like *that*, and be welcomed back like you didn't betray us!" He snarled.

I flinched, and Sage immediately stepped between us...defensive.

"Now isn't the time," Sage said, subdued. "*I* was the one who suggested her get you gifts. I picked them out. I just felt awkward giving them to you," he said.

Quill looked at Sage, and he sighed. "Alright, then," he said, opening the gifts.

Sage had lied, but I was fine with it.

He simply knew that Quill and his mate wouldn't open them any other way, unless he pretended that I gifted it under the pretext of Sage being the gifter himself.

My brother opened the large, sharp knife, with the saw on the back, and studied the blade.

"This is high quality," he said. "A good choice. Thank you, Sage, you have good taste."

At least he thought it was in good taste...even if he would refuse it from me.

My sister-in-law looked at the pretty necklace I'd gotten, and though she didn't say anything, she smiled at Quill as she held it up.

"That is pretty. It matches your eyes," he said, pointing out her honey-colored gaze.

That was why I had chosen it in the first place.

"I hope you like them," Sage said. "We'll get on back to the den, now," he told them.

"Don't come back," my brother spat, glaring at me.

Making eye-contact with me for the first time since I had been discovered as being mated with an enemy wolf.

"Wha—?"

"*Sage* can handle any business with us from now on. Don't...don't think you can come back here. I won't look at your traitor face again, you filthy whore."

I felt my eyes burn with tears, but I gave a nod, turning away. "Merry season," I told them. "I...love you."

As I walked away, I heard my brother's fierce snarl as he growled at me, "It'd be much *merrier* if my mother was here to celebrate with us! And I'd never want to be loved by you. Your love disgusts me! Look at what your disgusting, so called '*love*' did to this family, you dirty piece of shit!"

Tears streamed down my face as I walked with haste back in the direction of Sage's den...of the only safe haven I had left.

Walking, however, wasn't fast enough. So...I ran.

Sage didn't run after me. He continued at his own pace, letting me go.

By the time that Sage had reached the den, I had broken down and started to cry.

"Oh, sweetheart," Sage said, pulling me into his arms. "Please," he said, almost a whimper.

"Sage," I whimpered.

He lifted me, taking me to the bedroom.

He left the room, going outside of the den for a moment, before he returned and closed everything back behind himself before he came into the main bedroom, holding a large wrapped package.

"Merry blessing season," he smiled at me, a small smile on his face.

He brought it over to me, letting me rip into the paper, and I felt the breath leave me when I saw it.

● ● ●

It was a large, beautiful, framed photo canvas of me, my hands lying on my very-pregnant belly, looking out of the window.

I hadn't been paying attention, and he'd snapped the photo.

It was evening, the sunset light filtering through, and I looked like I was on fire, almost.

It was stunning, and tears formed in my eyes for an entirely new reason, this time.

"Oh, Sage," I whispered. "This...this is beautiful."

"So are you," he said, and I glanced at him to see his eyes blazing as he looked at me.

"...What...?"

He stepped up to me, taking the portrait and setting it to the side against the wall before he pulled me to him, cupping my face with one hand and my belly with the other. "You may not have been mine from the beginning...this pup might not be mine by blood...but I will give you both my all. My everything. If you let me, I will be the pup's father. They will never want for anything, and I will do all I can to keep you comfortable and content. I will heal you," he said, a plea in his tone.

"...Sage..."

I could see the war in his eyes.

He wanted me. He wanted this with me.

He had completely fallen into his role as my mate, and my heart tugged in my chest.

In that moment...I *wanted* to love him.

I wanted it so badly, for him to take this pain away from me, but my heart couldn't let go of the pain that North had given me, the betrayal...the rejection.

What if Sage rejected me too?

I couldn't respond, but Sage took a long moment leaning in, waiting for me to stop him...before his lips pressed to mine in a chaste kiss.

CHAPTER 10

Cedar...

Once Blizzard's Reign had arrived, I had hunkered down in the den and began the nesting phase.

I couldn't entirely say why, but I had the strangest feeling that my pup would be arriving soon.

I'd been stressed and depressed lately, but I kept feeling false contractions.

I knew, however, that I wouldn't have gone into labor unless I had all the signs, and I never did.

It was into Nivis's End when, one day around lunch...my water broke.

It was about a month early, and I went into a full panic.

I wasn't sure what to do, or what to think, even.

Was I in danger?

Was my pup in danger?

Since the Heaven's Gift holiday, Sage and I had gotten even closer...after how our families had acted toward me.

He made sure to take off work for me, to sit and be with me and try to make me feel better.

● ● ●

He went with me to the doctor and, though they insisted on no ultrasounds or positive treatment of the pregnancy...they at least didn't talk down to me the entire time I was getting my general health checked if Sage was with me.

Thankfully, it was around the time that Sage would be popping by for lunch, and all I had to do was wait.

I let out a sharp cry as a contraction began, and I tried to breathe through it.

I looked upward, my eyes closed, begging mother to help me through this...because I had no other family left.

It had been about twenty minutes of close contractions and feeling terrified before I heard the entrance door of the den open.

"Sage!" I cried from the bathroom, and I heard the pause before he rushed into the room, fully alarmed and alert.

"Cedar!" He said, looking me over and noticing the wet mess I was in. "Oh, oh goodness," he said, rushing to my side. "This is too soon, isn't it? I thought you weren't due for another *month*, Cedar..."

I groaned, nodding as another painful contraction hit me. "I wasn't."

He looked me over. "Are you *sure*? Are you sure you weren't pupped earlier—"

"I can't say," I cried, sobbing. "I-I don't actually know for sure! No doctors would actually look at me or do ultrasounds. It was all just a guestimate!" I cried out with a scream at the end.

He hesitated, and I could see the frustrated anger on his face, directed to the doctors of the pack, before he focused on the task at hand again. "It's alright," he said, bringing a cool washcloth he'd gotten at some point?

He wiped off my face, and the coolness was bliss on my hot skin.

"I-I'm scared, Sage," I sobbed.

"How far apart are contractions?"

"Almost constant. It is almost time," I heaved.

He gave me a tight nod, and lifted me up, helping me across the den and to the other bathroom, the guest bathroom.

He lay a bunch of pillows and sheets in the tub, and sat me inside. He situated the pillows behind my head and the sheet beneath me, having me pull up my sundress and peeking down...to my horror.

"Oh, gosh," he said, looking away quickly. "I can only guess it's time to push, because there is already a head starting to poke out," he said, trying not to look too long and glancing up at my face.

"Oh," I said, surprised.

I *had* felt the urge to push, but it all felt like fire ripping through me. I hadn't been able to really discern if it was time yet.

I took a deep breath, and began to push with all my might. I cried out, shouting and sobbing, as I felt myself expanding around the head.

I shrieked as I got the head and shoulders passed with his grossed-out updates and off-handed encouragements.

Despite how horrifying, terrifying and awkward it was, he was actually very encouraging.

I actually felt better.

He told me I could do it; *the head was poking out already. It is so dark and bloody.*

I could get it done; *the shoulders were already being pushed out. It is so slimy.*

Just a little more...*the body was almost completely out.*

● ● ●
334

He may have been a little grossed-out and gruff about it, but he was an ever-constant presence in the space with me, and an active and helpful participant.

I couldn't have asked for anything more from him, considering everything.

Then, he brought me a towel and a fresh, warm wet washcloth as I lifted my pup in my hands from between my legs, a bit unsteady, but with Sage at my side to help me with anything I needed.

I used the washcloth to clean the pup, careful of the head of thick, stunning black hair, and noting the pale skin beneath the blood and afterbirth matter.

Then I wrapped the pup in a towel as a doctor called from the front door, and I realized that Sage had called for the doctor in the pack link mind.

The doctor came in and looked things over, taking care of the umbilical cord and glancing with a sneer at the pup in my arms.

"A female..." He grumbled. "Better than a male from an enemy pack, at least," he said, before he had taken a wad of money from Sage and left on his way, as Sage grumbled at him and told him to get the hell out of our den with his horrid behavior, snarling and going on the defensive for us.

I glanced at my child...my *daughter*...and tears ran down my face.

"We...well...*I* have a daughter," I said, looking her over. "He...didn't want us, so...she's...just mine, I guess."

I wiped off her face, and I noted that most of her features favored *his*. Her inky, silky black hair. Her lips, her ears...her light, pale skin.

"A daughter who looks exactly like him."

Sage took her from me when I offered her, holding her, even as I sobbed into my bloody hands.

Would North hate her?

● ● ●

335

I saw Sage through my hands, and I watched as his eyes began to tear up, and a smile lit up his face. "Hi, there," he said. "I am excited to finally meet you, little wolf," he told her, pressing a kiss to her forehead. "Hello, baby," he cooed, looking at her like...

Looking at her the way that I wished her father would.

The way my father had always looked at me; completely hooked, line and sinker, wrapped around my finger and at my beck and call for any and all of my whims.

He was such a sucker for her already, and I was so thankful that I didn't have to do this alone.

I had been unhappy, initially, with the prospect of being arranged to him, in my situation...but I was beyond thankful and blessed that he'd been the male chosen for me.

None other would have been this compassionate and kind and forgiving.

None would be this gracious, surely.

I loved him dearly.

It might not be in love, but I wasn't far off.

I had an endless amount of respect and admiration for him.

He continued to coo at her for a moment before he tightened her blanket-burrito, securing her, and took her to her crib, before he came back and helped me wash up myself, bathing me with exceptional gentleness.

I basked in the warmth as his hands worked the hot water and soap into me, and he helped me dry off and dress in a fresh dress before he carried me to the nursery, where my pup was just starting to cry.

"Oh," I said, soft. "Come now, daddy was just helping mommy get a bath," I told her, and he and I both froze.

My face burned with mortification over just how natural it had felt to say that...

• • •

"...Daddy...?" He asked, a surprised and...almost hopeful expression on his face.

He was nervous, scared that I would take it back and hoping I wouldn't.

"Is...that okay? I mean, you don't have to...If...if you want, if you're okay with—"

"I already see her as mine," he said, eyes bright. "But I didn't...I didn't want to encroach on you, in any way. Yes, yes, I want to be her daddy."

I gave a nod. "Alright, then," I said, smiling when Sage handed her to me after I was situated in the rocker. "Let's get you fed, hm?" I asked her, pulling out my breast unabashedly and bringing her up, trying to help her latch.

He blushed a bit, turning his gaze away, trying to be respectful.

It took a few minutes and some frustrated crying on both sides, but I finally got her completely latched...and as she fed from me, taking what I could give...she finally opened her eyes as Sage kneeled by us, stroking her tuffs of ebony hair, and smiling down at her with a happy face.

I startled, sobbing, and crying and becoming an emotional wreck, when I saw that she had inherited her father's bright, stunning magenta eyes with hints of lavender around the pupil and bursts of burgundy throughout the iris.

"What—" Sage began, before he really saw her eyes up close. "Oh...Oh, I see."

"She...really looks just like him, Sage. She got his hair, his eyes, even his skin tone. She looks like him," I sobbed, kissing her little head of black hair. "*Just like him*," sucking in a sharp, shay breath. "Those...eyes...! How can I move on from him...when she looks and smells just like him?"

She smelled like him, too.

Sage didn't say anything for a while, but once I had finished feeding her and lay her down in her crib, he glanced at me.

He didn't comment on her appearance, or what I'd said.

Instead, he moved on.

"What will you name her?"

I had been thinking about that for a while. I had chosen a name for either gender a while back, when I was still angry...

It was a neutral name that could fit a boy or girl...and I'd made my choice.

"Ash. Ash Frost-Stone."

"...*Ash*?" He asked, and I knew it was, indeed, an unusual name for our pack, and for North's.

I was from the Terra-Forest-Stone pack, and most of our names were derived from plants or stones, items found in nature.

North was from the Glacial-Gem pack, and most of their names were derived from Nivis terms or gemstones.

"Ash...because her father lit my heart on fire, and turned it to ashes."

He stayed quiet for a long time, but gave a solemn nod.

"Ash," he whispered, looking at her again.

"Sage?" I asked, and he looked at me, question in his eyes. "Thank you...for everything. But thank you for today, especially. You have been more than I ever could have deserved...and I am thankful."

He blushed, but pressed a kiss to my lips...soft and chaste.

● ● ●

CHAPTER 11

Sage Onyx...

<u>Seed's Sewn, 1971 Imperial Lunar Year</u>

I was busy working on some paperwork from a criminal rogue I had just dealt with and gotten put in the cells, when Beta Cloud came up to me.

I looked up from my papers to see him looking...almost anxious.

"How is she?" He asked, looking away.

Ah...

He had done this several times since his daughter had come to live with me.

I knew that their family was still struggling with Dove's loss and that Quill, in particular, had cut off Cedar from the family...but no matter how betrayed the family felt, Cloud had always loved Cedar.

She'd always been a daddy's girl, as long as I could remember.

He was wrapped around her finger.

I understood the feeling, now that I had my own daughter. I, myself, simply couldn't begin to even imagine cutting her off, no matter what she did.

● ● ●

Cloud, as her father, didn't find it as easy to cut her cold turkey the way her brother had.

"She is doing well. At home resting."

"How is she? Is she struggling to recover? I know it's probably been a few days, but it all went well, didn't it?"

"Huh?" I asked, a little confused. "Days? What do you mean?"

"Didn't she give birth within the last week or so? I thought this was the time she was due."

"She gave birth early...*last month*."

He startled. "*What?* Is...is she alright? What about...the pup?"

I clasped my hands, a bit perturbed. "You could have asked her all of this."

He sighed, looking stressed. "I couldn't..."

"You *could* have, but you come through me because you're too upset to face her yourself. You're still mourning, *and that's okay*, but you feel conflicted about Cedar. Don't pretend you were busy and didn't have time to go talk to her yourself."

He glared at me, but didn't respond.

"She and the pup are fine. She gave birth a bit early, but a doctor did confirm that they are both in good health. The pup was a little underweight, but she's remedied that easily enough herself. The pup feeds quite well."

"I see," he said.

"Cedar's original scent has returned to her. The pup smells like a good mix between her mother and father."

"'Her?' It's...it's a girl?"

I gave a nod. "Yes, the pup is female."

Cloud nodded, looking away with a tearful expression.

Both of Quill's children were males, and his mate had already had her core—*the organs to reproduce*—removed, due to complications and a miscarriage at the time that they had their second pup.

Cedar had probably never thought he'd have a granddaughter.

He gave me a nod, and turned. "What does she look like?"

I paused at that. "You could go see her..."

"I might, *someday*...but I can't right now."

I sighed, cursing in my mind ,and rolling my eyes, before I gave him the answer he sought.

"She looks just like her father...all but her mother's nose."

He whirled around with wide eyes, looking at me. "*What?*"

I nodded. "I know your bloodline and Dove's are both dominant lines...but her father, from what I've learned through reports and intel, is the nephew of both the beta and the alpha of their pack. His father was the Offensive Gamma. He is now the Offensive Gamma and the beta heir, because he married the beta's daughter through an arrangement."

He looked at me with calculating eyes. "You've done your homework..."

I nodded. "I wanted to know more about the wolf who fathered my pup," I told him.

"*Your* pup...?" He asked, surprised.

I gave a tight nod. "I realize that it is rare for a male to claim a pup he didn't father himself...but I have claimed her as my own, before Cedar even asked me to. I will act as her father. I fell in love the moment I helped with her birth."

"I see..." He said, awed.

● ● ●

"I wanted to know about her biological sire, to know what to expect, at least," I explained. "I got the answer. She is the pup of North Frost, a powerful, prominent figure in his pack."

He looked away. "Yes."

"The pup's name is Ash. Ash Frost-Stone."

Without another word, he nodded, turned, and left my office.

I let out a sigh, leaning back in my office chair and running a hand down my face.

I didn't know why they had to blame her and the pup this way.

They acted like she was a criminal...but then, I wasn't exactly well versed in pack social norms; I was the Pack Hunter.

From what I had gathered, it seemed to be the Offensive Gamma Heir's fault to begin with.

He was the one whom hadn't rejected her, knowing they were true mates from enemy packs that wouldn't ever be able to work out. He had started to initiate a romantic relationship with her, kept it going for years, and didn't reject her right off the bat.

There was no reconciliation to be had with our packs.

Surely, he had to have known.

She could have rejected him if she were more powerful...but only an alpha-level female—or extremely powerful beta-level female—had the ability to do such a thing.

For females, the rejection was only an option if her mate was unfaithful to her, or if he tried to kill her or harm her in other ways.

For Cedar, it wouldn't have been possible for a while, because she hadn't even been aware of who, exactly, he was. Their first months of being true mates, he'd been a wolf.

He had stayed in wolf form, not letting her know who he was, so she couldn't have rejected him even if she had wanted to.

Very few females in history had ever rejected their males, and none in history had rejected her *true mate* first, without already being in an arranged marriage the way that Cedar's mother had been.

It was almost unheard of for an unmated female to reject her true mate first. It was extremely rare for males to reject their true mates, either, unless they had dangerous positions like me, or if they were rogues.

There was nothing for it.

The pack wouldn't change their mind, and she wouldn't be able to repair her relationship with them.

They shamed her and threw things at her each time she went out into the pack, so she couldn't even work off her traitor status.

I had always thought fondly of Cedar.

My father had always been angry, bothered that his true mate had already been mated to another male when he came of age...and therefore, he took it out on Cedar, being the child of his true mate and the mate who had taken her from him.

This child?

This pup was innocent. She couldn't control who had pupped her mother.

I hoped that the pack would see that someday.

Now that Cedar's father knew that she'd had the pup, it was likely that the entire pack would know soon.

Nobody had seen her in a couple of months, meaning that nobody had known she'd had the pup already.

• • •

I finished my work early, and I stood, stretching, and re-tying my bootlaces before I headed out of the pack house, going home.

When I reached the den...I found something I hadn't expected.

As I was arriving, I heard shouting, angry yells and obscene language.

Beta Heir Quill Stone outside, yelling through the entrance door...

"You can leave the pack with your enemy traitor's nasty spawn now, yes? I heard you were both safely through the delivery. It's time to *leave!* Get your things and go, and leave the pack like the *bitch* you are!" He shouted.

"What's this?" I asked, and he started, turning to face me...when I noticed a gallon-jug of vodka in his hand.

*It took much more alcohol for us shifters to become inebriated, but that amount surely ought to do it, and inebriated he **certainly** was.*

"You helped her finish her pregnancy with that bastard pup and give birth safely, but don't worry! I have your back! You did your part, like the honorable wolf you are. You don't have to deal with her anymore. She'll be going now that she's not so vulnerable, and I will help you! I'll make sure she gets out of your fur. You've done more than enough," he said, turning to the door again. "Isn't that right, traitor whore?!" He shouted the question.

I could feel the sadness rolling through my bond—my small, weak, but still meaningful-to-me bond of matehood and friendship from marking Cedar as my mate—and anger burned through me because of it.

"How *dare* you come here, to *my* den, when I'm not even home...and cause issues this way?" I snarled at him.

"Whoa, whoa, *whoa*...it *almost* sounds like you're defending that beast. You aren't defending that two-faced, enemy-fucking traitor slut, are you?"

I hesitated. "I think you're drunk...and I think you need to leave my property, before we have a problem."

He chuckled darkly. "Yeah? Is my being here an issue?"

"Interim Alpha Sierra, this is Pack Hunter Sage Onyx. Please come remove the Beta from my property before we get into a fight and I hurt him," I spoke through the pack link mind.

I got an immediate response. *"I happen to be nearby, already alerted to the disturbance by your neighbor. I'll be there in just a few moments."*

I turned my attention back to Quill. "Your mother wouldn't want this, you know."

I felt the blow to my cheek, but I didn't respond even as he snarled in my face. "You leave my mother out of this. My mother...she was convinced that Cedar was cursed, and she was right! Once that curse is taken out of this pack, all will be right again!" He shouted.

"Hey, now," we heard Alpha Sierra's voice come in, rushing to get between us. "Let's just cool down, yeah?"

Quill turned to him, a sharp expression on his face. "You're taking her side too? She can just stay safe and sound during her pregnancy and then give birth to an enemy's pup and that's just hunky dory to you?"

"**Stand down**," he ordered Quill. "You're drunk, and it is my decision whether or not to allow her to stay. I am alpha here. She has been silent and bearing her punishment without complaint. Perhaps you should keep your mouth shut, too."

"Punishment? What punishment?!" Quill cried. "She was mated to a powerful Pack Hunter, fed, clothed, housed, and allowed to bear that, that...that evil devil pup! They're both a disgusting curse, an affront on this pack! I refuse to tolerate their existence, here! They're the root of all evil in this pack and they deserve the worst of punishments for having the nerve to try to live here in peace after their sins!"

"She's a weak female!" I snarled at him. "Did you expect her to have the strength to reject her true mate? Enemy pack member or not...he didn't reject her first. She was bonding to him. And the pup? Completely innocent, unaware of anything to do with this, and has no control over her parents. She's a baby!"

"Oh," Quill said. "At least it isn't a *male* pup, who we have to worry about trying to rise the ranks and take over and destroy the pack, I suppose. Just another gutter whore like her mother, to take whatever mate she can get and put out, hm? Another traitor to spread her legs and take some poor, unwitting sap's cock—"

I couldn't help it. That was my adopted daughter he was slandering.

I slugged him right across the face.

"Alright, **that is enough**!" The alpha commanded us both. "You both got a hit in. *That's it.* Move on, let it go. Quill...if you want to remain as the beta, I suggest that you **let this go**, **pull yourself together**, and **get out of here**. *Now*."

Quill took one last look at me. "You can tell that traitor that she's dead to me...just like our mother."

Then he turned, and ran off into the forest.

Sierra stood there, sighing, rubbing his fingers over his temples.

"How did it come to this?"

I turned without another word, and I left him standing there as I entered my den.

I followed the scent of my mate, stepping through the den. I found the living space, kitchen, and nursery all empty.

I stepped into our shared bedroom, and followed the scent to the bedroom's walk-in closet...where I found her.

She was sitting in the floor, *behind* a lower rack for pants and jeans, and she was rocking Ash in her arms, tears streaming down her face.

● ● ●
347

She was completely terrified, in fear of their lives.

That only served to speak to the hostility she felt from her own brother.

When I stepped through and squatted down in order to better see her, she looked at me with dead, dreading eyes.

"Cedar...?"

"...How soon do I need to have my things out of here? If-if you want, I can just burn most of it. I can't carry much anyway, but I can be sure to be out by the time you come for lunch tomorrow—"

"I don't want you to leave," I told her. "I am not bothered by your presence here...and your brother is a drunk asshole who was being a dick. I got a good punch in on your behalf."

A small laugh escaped her, and I took Ash from her as she stood on shaky legs, before we walked to the bed.

She got comfortable, and I lay the slumbering pup between us as I propped my head up on my hand, looking over at Cedar as she continued to sob softly.

"You don't have to go anywhere. Don't feel obligated to leave. This...this is your home."

"You are too kind to me, Sage," she said. "I bring you far too much trouble, way more than I'm worth. What if you get tired of me and tell me to leave?"

I shook my head. "You're fine here," I told her. "That will never happen. I promise."

I said that because I meant it.

No matter what anyone else said, I meant what I told her.

● ● ●

Year's Fall, 1971 ILY

"Our pack...has decided to move."

All of us were in surprise by the announcement, as interim alpha Sierra spoke to us.

"A separate pack from the Central Kingdom has faced almost complete annihilation. They only need a space about this large to rebuild, whereas our pack has gained quite a bit in number over the last couple of years. Many new pups have been born. The Head Alpha has decided to give us twenty new wolves to add to our pack, as well, to help us extend bloodlines because we had so few lines left and we don't want to start interbreeding. So, he has given us a plot of land—fifteen miles across. The pack that was located there before has relocated to new land because they expanded...through marriage to the Head Alpha's pack."

"What?" Many of us were shocked by the news.

"The Head Alpha's son, of the Aurora Peak Pack, was found to be true mates with the Death-Shadow pack's alpha's daughter during one of their peace-keeping meetings. So, the pack has joined, and now the entire pack is renamed as Shadow-Aurora pack and is relocating."

This was big news, indeed. A truly momentous union.

"When are we moving?" I asked. I shifted the pup in my arms, trying to tuck her into me.

To be sure that the pack saw us as a family unit, to show them that I viewed them as my own family, I had decided to hold the pup myself.

"We will begin the move after the Heaven's Gift holiday season," he said, glancing at Cedar and our pup.

"Cedar...has the Offensive Gamma of Glacial Jewel made *any* attempts to contact you in regard to the pup?"

The entire pack went silent, save for the tense density that seemed to settle over us.

She cleared her throat, looking to the ground. "No, alpha."

"That is too bad. I had hoped he would have contacted you, asking to have the pup, but..." He sighed "That is also good, then. We don't need to move and it cause issues to rise with their Offensive Gamma, at least. We're just starting to get the pack starting to bloom again. Perhaps it is a blessing he doesn't care about her, and we don't have to get involved with their pack."

"Yes, alpha," she said, voice dead and monotoned.

Whispers ensued, but we paid them no heed.

Former Beta Cloud stepped up to us, looking at the pup in my arms.

He didn't say anything...but I could see him analyzing her face.

This was only the third time that he'd seen her, in her life.

She was now ten months old, and quite a happy pup indeed...even without a close family.

Cedar and I tried to be good to her, let her feel loved.

I had watched Cedar struggle a lot...she would cry often, and have to shut herself in the bathroom away from Ash fairly often.

She struggled with her striking appearance to her father's, her scent that was so much closer to his...

Truly, the pup barely resembled her.

She got her mother's nose and thick, full pouty lips. The eye-shape, eye-color, hair-color, and skin color were all completely different.

I, truthfully, handled most of her care whenever I could.

Cedar spent most of her time mourning the bond, and I could feel her wolf weakening more and more by the day.

"Hello," Cloud said to her, voice soft.

He had been kinder since he had fully retired as beta, and had started making an effort to rekindle his relationship to Cedar...but it was too late.

I couldn't bring myself to tell him that Cedar was dying.

Her wolf, Pepper, was dying rapidly, and when a shifter's animal passed away...so did *they*.

"Hi!" Ash replied, happy that someone was speaking to her.

"Growing fast," he commented. He looked to Cedar, noting her haggard appearance. "You look so tired," he said, sad.

She didn't really respond...just gave a have-hearted shrug and a small nod.

He glanced to me; eyes full of worry.

I knew that no matter how angry he'd been at her, how upset and disappointed...she'd been his little girl, and he'd been a sucker for her from the moment she was born.

To see her in such a condition was horrifying for him, I was sure.

Nivis's End, 1972 ILY

The move to our new territory was uneventful, and truthfully, being in this new place with new air and new surroundings...it was like the pack-wide healing we had needed.

Cloud, and even Quill, seemed much lighter, and though Quill wasn't willing to reconcile with Cedar...he had come to me to request a meeting with the pup.

He vowed that he wouldn't harm her, and meant us no ill-will.

He had met her, and though he hadn't been very excited, he had admitted that she wasn't the evil demon spawn he'd thought.

She was just an innocent little pup with no sins that she'd made yet.

Now, she was turning a year old, and we celebrated with a completed den and a decked-out toddler bedroom.

She had squealed and laughed, giggling into fits at her new toys, while her mother and I watched on in content silence.

Shortly after cake and ice-cream, Cedar had excused herself to go and cry in our bathroom, and I took care of Ash as I gave Cedar the space to do so.

The Head Wolf pack, the Shadow-Aurora pack, had indeed sent twenty new shifters to join our pack.

Ten omegas—five males, five females.

Eight Deltas—six males, two females.

• • •

Lastly, he had sent two gamma's children...a male and female.

They were second and third children, and thus not eligible to become gamma heirs in their pack, but they were more powerful than average deltas.

Nineteen new bloodlines to add to our pack, being that the two gamma children were siblings...and they were teens already.

Things were looking on the upside for our pack, and I hoped that things continued to improve.

The only thing that was iffy was that one of our new pack members was originally from Glacial Jewel pack, and it was certainly a tough thing, adjusting to her scent around the pack and getting accustomed to it.

Nivis's End, 1973 ILY

"Get back to your positions!" I shouted at the line of warriors. "We cannot let the line fall. Fight these rogues!" I shouted.

I was already distracted...I'd had to leave Cedar and Ash at the den, and my mind flashed to earlier that day.

*Cedar and I had been talking, and I had **finally** broken down.*

*"Why can't you just...love me?" I'd asked her. "Let him go, Cedar. Choose **me**...give yourself, your heart, to me. Don't you want to watch Ash grow up? Be here for her?" I asked. "If you mark me—even if we don't mate again—you would be able to come back to life. Pepper would get strong again, you would be free of the pain his rejection causes you each day. Please, stay for me. Stay for Ash!" I begged.*

She looked at me, eyes dead.

I could sense Pepper wheezing in her, and my wolf whined and cried sadly inside of my own heart.

We wanted her.

We loved her...but she would not spare her own life to be with me.

She wouldn't mark me.

Pepper was on the brink of death, now...and only her human letting go of that suffering and marking me in return could save her.

Back during Heaven's Gift season—our third merry season together—she'd given me something I'd never thought I'd have with her.

She had mated with me, in a tender, soft, emotional night of crying and fear and pain.

We'd shared a few kisses and hugs, hand-holding, but that season, we had made love…and it had been amazing. Even she had enjoyed it, physically, even if she had cried afterward.

She had not, however, marked me in return…because she wasn't in love with me.

I knew she wanted to be.

She claimed as much, told me so…but she wasn't. She loved me, even romantically, but she couldn't let go of her pain.

A rejection to a wolf as weak and pitiful as hers? I couldn't imagine how much strain it put on her.

Rejection after growing and forming an attachment and securing a bond through mating, and especially bearing a pup together…it was a wonder she had survived this long.

Now, she was lying here in bed, dying.

I had clasped her hands, begging her…but she had just smiled and patted my head.

"Take care of Ash for me," she had whispered.

That was it, then.

She had made her choice.

Despite all our family memories, the joy I had seen in her, the happiness our family gave her so much of the time…she couldn't let her pain go.

She was going to let herself die, because she was wallowing in it, rather than focusing on getting better…rather than letting herself love me.

● ● ●

Rather than letting herself live for her child.

His child…

After I had left her, I had gone to Ash's room and given her a hug and a kiss.

"No matter what anyone says…I look at you like my own," I had whispered to her slumbering form. "Be a good girl…daddy will return. I love you so much, princess. Daddy will be back to celebrate your birthday tomorrow, okay?" I spoke into her hair.

That's right.

My little girl was turning two the next morning, and I was so excited.

She was so smart for her age, and so well behaved.

I loved bragging to everyone about her.

I had thought over the first time she had called me daddy, and her mother had locked herself away for three days, crying, while I had cried with joy.

Cedar had agreed with me that I would be her daddy…but to hear her actually say the word, refer to me that way…it was hard for her.

All I felt was peace and joy.

Joy that this tiny pup had welcomed me into her heart, and given me a place as her most prized male model figure; her father.

That role had belonged to another, but like a fool, he'd given them up. So, now it was mine.

All I felt was joy.

Joy that I'd finally gotten to know what it felt like to be a father, and realized that I'd never known what I was missing until I had it.

I was daddy.

Our new home had been brought under attack, and I had been saying my goodbyes to my family.

It was dark, already into the night, and after I'd said goodbye, I had left them to fight the large band of rogues marching on our pack.

I'd fought so hard already, but I could feel Pepper slipping.

With every punch and cut I received, she got weaker, herself. She wouldn't last much longer.

"I love you," I had told her...because I had grown to love her.

Even if she never returned my feelings.

I continued to fight, pushing and pulling, stabbing, parrying attacks...

It seemed endless.

I was on autopilot, and my mind was struggling to keep up. For some reason, a reason I couldn't understand, I was seeing my whole life play out in my mind.

Especially the last few years.

Every moment with Cedar, Pepper...every moment spent with my beautiful, glittery Ash.

The princess she was...

I wanted her to be someone's queen someday.

Find her true mate, a love unlike any other.

Perhaps reunite with her birth father, and rub it in his face, the life he missed out on.

Brought back to the here and now, I startled as I got a punch to the face, and then everything stood still when I felt it...

Pepper was gone.

She had slipped away, and I felt the bond snap and shatter as, too, Cedar passed away.

Tears ran down my face, and I let out a painful, wailing howl.

I had lost my mate.

I gasped as I heard shouts and cries around me, and for a moment I was confused.

Were they mourning with me?

...No...Ash...my princess, my wolf whined pitifully, realizing the situation.

Looking down at the spear that protruded through my chest from behind, realizing that the leader of these rogues had used my distraction from Cedar's death to bring me a fatal blow.

I realized that I was dying, now...

As everything spun and went back around me, all I could think in my mind was,

"Who is going to watch over Ash, now? What about my little princess Ash?"

Because daddy wasn't going to be able to make it home, after all.

My last lingering thoughts, as tears leaked down my battered face, were of her sad, heartbroken face when she realized that daddy wasn't coming back...and even worse...tomorrow was her birthday.

I promised I'd be home to celebrate her birthday, I sobbed in my mind.

Fear ran rampant in my mind as I tried to imagine...what would happen to her now...?

-Fin-

.........Stay tuned for the exciting conclusion coming in:

The Rejected Lady, Parts 3 & 4

Coming soon!

Book Excerpt to follow

KRISTEN ELIZABETH

The Shifter's Saga, Book 1.5

The REJECTED Lady

PARTS 3 & 4

Self & Daughter

Arranged Marriage, Forced Proximity,
Enemies-to-Lovers,
Forbidden Relationship, Passionate, Steamy
Wolf-Shifter Fantasy Romance

1st Editon - Author's Art Edition

Quill Stone...

I watched as Sage took that spear through the chest from behind, and the look of horror that flashed across his face.

He looked to me, and I could see his eyes full of fear and tears.

Then, he was falling.

Strangely, I didn't feel the family-bond break.

I only felt the pack-link break for him.

Then, I remembered...I had disowned Cedar.

I said she was dead to me, and I'd never claimed her as my family again.

That had cut our family bond at that point in time.

There was nothing for it, I guessed.

I knew I would have to face her eventually, to tell her about what happened.

Father hadn't seen it directly, and I was sure she'd want to know that he fought well until the end.

However, first I'd give her a few days to mourn, and then I'd go check on her and the kid.

"We haven't heard *anything* out of her?" I asked father.

"I...I felt the family bond break when Sage was killed," he said. "I wonder if the loss of the mate bond hurt her, too."

I shrugged it off. "She wasn't in love with him, anyway. I'm sure she's fine."

He glared at me. "Go visit her soon," he told me. "I have to go out of town for a pack meeting to discuss the losses and re-up our supplies, discuss a union to strengthen us. I don't have time to go check it out."

I sighed, rolling my eyes. "I'll go soon," I said.

"Has anyone heard from Sage's mate?" The Defensive Gamma asked. "I know that I tried to reach out, but nobody answered the door," he asked me.

It was two days since Sage had died.

"My father wanted me to go check on her," I said, conceding. "I thought I'd give her some time, though."

"I haven't heard anything via the mind link, either," the alpha said, considering. "She usually never ignores me."

I shrugged. "Her mate just died. In love or not, it had to be a tough blow, even if just to her pride."

"You don't know what you're talking about," the defensive gamma said, frustrated. "That woman and her brat were *his whole world*. Just months ago, he came telling me all about how she called him daddy and he was lit up like a sunbeam. He was head over heels. He told me that Cedar was one of his closest friends. I don't think their relationship was quite as cold as you might believe."

I considered that.

I hadn't really thought about her as having genuine feelings since the situation with North had happened, but she was a mother and a mated wolf, now.

Perhaps things...had changed...?

"I'll go by there in the morning, and I'll let you know how she's doing."

The following morning, I had a strangely eerie feeling.

Jasmine felt it, too.

"Doesn't it feel spooky?" She asked me. "I feel like something is off."

I shrugged. "I'm not worried. I'm sure she's fine."

We got ready, and we left the den.

Even the air was thick, almost...*bleak*.

Something was definitely wrong, but as my mate looked around, uncomfortable, I tried to keep a brave face.

We made our way to the den where my dead-to-me sister and her mate and child lived.

The air here was absolutely the source of foul air in this part of the forest.

It was thick, stunk, and felt physically *heavy*.

I hadn't felt this since we'd had to go to the morgue to make sure mother's body was prepared the way we wanted before her burial...

What *was* this?

The air felt almost...angry.

If I hadn't seen him die with my own eyes, I would have thought that Sage was standing behind me, fuming at me for something.

His ghost was probably fuming at me for waiting three whole days to go and check on his mate and her child—the child he viewed as his own.

I still couldn't understand that, but to each male his own, I guess.

Most male wolves had a hard time accepting a female's pups from previous males, but Sage hadn't been bothered in the least.

He'd stepped right in and claimed her as his, making everyone in the pack question his rationality and sanity.

Had he gone mad?

He was wrapped around their fingers, but he just smiled and laughed like it was the jolliest thing.

Whether he had made my sister happy or not, they had certainly made *him* happy, and there was something to be said for that, at least.

I reached out a hesitant hand, before knocking on the door.

We heard the pitter patter of child feet, and I heard a timid voice call out.

"Daddy?"

My heart tried to break, but I felt my wolf, Nickle, stacking the pieces back up and gluing them together, determined to get through this.

...

....

....

................Want to keep reading?

Be sure keep an eye out for the release of
The Shifter's Saga, Book 1.5:
The Rejected Lady, Parts 3 & 4

It only gets better from here, and let us not forget: STEAMIER.

...Y
U...
...M

EXTRA CONTENT

Extras:

Character illustrations:

Dove:

Silver:

Cloud:

Slater:

Quill:

Nickle:

Cedar:

Pepper:

North:

Coal:

___

Sage:

Smoke:

Ash:

Books by Kristen Elizabeth

The Royal's Saga

The Apathetic Knight, Part 1 – The Crowning
The Apathetic Knight, Part 2 – The Burning
The Apathetic Knight, Part 3 – The Freezing
The Villainous Princess, Part 1 – The Trapped
The Villainous Princess, Part 2 – The Freed
The Disregarded Dragon
The Hidden Queen
The Conquering Empress
The Abandoned Prince
The Decoy Duchess
The Empathetic Brother
The Anonymous Writer
The Luxurious Slave
The Incensed Guardian Novella
The Royal's Behind the Scenes Finale Novella

>The Shifter's Saga<

>The Rejected Lady – Parts 1 & 2<
The Rejected Lady – Parts 3 & 4
The Hunted Cat
The Damned Wolf – Parts 1 & 2
The Justified Siren
The Lost Heir & Heiress – Parts 1 & 2
The Trapped Son
The Shifter's Behind the Scenes Novella

The Lover's Saga

● ● ●

Titles coming soon!

Acknowledgments

A special thanks to my proof reader & good friend, Trisha, for reading through the novels and helping me with the grammatical and spelling aspects. Without your help, there were a lot of mistakes that would have made it into the books, and you encouraged me a ton. Thank you for your interest and investment in the story! I love you.

A thanks to the Ghost-Writer who helped me with some editing, some of the ideas, and some of the bonus content added to the original story. You rock, and I appreciate that. Thank you so much!

A special thanks to those who supported my work, including but not limited to, Sammie-Anne, Shannon, Amber, and so on. Several people who really encouraged me to write, publish and seek higher things. You guys inspired me to make this possible. I appreciate it so much. Special thanks goes to my most avid of fans, including Christine, Jeanna, and a few others who had been following my work and have gone to extra measures above and beyond to support and read my works.

All of you aforementioned people make writing the books so much more exciting so that I can see your reactions and give you good books to read!

Thank you all for being amazing. Without you, there is no way I would have gotten such a great start!

A special thanks to my husband, Reece, for allowing me to take so much time to write and keeping everything running, and not complaining a ton.

You wanted me to pursue my goals, and I needed that extra push because I'm bad about procrastinating on things. I love you, handsome ;)

Lastly, I want to give a special thanks to my mom. You don't read my work or really think this will go that far, but you love me and try to support me the best you can. Thank you for everything, and I love you.

Thank you again to all of you readers!

You are amazing, and I hope you enjoy the rest of the novel series!

Please review the story, and please share with friends! One of my biggest dreams is to see people unboxing my story and enjoying the worlds that I take them to within it.

Much Lovely Madness to you all!

#TheShiftersSaga

#TheRejectedLady

#SteamyRomance

#KristenElizabeth

#LovelyMadnessFantasies

About the Author

Kristen Elizabeth is now on social media! Follow on Instagram and Tiktok! Handle for both apps is

lovelymadness92

She also has an author's page on Facebook! Check her out at

Kristen Elizabeth
(Lovely Madness Fantasies)

Follow for more bonus content, updates, and publishing schedules!

You can also now purchase the special Book Box Set of The Royal's Saga! Contact me via Email to place an order @t:

i.write.lovely.madness92@gmail.com

This is my professional author's email, specifically created to allow fans to contact me directly!

Kristen wants to share her unique worlds with those around her. She hopes someone out there will enjoy her creations as much as she does and use her creations to escape from the mundane everyday life. Kristen's biggest goal is to fit somewhere outside of the norm, and to broaden horizons in the world of fiction.

Life isn't always happy endings, sunshine, and rainbows.

Sometimes, life is an utter freakshow and things don't work out the way you hoped.

That's something that Kristen wants to bring to her writing.

Let Kristen help you fall into her world of Lovely Madness ;)

None of this happens without the readers! Please help me by sharing and spreading the word means so much to me! Thank you so much!

I hope you tune in for Book 1.5:
The Rejected Lady, Parts 3 & 4!

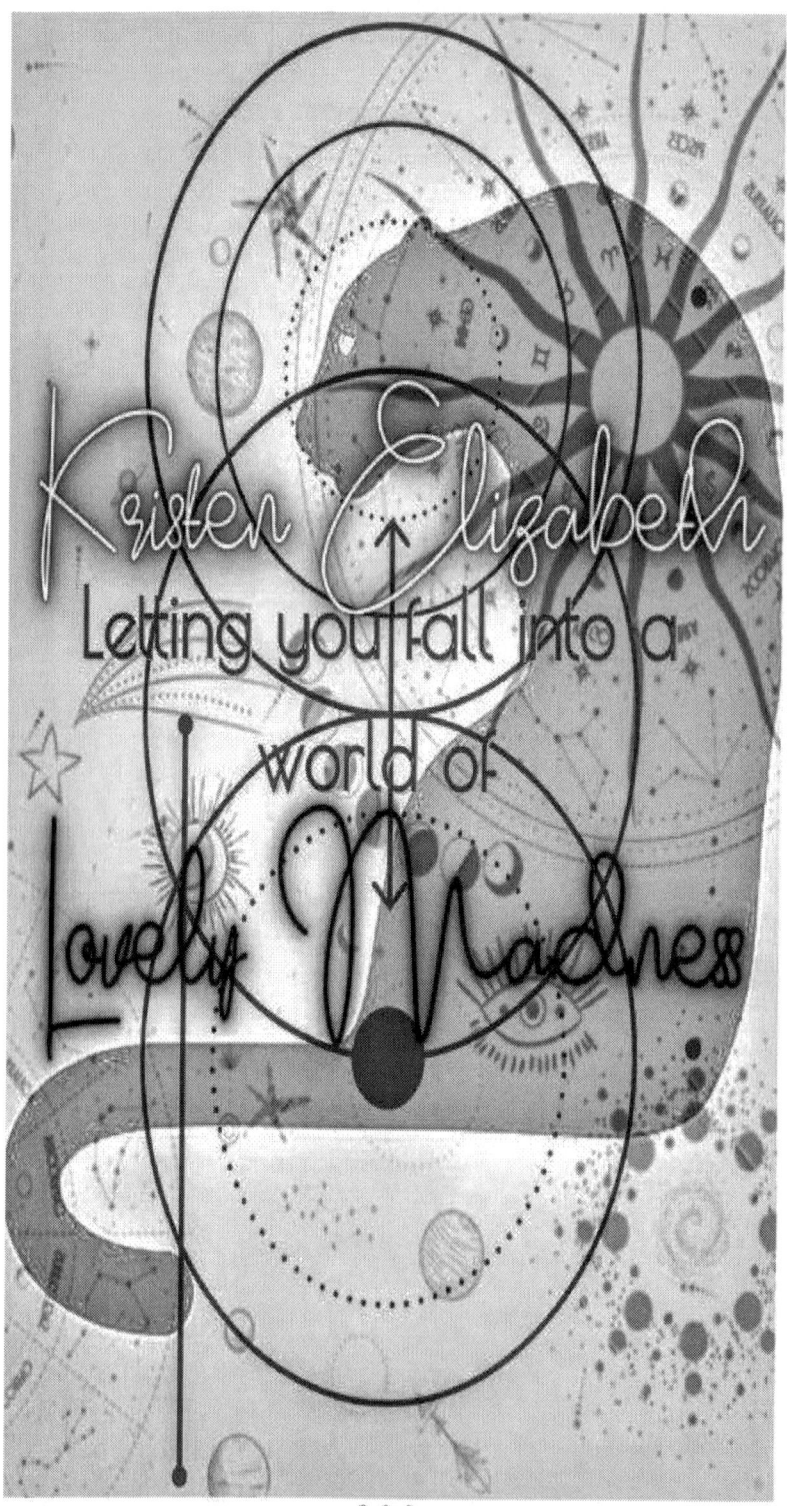

Kristen Elizabeth
Letting you fall into a
world of
Lovely Madness

Final Remarks

Thank you so much for
reading Kristen Elizabeth's
novel world of Lovely Madness

The Shifter's Saga, Book 1.0:

The Rejected Lady, Parts 1 & 2

1st Edition;

"Author's Art Edition."

Lovely Madness Fantasies

Kristen Elizabeth

FANTASY ROMANCE AUTHOR

Made in the USA
Middletown, DE
28 May 2024

54949504R00216